Twins in Time

A NOVEL

SHE CAN'T GO BACK …

Natalie Griffin

WINDY OWL PRESS

To everyone who refuses to let go of their dreams.

PROLOGUE

1894

Elizabeth stood at the edge of the river, hands at her sides to avoid fidgeting. Her toes had no such restraint. They curled in her boots, nearly as hard as the anxious knot in her stomach.

There was no real way to tell him what she wanted—that she refused to go through with the marriage. There were plenty of reasons to continue with her predestined path, to simply go along with what her father said.

In her mid-twenties, she was far too old to have the privilege of marrying for love. She wanted children; she could see their squishy cheeks every time she fell asleep. That was what made her say yes in the first place. But the biggest reason was, the wedding would create peace between the two families.

It would be fine in the long run. She'd have her brood of children, a house of her own, a full life. Even so, she couldn't stop thinking of that one time . . . that one time he'd gone too far. The one time his temper got the best of him.

If Pa hurt Momma, would she have gone through with the marriage? The thought whirled through her head like a tornado.

His footsteps echoed off the gangly trees as he approached.

The answer never changed. Her mother would never have married someone who would injure her, or her family, so easily.

And that was why Elizabeth stood there, waiting to have the most difficult conversation of her life.

"Why'd you want to meet me out here?" He leaned against the tree and stuffed his hands into his pockets.

She said a silent prayer, rocking back and forth as she did before turning to face him. "I don't think I can do this anymore."

One eyebrow rose in confusion. "What are you talking about?"

Though it was a warm spring morning, she rubbed her hands over her arms to hide the fact that they were shaking. "I don't want to marry you anymore." She expected him to argue, to tell her how he would behave better, how the wedding was far too close to call it off. Instead, pure, menacing fury took the place of his calm, blue eyes.

"No." His voice was firm, certain it would be the final word in any argument.

"I've made up my mind. Listen to me, please. We just aren't a good match. Just as you said before, I'm far too strong-willed. I'll never make a good wife." She silently prayed it would be enough, that he'd simply shrug and walk off.

"I made a promise." He looked like an angry dog, standing taller in order to appear as oppressive as he possibly could.

"A promise?"

"I made a promise to your pa. I swore I'd never let you go." He closed the distance between them with a single step, looming above her.

"That promise was to take care of me. To ensure nothing ever happened to me." Her fingers squirmed, rubbing the fabric of her skirt between her fingers. "Sometimes that means to let me go."

He tsked and ran his finger along her jaw, pausing at her chin to guide her gaze to his. "You're as good as mine. The land will be mine. I chose you, and that's that."

She opened her mouth without thinking. "Our parents made the decision for us. This wasn't *our* choice."

"How cute, you think you have a say in all this?" A sickening sort of grin snaked across his face. "I don't plan on lettin' you go that easily." He leaned in for a kiss. As his lips tickled hers, her self-control cracked. With as much force as she could muster, she kneed him straight between the legs.

He crumpled forward like a rag doll. "Why'd you do that?" he demanded, hands clutching at his prized jewels.

"Perhaps it's because I don't want you kissing me." She fought against the tremble in her voice and crossed her arms over her middle, mainly to hide her anxious fingers as they fiddled with the corset boning beneath. "I'm not going to marry you. I've made my decision."

He stayed quiet for a long while before he said another word. He spoke through his teeth. "You'll learn. And you'll learn right this moment." Before she could say a word, the first blow landed directly below her collarbone. As her hands flew to the pained area, he grabbed her forearm and shook her.

"Let me free. The bruises will show!" She pulled back, feeling his fingers sink even farther into her pale skin.

"You think you're gonna leave me, now, do you?" He laughed, low and menacing. "You will *never* leave me."

And he threw her to the ground. The breath she had been holding rushed through her teeth as she hit the dirt. Before she could consider getting up again, he was straddling her, hands pinning her arms above her head.

"You. Will. Never. Leave. Me!" he shouted, shaking her so hard, her head hit the ground. Once. Twice. Again and again. Each time with the sole purpose to drive his point home.

She gasped in pain but otherwise stayed silent. She would discuss the matter with her brother when she got home. He'd stop. As long as she remained a submissive, quiet girl, he was bound to stop.

But he didn't. Her vision blurred and her mind became fuzzy. Almost numb. She hardly noticed each blow to her face, her chest. The trees turned dark as her vision caved into an ever-narrowing tunnel, closing faster and faster with each passing moment.

Fear gripped her for only a second. What about her father? Would he be okay without her? Her brother?

But it all faded to an unfeeling sort of peace as she slipped away, the blood from her head flowing into the river below.

CHAPTER ONE

"One large, iced, half-caf, soy macchiato?" I held the cold beverage out the drive-through window to the dull-looking man in the yellow sports car. He took his sweet time turning to face me, reminding me of some kind of evil sloth that took pleasure in watching the sleet fall from the roof onto my head.

"Excuse me?" He raised one eyebrow.

"You ordered a large, iced, half-caf, soy macchiato?" I kept my customer service voice in full swing, though I knew exactly what was coming. It was probably the biggest issue with my job. All the caffeine in the world wouldn't make it easy to be nice to assholes.

His eyebrow fell back to its rightful position, leaving a scowl on his face. "No," he said curtly. "I had a large, iced, half-caf, soy macchiato with *two pumps of caramel.*" He spoke the words slowly, as though I had to be an idiot to have missed such a thing.

I took a second to let my eyes close, then inhaled deeply. Patience . . . patience . . . "Oh, I'm sorry! I'll fix it for you." I backed into the heated building and set the cold drink beside the order screen.

"You've *got* to be kidding me," Trisha muttered from her position in front of the espresso machine. "What was it? I'll make it again."

I repeated the order, and she eyed the offending drink. "I could just add two pumps to that."

"Don't, he's watching," I cautioned. Like a switch, the customer service demeanor turned back on with the ding in my headset. I could only imagine the customer leaning out her window, shouting through the torrential sleet. These people were certainly desperate for their afternoon pick-me-up. It was nice to know it wasn't just me suffering each time I stuck my head through the window.

The shift was long. The weather seemed to make everyone grumpier than normal. If I drank all the returned drinks, I could have bounced to the moon with all the caffeine.

Mercifully, closing came at eleven. I had a long night of studying ahead of me, so I made my own concoction of hazelnut, mocha, and a whopping three shots of espresso to help me survive.

"You doing anything tonight?" Trisha tiptoed on the counter, packing the sealed bags of coffee beans into their respective, high-up places.

I interrupted a yawn with a gulp of coffee. "Yep. Booked up. My bed will be angry if I decide to stand him up."

"Your bed . . ." Trisha shook her head. "You're a college student. Your bed shouldn't have a persona until you have a good two kids."

I rolled my eyes and grabbed one of the boxes strewn across the floor. Stubbornly, I fought to flatten it into submission. I *refused* to search for the box knife. "I'm not a normal college student. You know that."

"We haven't been out in so long! If you even *think* of telling me you have some assignment you haven't finished, I'll jump on down and tape your mouth shut." As evidence, she held up the piece of tape she'd just yanked from a box.

I smirked. "I technically do. I have a test at nine."

She groaned. "Ellie, come with me. You need something other than school and work in your life."

"Trisha . . ." I complained. "I really just want to study, then go to bed."

"You will. After we party. Come on." She hopped down in one fluid movement. "I'll drive. You don't have to worry about a thing."

"You're my ride anyway," I muttered. "You can go. If you hadn't noticed, the sky's been throwing ice at us all day."

"Come on, don't be a sheltered little—"

I took a moment to calm myself before responding. "Thank you for the invite, but no." In all honesty, even if I didn't have a test in the morning, I wouldn't have gone. The few times I had ever gone out with her, I ended up in the back corner of the bar with only my drink for company.

"Fine," Trisha grumbled. "Come on then. I've got the keys to lock up."

After securing the tiny coffee shop, we sprinted through the icy rain and piled into her 1980s Cadillac. As it roared to life, the sugar-sweet voice on the radio warned of the potential of ice on the roads by morning.

One of the issues I had with Trisha's car was the seat belts. The one on the driver's side was the only one in working order. With the weather, that just made me extra nervous.

I didn't like that the sleet had turned to rain over the last hour, but at least I would be home soon.

We drove north out of the main part of Woodward, Oklahoma, without an issue, heading in the direction of my garage apartment. At nearly midnight, the streets looked like they had come out of a ghost town.

When the car slid past the stop sign, my anxiety took over. "Careful, don't go so fast. If there's that icy spot, I'm sure the bridges are already trashed."

"Chill, it hasn't been raining very long yet," Trisha said. "You're giving the northerners a reason to laugh at us."

With each mile, I stiffened some more. She wasn't known for her decision-making.

As we geared up to cross the river, I sat a bit straighter to try to glimpse the water beneath. It had rained almost all week before the cold spell, sending all the creeks and rivers into full Oklahoma-style rapids. Of course, nothing could be seen. The barely budding trees were too thick, and the night too dark.

A curse from Trisha was the first sign that something had gone wrong. The car slid to the left, then jerked the other way as she tried to correct the error. The rolling coffin wasn't having it.

She's got this, I lied to myself, grabbing on to the door handle with a death grip.

The car spun like slow-motion ballet, the sleet pelting the windows with an elegant, teasing force. It was like the droplets were laughing at my misfortune.

The car hurtled toward the ditch on the right side of the road. I knew the trees were short by most standards, but they no longer looked that way as I braced for impact.

Trisha yanked the wheel to the left.

"Watch out!" I heard myself scream.

The car smashed into the guard rail.

Everything after that was a blur. I didn't have time to marvel at the flying cell phone, or all the glass that followed it. Panic filled every inch of my body as we crashed toward the river, hitting who knows what on the way down.

It was impossible to keep track of everything. Screams came from nearly every direction, echoing in and out of focus and drowning out even the rushing of the river.

Something told me how I should know better than to get into a vehicle without a working seat belt, but another part was still confused as I hit the water—completely free of the car.

I gasped as the cold seeped into my clothes. It was impossible to stand, no matter how many times I kicked my feet. The water dragged me down into its murky depths. All the muck from the week's storms rushed about me in all directions. It was impossible to tell which way was up or down, which way was upstream and which downstream.

My mouth opened to scream, and my mind tried to regain control. Nothing worked. I was swept on, pushed out of the water for a breath here, and a breath there, but it was never quite enough.

Each time I got the smallest bit of oxygen, I was shoved right back down. My side slammed into a rock, my shoulder into a limb. Each object sent more precious air bubbling up to freedom.

Suddenly my body took over. It gasped for breath. The firewater burned its path all the way down my windpipe and into my lungs. I smacked into another hard object, my body becoming as heavy as a rock. My lungs gasped for more air, and I sank faster, all the while being swept around in the swirling water.

Then black.

CHAPTER TWO

There's no telling how long I lay on the side of the river. I have no idea how I even got out of the water. But when I opened my eyes, they burned in the bright sunshine.

I smelled vile. Like puke and pond scum combined.

The realization of what happened was slow, creeping into my mind like a snail invasion. The car accident, the river, the ice, breathing the water in—

I gasped and sat up. The coughing was relentless, ejecting water all over the tightly packed dirt. Where was Trish? Would they let me retake my test?

Watered-down blood dripped from the tip of my nose, staining the ground. Alarmed, I smacked my hand against the offending wound on my forehead. The blood welled around my fingers at an alarming rate.

Logic told me head wounds bled a lot, and I didn't have reason to panic, but the blood running off my chin terrified me.

I needed to find my way home. To someone. To a hospital. To find Trisha.

Surely the first responders had already located her. If I had survived and traveled so far, maybe she did as well. But those screams had insisted otherwise.

Forcing myself to my feet took much more effort with the dizziness. The throbbing of my head caught up with me the moment I stood upright. I glanced around desperately.

Nothing.

I was in the middle of absolute nowhere. Probably a farmer's field. Or ranch. Or something. There were no fences, no cows, no buildings. Only trees that lined the river and rolling hills that continued on until they disappeared into the cloud-dotted sky.

I dug into my pocket for my cell phone but found nothing. Not that it would have been likely to work after swirling around in the water, but it had certainly been expensive. Besides, there would have been that *tiny* chance that I could call an ambulance.

I tugged at my sweater, hoping to make the hem into a bandage for my head, but nothing budged. How did they manage such things in the movies?

Of course, I had traveled downstream. Ideally, I would only need to head back the way I'd come and hold pressure on my head.

Easy.

Hopefully Trisha hadn't been swept away. But if she had, she was likely to be along the riverbank. At the very least, there was bound to be debris from the car.

I silently prayed she had made it to safety and was hunting for me.

But those screams . . .

Panic swelled in my chest, threatening to take over. My breathing came faster by the second, causing my vision to go fuzzy.

Breathe . . . breathe . . . I placed my hand on my chest to focus on its rise and fall. Hyperventilating wouldn't help me.

It took awhile, but when all that was left was the dull pain that radiated through my body and the killer headache, I began to walk. One step in front of another. It felt like I had just run a marathon completely untrained at some kind of record pace. With werewolves on my heels.

Within a few minutes, ominous blood splotches appeared on my jeans. I refused to pull up my pant leg to check on the injuries. If

I didn't see what was going on, maybe I could ignore it until I found help. That was the hope anyway. Wounds always seemed to hurt worse once I saw them. These were no exception. It was as though my brain had some kind of radar, latching on to each of the bloody zones and awakening the throbbing pain.

I wrapped my arms around my shivering self and continued on. A farmer's field couldn't go on forever. There had to be a fence hiding somewhere to follow toward a road. *Something.*

The river meandered on its merry way, showing no trace of its earlier malice. It was much warmer than it had been too. Likely the upper fifties, low sixties. I wouldn't freeze, though my body still shivered.

I finally came across a road when the sun was high in the sky. An old, dusty path with two bare spots for wheels. I figured there was a fifty-fifty chance one way would lead to the farmer's house, the other would go off to an abandoned shed.

The wound in my head had slowed to a trickle, though each step threatened to reopen it. Hopefully it wasn't as bad as I had originally feared.

Time seemed to stretch out indefinitely. My footsteps got slower and slower. Until I saw buildings in the distance. It was as though someone injected caffeine into my body. Surprising even myself, I ran for them.

It was a town. A very tiny one, but a town nonetheless. It didn't even have a Sonic. Or power lines. Or even streetlights, for that matter.

I didn't completely realize how much was off until I stood next to the closest building, looking on to Main Street. It was the perfect replica of one of those ghost towns in a TV show, only with plenty of movement. The women bustled around in bulky, multilayered dresses. Some had on bonnets, some had heavily ornate hats to enhance their fancy look. The men wore long-sleeved shirts, high-waisted pants, and the classic cowboy hat, and most of them had suspenders or vests on.

Bonnets? There was no possible way they were back in style.

I moved into the street, blown away by the perfection of the horses and wagons, all the men hoisting hefty things and the women gossiping in the corners. Whoever put this together was a genius, and I felt bad for interrupting the production.

But I needed help. A hospital, preferably.

"Elizabeth!"

The sound of my full first name piercing through the air hit me with both hope and apprehension. I whirled toward the voice coming from what looked like the general store. The tall man rushing my way had brown, tousled hair and was dressed just like the other men, only slightly dirtier. The biggest difference was the stressed-out look that reminded me of a parent who was about to navigate their toddler's fifth tantrum of the day.

I automatically backed up a few steps. I had never seen this man in my life.

"Where have you been? Do you have any idea how long I've been looking for you? And what happened to you! And . . . what are you *wearing*? Why are you dressed like a boy?" He paused, eyes narrowing as he fought for the words. "Where'd you get those pants? They're way too small. You can hardly move. And is that a sweater?" His jaw went slack as he stared at my blood-streaked face. "You cut your bangs. Why would you do *that*? You look like some cheap—" He cut himself off, confusion contorting his expression in waves.

A lady whispered into her husband's ear, a scandalous expression taking over her pinched face.

I glanced down at myself. A low-cut, oversize sweater, now torn to shreds and hardly blue anymore with all the blood from my forehead, then my equally as destroyed jeans. For this fantasy land, I could see the outfit being somewhat of an issue.

He didn't wait for a reply before he pulled off his jacket and wrapped it around my shoulders.

"What happened to your head? Where's Rose?" He wrapped one arm around me and ushered me toward a beautiful black mare.

Something twitched in the back of my head, reminding me that strangers were no good. Especially when you got into a car with them. Or horse, in this case. Apparently, the car accident wasn't enough to teach me that lesson.

His solid hold cautioned me against jerking away, but it still somehow felt protective. For the tiniest of moments, I somehow felt like I was completely safe.

"Why is everyone dressed up?" I managed to ask.

He shot me a quizzical look. Before I had a chance to react, he hauled me up onto the horse. Instantly, I leaped for the ground. I didn't plan on being kidnapped. Especially not on horseback. My landing was horrible, giving him enough time to scoop me under his arm like a football.

"Come on!" He let out a grumble and set me securely on the horse again. This time, he swung up behind me before I could try to escape. His arms stretched on either side of me, effectively caging me in. He moved with the same ease I had when getting into the seat of a car, as if he did it a million times a day.

"You'd better come up with where you've been. Pa might as well shoot you."

"Pa?" I blurted. Every word he said felt like it hit some kind of brick wall before bouncing off into some confusing swarm of gnats.

"I don't think—" I cut myself off as the perfect set of gallows came into view, placed right next to the even more perfect jail.

The confusing gnat swarm started to come together. It finally clicked how *wrong* the entire situation was. "Where the fuck am I?" I demanded. Unwisely.

He yanked the horse to a stop and turned in such a slow fashion, I envisioned a vulture narrowing in on his prey. "Pardon me?" he asked, one eyebrow raised, pure shock written in his blue eyes.

"You haven't heard a girl curse before?" I snapped, the bravery coming out of some hidden part of me. I was sure he could tear me to shreds in an instant, and with the look in his eyes, I was wondering if he would. "I need answers. Once again, where am I?"

He shook his head slowly. "Never heard a girl like *you* curse before. Any girl I've ever heard with that sort of language was wearing a damn sight less than even you right now."

I stared at him, shocked into silence. Did he just call me a whore?

"And you're wrong. *I'm* the one in need of the answers," he added before I could gather myself.

I crossed my arms around my middle as I tried to create a comeback. He turned back around, and with a kick and a sort of clicking noise, we started off. I grabbed the back of the saddle before I could fall.

There was no way around it: I was going to miss my test.

CHAPTER THREE

A narrow, dirty road opened to the right almost as soon as we passed the last building. The man turned there, body stiff with worry. Or anger. It was hard to figure out which.

"We need to get you fixed up," he said.

"I need a hospital. Take me back to town." I turned in the saddle to peer back at the buildings in the distance.

"The closest thing you can get to a hospital 'round here is Mr. Spencer." His tone left no room for argument.

I touched the clotted wound on my head. Whoever Mr. Spencer was, I doubted he had what I really needed.

A two-story, wooden house came into view right as the town faded behind the hill. Painted white with a big front porch that spanned the entire front, it looked like one of those houses that would be preserved by the historical society.

The man dismounted and reached up to help me down. I didn't budge.

"Take me to a hospital, please," I said, lifting my chin and forcing myself to make eye contact.

He leveled his gaze. "As I said, this is all we've got. Come on." He scooped me up like a child, one arm wrapping behind my back and the other snaking under my knees.

"Put me down!" I shouted, kicking at whatever part of him I could.

"Hush, look, you've made it start bleeding again with all that strugglin'."

As if on cue, a droplet of blood fell from my chin and onto my chest.

Letting out an irritated sigh, he walked me straight up the steps and to the door. He knocked with the toe of his boot.

"I'm comin', I'm comin'!" came the bright, feminine voice from some hidden corner inside the house. The moment she laid eyes on us, her face transformed from a pretty shade of pink to as white as a sheet.

"Elliot! Elizabeth!" She let the door fall all the way open.

My captor—Elliot, I assumed—hurried inside without a word, leading the way to a room on the right. The woman fluttered along behind.

The inside of the house matched the historical perfection of outside. It was a place that needed to be taped off with big signs threatening death if anyone was to cross. However, everything was well worn and still in use. Even the Victorian-style settee in the parlor.

The room Elliot brought me into matched the time period but not the decor. A black, padded bed stuck out from the wall next to a clear cabinet filled with tools and medications. A chair rested beside the door, but otherwise, the room was empty.

Elliot ushered me to the ancient exam table with such care, I felt like I had gone back to being two years old.

Before he could get out of reach, I grasped his shirtsleeve. "I need a hospital."

He smiled sympathetically. "This is the best we have. You know that." He patted my shoulder.

He pried my fingers from his clothing and sidestepped my attempts at grabbing him again. Before I could protest, he left the room, shoulders visibly relaxing as the stress melted away. He was perfectly okay with leaving me with this strange, middle-aged woman. I could only assume she was Mrs. Spencer.

Before I could consider getting off the table, she rushed over and started her examination. Her eyes traveled every inch of me, focusing on every bloodstain and scrape. "Poor dear . . ." she cooed. "Let's get this off you so we can get you cleaned up."

There wasn't much else I could do other than let her try to help me. She pulled the sweater off with the care of a grandmother, but it still pulled at the dried blood and glass shards that hid underneath.

I closed my eyes against the pain. If I didn't fuss, maybe she would be more helpful.

Her questions flew through my head faster than I could hear them. The only words I caught were the basic who, where, when, and why. But none of my answers had a chance to form on my lips.

She let out a scandalized yet somehow dainty gasp as she got the shirt over my head. I subconsciously glanced down, hunting for the cause. I halfway expected to find a gash in my abdomen by the way she looked. I had plenty of scratches, but there was nothing too major.

She focused on my foot, the cabinet, anything but my lacy bralette. It would have been the perfect reaction for a hidden camera TV show. "They're not the most supportive things, are they?" I laughed awkwardly.

She got over her shock quickly and started to clean the wounds with a wet rag. She pulled out whatever pieces of glass she could. Though she was careful, it took more effort than I expected not to whack her away. My body seemed to have a mind of its own, twitching in self-defense with each sharp pain.

Her hands were cold, a relief to the hot, swollen skin around the glass and dirty cuts. She worked efficiently, talking about all kinds of things as if she weren't mutilating my body for a cause. She told me about all kinds of people in the town and what they were up to, but I didn't register any of it.

Only when she was satisfied with my torso did she move on to my forehead. I fought to stay still as she pulled miniscule pieces of glass out of my hairline. She went mostly quiet as she worked on that one, only making scolding *tsk* noises when she found things she didn't like.

She cleaned that wound with agonizing slowness, drawing a few squeaks out of me with the poking and prodding. Eventually, she pressed the rag against my forehead and directed me to hold pressure. I obeyed.

Not as much glass made it through my pants. Thank God for denim. Most of them were easy to clean and not very deep. Something had slashed through the upper part of the jeans, leaving a larger cut on my inner thigh. She took her time cleaning that one but bandaged it without much fuss.

Satisfied, Mrs. Spencer pulled a well-worn, off-white slip sort of garment from the chair beside her and slipped it over my head, making sure not to bump the gash. A knock sounded on the door, making both of us jump.

"Give us just a moment!" she called, supporting my upper body as we let the garment fall over my skin. I was grateful for her concern for modesty as she pulled the slip down to my knees.

Satisfied, she turned toward the door. "Phillip, come on in!"

A larger, husky man came in at her call. He had a dark brown beard and mustache, one that would certainly be the envy of many guys with the beard craze back home. The only thing was, like the house, he was definitely not dressed for the twenty-first century. He wore the same light-colored pants held up by suspenders and a shirt the color of dark moss. He covered it all with the white lab coat that hung on a peg by the door.

My stomach caught in my throat as he rummaged through his medicine cabinet.

"Miss Elizabeth," he began, shaking his head slowly. "Getting yourself in trouble, I see?"

Elliot slipped in behind him, moving like a ghost to stand by my head.

"Ellie," I muttered, mainly to myself. I should probably have asked how they knew my name, but I didn't have the energy. "And accidents happen." My throat felt dry and scratchy after my prolonged silence.

"Of course they do." He turned back to face me with a leather-bound roll of tools in his hands. "If they didn't, I wouldn't have a job."

In old historical films, it seemed like doctors loved to shove leeches on their patients. What if they were committed to their charade enough to conduct their medical care in an old-fashioned way? "Please don't put leeches on me," I pleaded, voice high-pitched. I couldn't get the thought out of my head.

Elliot laughed first, sending the happy sound circling around the room. I didn't join in. None of this was funny.

"No leeches," Phillip promised. He motioned for me to lie down. I did, though my muscles shook in nervous protest. He placed the roll above my head and unrolled it, humming as he did so.

I tried to crane my neck to see the contents, but I couldn't see anything except for the worn leather.

Elliot cleared his throat to get my attention. "Do you remember what happened?" he asked.

"I was in an accident," I said absently.

"What about Rose? And Luke?" he prodded.

I didn't get a chance to come up with an answer. The doctor stood up straight, holding a long needle and thread.

"Nope!" I sat up with all the umph I had and turned to swing my legs over the side.

Elliot placed his hand on my shoulder and pushed me back down. He was careful not to apply too much force, but his grip was still strong.

"I need to be in a hospital for this bullshit," I snapped. My heart pounded in my ears and my breathing came fast. "I'm done playing your games. Take me to a hospital!" I pushed hard against him, but he didn't move an inch.

The doctor didn't react to my words, but Elliot visibly flinched.

"The nearest hospital is in Kansas. This is nothing Mr. Spencer can't take care of on his own," Elliot said with a forced calm.

He held pressure on my shoulders as the man came for my forehead. Mrs. Spencer stood opposite him with a wet rag to dab at the wound as needed.

"Let me go!" I shouted, kicking weakly at the doctor. "Let me the fuck go! Dammit! This is not sanitary!" The infection would set in rapidly, I just knew it.

The door burst open, and a taller, older version of Elliot walked in. They looked so much alike, other than the gray hair and the long, gray mustache that took over the new man's face.

"Elizabeth," the man said, rushing to my side. He looked me over with a brooding expression so much like one my father would have had; it sent a pang of sadness through my stomach.

"I need to go," I said, holding in the question of who he was. It didn't matter.

"She's not cooperating," Elliot tattled. I shot him a glare and yanked away, taking advantage of his distraction. He just moved his grip to my forearms and held tight. The new man wordlessly did the same to my legs.

I cursed and screamed at them, but they ignored me. This ridiculous act needed to stop. I didn't deserve to be thrown into this charade.

Nothing about me was silent as the doctor prodded at my forehead. With every movement he made, I expected the needle to prick into my skin.

"This is madness! Just let me go! Let me bleed to death!"

When the needle finally began its horrifying job, I sucked in a sharp breath and whimpered. The pain stole the fight from my body and pushed me right into helpless submission. That wasn't to say I stayed quiet. Every word I said was a curse of some kind, whether made-up or completely understandable. Each time my body tensed, the men holding me down tightened their grip.

Thankfully, the doctor was fast. Either that, or the wound wasn't as large as it felt. The moment he snipped the thread, everyone collectively let go and breathed a sigh of relief. I didn't blame them; even I had fully planned to launch up like an angry cougar as soon as I was released. Instead, my hand shot to my head to feel the result. It was a good two inches long, hiding right along my hairline. The doctor had done delicate, precise stitches. That was a good thing, right?

Other than the infection risk, of course.

"Were there any other places that need stitched?" Phillip directed his question toward his wife.

I answered first. "No."

"Her left thigh had another large wound, but I believe bandages do the job nicely," she said.

With those magic words, I relaxed.

"Now, drink lots of water, okay?" Phillip said sternly. "And rest. Lots of rest. As for your wounds, just keep them clean. I don't want to perform an amputation on you."

Even though it was said with a teasing smile, I flinched at the word. I was going to get all kinds of infections from that needle. I needed a hospital.

"Elizabeth," the new man said, voice just like a cautioning parent, reminding me there were still other people in the room. "What happened to you?"

Lips sealed, I didn't say a word. I didn't turn to face him, didn't look up at anyone. I needed to get home. To a hospital. Anywhere else.

Apparently giving up on me, they turned their attention to the doctor, giving their thanks and gathering instructions for my care. I tuned them completely out and stared straight at the wall.

After a few minutes of chatting, Elliot scooped me into his arms. Whether it was the instinct that told me he meant no harm, or the fact that I was beyond exhausted, I rested my head against his warm chest. It felt comfortable, despite all the warning bells going off inside my brain.

"Wait!" Mrs. Spencer said, rushing to Elliot's side and nodding to me. "She can't leave like that."

"We can't take clothing from you," the father figure said.

"Nonsense." The woman fluttered her hands at him and rushed to the hall closet. She came back within a few seconds with a long, blue coat. "I can spare this for a time, I think. And it will save her dignity. She can bring it back when she's feeling up to coming into town again."

Elliot set me down and helped wrap me up in the too-large coat. Mrs. Spencer was large enough that it could probably wrap around my middle a good one and a half times with the hem dragging the ground.

Once outside, my brain fogged over the rest of the way. I sat on the front of the horse this time, Elliot swinging up behind me and putting his arms on either side like a cage. They chatted with Mrs. Spencer for far too long. My eyes slipped closed against my will, only to snap open again in a panic. I had to stay aware of everything. I couldn't fall asleep.

We only took off when the sun threatened to sink below the horizon. The father kept his horse even with Elliot's, and no one said a word.

The landscape moved by ever so slowly. We weren't far from the river. Every once in a while, I could hear its tinkling song as it meandered through the trees. We passed a few tiny sod houses. Many of them were so new, the ground around was still torn up. Each house was acres and acres away from the next.

Children peered out of the doorway of one of them.

"Ma!" The littlest one's voice came as a startling screech. "They found her! Elizabeth! Come see!"

There was some scolding inside after that, and before the child could take two steps out the front door, arms pulled him inside. I caught the words "be polite" but otherwise couldn't understand what was said.

In reality, the only thing that pierced through my exhaustion was the ever-present panic. My heart beat with a steady, decisive thud. With each step the horse took, the fear threatened to break through.

Everything seemed less like a charade the farther we got from the river.

By the time we reached a tiny, two-story house, the light had turned to that of an oil painting. Everything had a romantic, yellowed feel as the sun began to set. The house wasn't nearly as spectacular as the doctor's home. It sat at the bottom of a hill, dwarfed by a patch of trees off to the side.

The house didn't look like it had been constructed by anyone with experience. The first floor was a simple rectangle with a lean-to attached. A smaller rectangle had been plopped on top. Nothing looked like it would survive all that long.

All the wood was freshly cut and placed together; it didn't have the weathered appearance of a classic old cabin I'd seen while driving through the country. Extra panels and logs sat close by, stacked beside a startlingly small sod building. It didn't look much bigger than a walk-in closet.

Elliot dismounted in front of this earthen structure and handed the reins to his father before helping me down. He carried me inside easily.

Inside was about as cozy as it could be. There was a staircase to the left with a door underneath it that led to whatever room the lean-to held. To the right there was a fireplace, woodstove, rocking chair, and a few benches around a table. Knickknacks hung all around, including a broom and a shotgun that rested in a cradle above the door. There were cabinets beside the stove but no sink. All the furniture was crammed together, making the space feel like a dollhouse.

Elliot didn't give me a chance to process the room. He carried me up the narrow stairs to a very claustrophobic hallway. The ceiling was so sloped, he had to stay on the side of the rooms. He opened the door to the second one and went in.

It was equally as simple and cramped as the rest of the house. A dark wood vanity sat against the left wall, a chest beside it. A nightstand with an oil lamp and a rickety old metal bed sat next to a window. Everything was so . . . wooden. The walls were panels, the floors were panels, the ceilings were just as sloped as the hallway with the large beams holding the entire household.

Elliot set me on the quilt-covered bed and lifted the glass cage around the oil lamp. With startling ease, he lit it and a warm glow cast across his face.

I hadn't seen anyone mess with one of those since my grandmother. She had one and lit it a few times at my insistence. But this man did it so easily, he had to do it every day.

The movie set idea was becoming less and less of a possibility.

"Are you going to tell me what happened?" Elliot asked, pulling me out of my thoughts. His voice was gruff with some hidden turmoil. He didn't look up at me, just stared at the flame as it danced inside its cage.

"You won't believe it," I said.

"If we are to do anything to help you, we need to know."

I sighed and lay back, relieved that the mattress wasn't too horribly uncomfortable. There was no user manual of what to do. Was I supposed to tell him the truth? Pretend I knew what was going on? Impulsively, I chose some kind of middle path. It was the only way I could see making it through without as many snags. "I don't know who you are," I finally admitted.

He couldn't hide his sharp inhale. It took him a long time to say anything, let alone breathe. The flame could have caused eye damage with how hard he stared at it. "Elliot. I'm your older brother, Elliot." His voice turned in to that of a strangled man uttering his last words.

My eyes snapped shut as unexpected emotion slammed into me. A brother. "My brother died a year ago," I whispered, not sure if it was wise or not. He flinched but said nothing. "The other man—he's your dad?"

"Yes." His voice cracked, forcing himself to pause. "Newton Hersley. Your father." Each word took obvious effort. A crunch split the silence as he crushed the box of matches in his hand. "You need your rest," he choked out. Without the slightest look back at me, he left and the door clicked behind him.

The light danced across the wall, telling stories with the shadows that happened to pass. My head ached with more than the stress and injury. The confusion swarmed so violently, it made it hard to focus.

Tears made trails along my cheeks before dropping onto the pillow. My brother . . . Travis. Though I'd done my best to move, to start a new life without him by my side, it had been nearly impossible. He'd been my roommate as we struggled through our college courses and worked full-time, menial jobs. He'd been my only confidant when our parents died in the fire.

Until he'd chosen to end it all.

It was a blessing I wasn't the one who found his body. Or at least everyone else thought so. To me, it was more of a curse. If I had been there, I might have been able to stop it.

Balling my hands into fists, I roughly rubbed them against my eyes, trying to avoid falling down the emotional rabbit hole.

I didn't have a brother.

Travis Hersley was dead.

It was all a big trick. It had to be a trick.

But somehow, I knew it wasn't.

CHAPTER FOUR

"**D**on't you *dare* even *think* about doing something as idiotic as going after them!"

Faint light flittered through the window, brightening the room just enough to show me I *wasn't* home. I pinched my arm roughly and groaned. Reality.

The shouting continued downstairs, shattering my disappointment. "You mean, don't defend your daughter's *honor*?" Elliot's voice soared through the floorboards, full of venom.

"We don't even know if it was them!"

"How could it be anyone else? Do you know of anyone who would have anything to gain from hurting her?"

"We don't know what happened, Elliot." Newton's voice held the unwavering no-nonsense edge but seemed more calm than before.

"We know something happened. And I'm not just going to sit here and let them glory over stealing away—" Emotion cut Elliot off, leaving an awkward silence in the air.

Forcing my body out of bed, I wrapped the quilt around my shoulders. The room spun slightly as I walked toward the door and down the rickety hallway, but I managed. As long as I kept an eye on my feet, my body stayed upright.

"Elizabeth," Newton said, as I appeared on the stairs. His gravelly voice reminded me of an old man pretending to be a radio host. "We should have done better at staying quiet. I apologize."

Tension hung heavy in the air as I looked between the two men. A lone tear sat on the very top of Elliot's cheek, but he didn't make a motion to remove it. Likely because it would draw more attention to it if he tried.

Elliot broke the silence. "Do you need anything to eat?" He hurried to the kitchen corner of the room, as if the sudden hunger had snapped him out of his daze.

"No," I said, tugging the blanket closer around my shoulders. "I'm not hungry."

I might as well have slapped them. The worry plastered itself to their faces almost instantly.

Newton broke the silence by grabbing his hat off the chair by the door. "We're going out to hunt for Rose." He pressed the hat on his head and grabbed the coat from the rack by the door. "We will be back by sunset. We got all the chores outside done already, so you don't have to worry about it. Just rest."

I nodded, not fully realizing he meant things like working with cows and chickens.

Rose had to be the horse. Either that or a dog. I couldn't imagine anything else would have been with the other Elizabeth. Maybe a best friend, but they would have been more worried about a human.

A nervous feeling swirled in my stomach. What were they talking about, after all? Me, obviously. I didn't have anything to worry about, did I?

When they never left the doorway, I hit me that they might want some sort of response. "I'll be okay," I said.

Newton smiled under his mustache and tipped his hat at me before escaping.

"Whenever you're ready to talk, I'll listen," Elliot said, leaning close to me so he couldn't be overheard. "I will do whatever is needed to make this all better." It was a vow I didn't fully understand, but the guarantee of violence was obvious in his eyes.

I nodded again, my blood turning to ice from the poison that coated his promise.

"Stay close, don't do more than you should. I reckon you're not feelin' so great yet." He followed his father out to the barn.

I watched them go. Watched every step until they disappeared into the sod barn. No part of me wanted to face what I knew to be true, but there wasn't much of a choice.

I turned slowly, breathing as steadily as I could. It was part of my dreams. That was it. A hidden camera, a sick, twisted joke from one of my friends. Perhaps I was in a coma in the hospital. I'd wake any moment.

Everything felt like a movie as my body made its way to the hearth. I hadn't told my feet to move—they just did. A nearly for-gotten childhood memory beckoned me closer.

My fingers traced the stones, each one placed in their rightful spot. Each one their own perfect art. No cracks, no imperfections, other than the slight scorch on the wall inside from the previous fires.

Even so, I knew the exact stones that had fallen to the ground. Which ones sat piled up where, and which ones had completely disappeared from our play area.

Many people in Oklahoma had fireplaces from old homesteads. It could have been anyone's that I remembered from childhood.

But I *knew* this one. Without the slightest doubt, I knew it had to be the one from my grandmother's acreage. What were the chances of it being such a similar fireplace?

What were the chances of these people having the same last name?

There weren't any chances.

It was the same place.

I raced back up the stairs, chest constricting at the sudden movement, sending a coughing fit my way. I ignored it as well as I could and hunted for my normal clothes.

Digging through the dresser drove me farther into the nineteenth century. The top one held a few hair items: an ornately decorated brush, hair pins, ribbons, and a dainty hand mirror. The others held neatly folded undergarments: stockings, chemises, underwear—or rather, bloomers.

Frustrated, I shoved the drawers closed and went for the chest. It wasn't much help either. Dresses. There weren't many, but they took up a decent amount of space with all the fabric. There were a few petticoats folded along the sides.

When my fingers brushed the bottom, I was about to give up and choose a random outfit. Then, I felt a delicate lace.

I pulled out the item in confusion and let my fingers trace the garment. It appeared nearly finished—long, white lace with intricate flowers decorating the edges all the way down, then along the curved back. At the top was a comb to attach it to the hair.

"Shit."

The beautiful object could have been a rattlesnake with how fast I dropped it into the chest and bolted for the door.

A veil. That could only mean one thing. At least it did to me. What else did women wear white veils for? Weddings. Why did nineteenth-century women have a half-sewn one? To wear one in the near future.

Curses flew out of my mouth as I blindly rushed into the next room. It smelled of man sweat and dirt. It had to be Elliot's. In an ordered, chaotic kind of way, it was clean. The bed was haphazardly made, and random, roughly folded piles of slightly used clothing sat on different surfaces. The room contained only a chair, a bed, a chest against the wall, and a strange wooden device to help get boots on and off.

Not allowing myself time to marvel at the strange world I had walked into, I ran to the chest and dug through it. There was no point in secrecy, so I just yanked out the first shirt and pair of pants I came to.

I changed right there, pulling the shift off my body and replacing it with the shirt. It would have worked nicely as a nightgown, it was so large on me. For my rash escape, it didn't particularly matter.

A veil. A wedding.

I needed to get home, and I needed to get home *immediately*.

Pulling the pants on and tucking in the shirt, I hunted for something to help keep them on. Grabbing a rope lying on the floor by the boots, I tied it around my waist. I could imagine it would have been used as a belt anyway.

My stomach was fluffy enough to make me hide it from the world, but it certainly didn't help keep a taller man's pants on without help.

Rummaging through the shoes, I determined they certainly wouldn't work. Every single pair would cause more twisted ankles than if I went barefoot. Instead, I hurried back to my namesake's room. I grabbed the first pair I came to and yanked them on.

It should have been a difficult task. I imagined the leather pinching my toes painfully. Instead, it was as though they were made for my feet.

A coincidence.

Pushing the suspicious feeling away, I raced downstairs. The room was fuzzy, everything was spinning, but there wasn't time to waste worrying that either. I hadn't passed out yet, so I'd be fine. The coughing had returned with the quick movements, and that concerned me more.

Before I could concentrate too much on it, I bolted into the chilly spring air and looked around. To my dismay, everything looked just as real as it had the night before. No stage lights or painted backdrops.

The outhouse to the right of the house caught my attention. It was very obvious, sitting by itself with the moon shape cut into the front door.

My bladder throbbed at the idea, but I chose mind over matter. The final decision made, I ran in the direction I thought I had heard the river the night before.

All I needed to do was find the river and hop in, and the cold water would simply force me to wake up in a hospital bed back home. Anything except this.

I ran blindly, traversing the tall grass like it was a normal activity. There were patches of trees every once in a while, working hard at looking like an imposing forest. But they weren't nearly big enough. All the trees were thin, and everything underneath their protection was more dead and broken instead of green and thriving.

Though I tried to keep the pace, I couldn't run long. My chest burned within a few minutes, despite my best efforts to fight through the pain. The coughing caught up with me a short time later, my body exhausted, my head pounding. My heels had blisters from the shoes, despite how well they fit.

I slowed down, pounding on my chest to get the coughing to subside. Gunk came up with the more violent of coughs. When I let myself slip down to sit in the field, it graciously slowed.

I'd just rest for a minute.

Then I'd go home. I'd just jump into the water and be whisked away back to my own time—which would probably be a hospital bed.

I looked off to where I came from. The house sat in the distance, small and far from terrifying. It could have easily been a mile away. I almost wanted to go back, to curl up in that bed and take a full nap. At least I knew they would take care of me, keep me from ending up with pneumonia.

But all that I needed was to make it to the river. It couldn't be too far. It had to be nearby.

You almost drowned, you idiot, I scolded myself. *You can't go running blindly to find a river. Especially to drown yourself* again.

I groaned against my self-scolding. Of course I knew that running off was an idiotic move, but I didn't know what else to do. I wanted to go home. *Home,* home. Not just my apartment over a garage. I had surpassed that. I needed my momma.

But I knew that could never truly happen again. She was gone, and nothing could change that.

The coughs that tackled my body meant I couldn't finish any of the plan.

At some point, my body gave in and I fell asleep. To me, I simply blinked. However, when a cold nose nuzzled my face, I jerked back into reality.

There was no wondering where I was, or what was going on. As soon as consciousness took over my body, I knew. Stars littered the sky, no light around to interrupt them. It felt like we were living inside a fishbowl.

When my eyes found a tall, shadowed figure standing only a few feet away, I jumped. He was so silent, he was almost invisible.

The fluffy dog nuzzled my shoulder as I propped myself up on my elbows to debate on an escape route. The quiet man watched me, sending chills up my spine. He was likely only scary because I hadn't realized he was even there.

"Who are you?" he said, his voice melodic, an up-and-down cadence that reminded me of a lullaby. I could instantly place the accent. Native. What didn't fit was his outfit. He was dressed just like the men I'd seen in town: a worn suit coat, off-white button-up shirt, and dirty pants that might have once been cream. His hair was short, face shaved. He looked like a man trying on someone else's life. With a sinking feeling, I knew that was exactly what it was. Only a forced version.

Assimilation.

I made a gruff sound to try to clear my throat. It was sore and scratchy, and I wished for nothing more than a good cough syrup.

He scrunched his eyes up at me, only partially visible in the moonlight. "That doesn't sound good," he pointed out.

Without asking, he scooped me up and walked in the opposite direction of the house.

I weakly pushed at his shoulder. It didn't faze him one bit. "Where are you taking me?"

"My family," he said simply.

"I'm supposed to be back that way." I nodded in the general direction of the house.

He just made a noise of ascent but otherwise ignored me.

His horse stood on the other side of a tree, ready and waiting for his return. He hopped up easily and took off, the dog running happily along beside us.

My stomach swirled with nerves. It was dark. They would know I had disappeared. They would be worried.

I hadn't been sure what to expect, likely some stereotypical home. To my surprise, he brought me to a sod house near the river. He hopped off the horse and brought me straight inside.

A stop-and-go sort of language flowed from him easily as he set me in front of an old, iron stove. A withered, older lady stood beside it, stirring what I could only assume was their dinner. She responded in the same language, eyes glued to me.

With a flurry of words, she directed him to grab some things from a shelf on the dirt-and-grass wall. I watched, only partially paying attention. My chest seemed to grind with every breath I took. If anyone could fix that problem, I figured it would be them.

Her rapid words turned to me, a lecture that even I somewhat understood. It could be nothing short of scolding me for running off when my lungs weren't healed yet.

"Who are you?" I finally asked, as the lady placed some of the unidentified herbs into a pot.

"Johnathan," the boy said. "This is Rachel, my *ulisi*. My grandmother."

The lady placed a hot cup of whatever she had concocted in front of me. Startled at how fast she had made it, or at how much time had just slipped away from me in my shock, I stared at it.

"Drink," Rachel commanded, tapping the bottom of the mug. "Your cough will take over if you don't."

I obeyed, and the bitter, hot liquid nearly burned my insides. Despite the temperature, it felt good as it coated every inch of my throat.

"Is this the girl you've been sneaking off to see?" Rachel asked, turning to Johnathan.

His face turned a shade of red. "N-No!" He shook his head. "Not Elizabeth."

"This *isn't* Elizabeth," she said confidently.

I spat the mouthful of tea back into my mug. "What?"

"You're not Elizabeth," Rachel repeated.

"How do you know that?" I practically squeaked. Could it be a good thing they knew? Or would it put me in danger?

She tapped right beside her eye. "We pay attention. They do not."

I took another careful sip, not sure how to answer such a thing.

"Will you tell us who you are?" Johnathan asked.

I pinched the bridge of my nose. Hard. "Waiting to wake up from this coma."

Rachel nodded at the drink pointedly. "Don't stop drinking."

Obediently, I took another sip.

"It's all real, I can guarantee that," Johnathan said. "What's your name?"

A panicked laugh erupted from me. "Also Elizabeth Hersley. Believe it or not."

Rachel squinted her eyes again as she thought. "Where is Newton's child?"

I shrugged. "I don't know. Elliot found me yesterday."

Rachel grabbed bowls from another shelf and spooned dinner into three of them, each movement more choppy than the last.

Johnathan asked something in their language, and she answered right back. He stiffened.

"What?" I demanded.

"You shouldn't be here," Johnathan said simply.

"It sounded like you said a *lot* more than that," I muttered, downing the last of the tea. My throat already felt a bit better, but I was sure it would disappear as soon as the heat from the tea began to wear off. My stomach made an irritated gurgling noise. It didn't seem to appreciate anything new as much as my throat had.

Rachel pointed her chin in the direction of the door. Johnathan followed the quiet direction and opened it. A young man stood in the darkness, only a few inches shorter than the native boy. His hair glowed like fire in the light, his expression strained.

"Sam!" Rachel beamed, hurrying to his side. "Come, come eat! I have plenty!"

The young man staggered inside at her request, his eyes finding mine. Emotions floated across faster than I could keep track. Relief, confusion, irritation, then blank nothingness.

He was probably a few years older than me, but not by much. His jawline was on the softer side of things, with a shadow of light hair scattered around. Scraggly, not something a man back home would ever consider a "real" beard. Maybe just a five-o'clock shadow. The brown tones to his shoulder-length hair showed up more inside. A true auburn.

He said, "I can't stay—"

Johnathan mouthed the word *rude*, which effectively shut him up.

"Thank you," Sam amended.

Rachel pulled her final bowl from the shelf and spooned a generous helping of the stew inside. She handed it to Sam with a huge smile. "I haven't seen you in quite some time!"

"Yes, I moved to the Holmes ranch. They took me on and gave me a place to stay," Sam said, taking a slow bite. His eyes didn't stop flickering to me. Did he notice a difference too?

I took a bite of the stew, watching him right back. The moment it hit my stomach, everything changed. Apparently, adding food to the mix was the last thing it wanted. Leaving no time for me to prepare, my insides forced an evacuation. I pressed my shirt to my mouth in an idiotic attempt to stop it. I didn't want the cleanup. I didn't want such a sweet woman to be in charge of cleaning my own puke.

But using my shirt to catch it was probably the worst idea I could have had. The only plus had to be that I hadn't eaten in so long, it was mainly burning bile and tea.

Both the men flinched back, but Rachel had everything under control. She rushed to my side, going straight into cleanup mode.

I couldn't keep track of what she did as she tried to mop what she could from the front of my shirt.

"It will wash," she cooed, patting me on the shoulder and wiping a tear from my eye. "Don't worry."

Why hadn't I just let myself puke on the floor? But then, would it really have changed the embarrassment level?

"I really should get her home," Sam said.

I glanced at him, noting the dirt on his shirt, the rips forming on his pants. I'd never been the best at judging people, but he seemed somewhat okay.

"They are likely missing her," Rachel agreed, standing up and packing some of her tea mixture in a leather bag. She pressed it securely in the palm of my hand. "Take this every morning and evening. It will help keep the cough out of your chest."

I nodded and tucked it into my pocket. Sam helped me to my feet, carefully avoiding the mess I had created of my front.

I took two shaky steps toward the front door and stopped. "Can you help me get home?"

Rachel's face fell. She shook her head slowly. "No, something happened. You can't go back."

Sam's eyebrows rose in surprise. "We need to go. Your father has search parties combing just about everywhere. You can't be found here."

I looked from Rachel to him, confused for only a brief moment. I understood the search parties, but the reason why I couldn't go home, not so much.

"Why can't I go back?"

Rachel said nothing, whether from not knowing herself, or from not wanting to answer, I couldn't be sure.

"We need to go." Sam pulled on my arm.

"Go home," Rachel agreed.

"But it's not—"

"It is," she said, setting her hand on my shoulder. "They need you there."

CHAPTER FIVE

S am quietly led me to his horse, his eyes on my every move. Almost as soon as he had me on the front of his horse, he spoke.

"What happened to you?"

I slumped on the horse, creating some kind of horrible posture that certainly wouldn't have been possible with a corset on. "I don't know." I barely managed the words. My stomach swirled and dispensed of whatever was left on the ground beneath us.

Sam jerked his foot out of the way, only barely making it. With the awkwardness of someone who didn't know how to act around a less-than-perfect female, he patted my back. "Did he hurt your head?"

"What?" I managed to ask. "Who?"

"How did you hurt your head?"

"I don't know," I repeated.

Sam sighed and patted my back. "You'll be home soon," he promised.

My body tipped precariously to the side. He pulled me closer to him, letting my head rest against his chest. "Just don't get sick on me."

I barely nodded, gritting my teeth against another swirl. "I don't think there's anything left."

I could hear the river meandering along. I'd nearly made it. It flowed so closely to Johnathan's house, I could have simply walked outside and been home again.

"Do you think you could do me a favor?" I asked, noting how my voice came out like that of an eighty-year-old smoker. My throat needed some more of the magic tea.

"Well, of course." Sam sounded shocked I would even need to ask. "What is it?"

I curled my toes under, as though it would force the courage to ask something so ridiculous. "Could you take me to the river?"

He exploded into a laugh, spittle flying in all directions.

"You want to go *where?*"

"The river?" I wiped some of the spit off the back of my neck with my wrist. I had thrown up all over myself in front of him, so the bit of accidental slobber couldn't come close to the same level of revulsion.

"Sorry," he said, placing his hands on my arms and pushing me to a more stable position in front of him. "I'm charged with taking you home right now. Taking you right back to where I assume you nearly drowned would only get me strung up."

"They don't even know you found me yet," I protested. My eyes felt as though someone had placed tiny weights on each of my eyelashes. No matter how hard I tried to keep them open, they only wanted to flutter closed again.

"They don't. But they will soon enough. Look." He nudged my shoulder and pointed off to the side. Two lantern lights flickered in the distance. Sam held up his own lantern to signal, and the lights started our way.

"Maybe I don't—" A yawn interrupted my complaint. "Maybe I don't want to go back."

Sam shook his head, his loose hair hitting the sides of my head. "Because your life is that horrible . . ." he said sarcastically.

"You know nothing about me," I shot back. I meant for it to come out harsh and ready for a fight, but the exhaustion had other plans.

He snorted but otherwise didn't respond. The others were too close.

Newton came into view first, the instant relief looking as though it would knock him out of the saddle before he made it to us. The other man I hadn't met yet. Large with a graying beard and sharp features. He looked around the same age as Newton, but much larger. And louder.

"What's she doing all the way over here?" he asked, looking past us in the direction of the sod house.

Newton held up a hand. "If there's anywhere I know she'd be safe, it would be there. If anyone could get rid of a cough, it would be that Rachel."

"All that savage mumbo jumbo." He scoffed. "For all ya know, they're the one who took her in the first place. Make a nice little gift for their family back east, now, wouldn't she?"

Sam stiffened, and his hands that had held me securely in place tightened just enough to make it impossible to ignore.

"I can go ahead and take her." Newton moved his horse directly beside Sam's and reached in my general direction.

"She got into a bit of a mess," Sam warned.

"I see that." Newton hooked his hands under my shoulder and helped pull me over to his horse. It occurred to me that I could struggle, but the exhausted fog decided I might as well wait until I had energy again.

"Good Lord!" the man said, shaking his head in disgust when he got a good view of me. "That girl'd better get her act together quick, Newton. There's only so much acting out that I'll allow!"

Newton froze for only the slightest of moments. "She will," he promised.

I scowled inwardly at the idea. *I'll be my own damn person, thank you very much,* I thought.

"Thank you, Samuel. I'll get her home from here. If you can go tell Elliot's team we found her on your way home?"

Sam nodded. "I'll send him your way. Rachel did send home some tea with her. Think she put it in her pocket."

With no other real choice, I gave in and let my eyes flutter closed and my head lean against Newton's chest. At least I knew I would be safe with him.

As long as he thought I was his missing daughter.

Newton shook me gently to bring me back to a fully awake state when we reached the house. He swung off the horse and pulled me down beside him. I felt like a child, holding on to his arm to stay upright.

The strange man was talking. "What are you going to do with her after she ran off like that? We can't have her—"

"Levi." Newton let out a sharp breath and turned to face him. "For now, we don't know what happened. I'm not planning on punishing her when something else entirely could be going on."

"Well, you know if she doesn't go through with it, I'll be forced—"

"That is not what's going on. Thank you for your help. I'll be taking her inside before she catches her death." Newton tipped his hat, wrapped the reins around the hitching post, and led me toward the house.

My stomach lurched with every step he took. I had certainly pushed myself much farther than I ever should have. We had only made it to the front steps when I had to drop to my knees and introduce the dry ground to a new kind of fertilizer.

Newton patted my back until he was certain I was finished. Only then did he scoop me up and carry me up to my room.

It astounded me how easily they all carried me around. I wasn't a size-zero human by any means. My curves came with weight. Even so, they acted like it was the easiest thing they ever had to do.

Before Newton could set me on the bed, Elliot rushed in. "Thank God!" He practically skidded to a halt when he saw my state.

"Good, you're here," Newton said. "Help get her cleaned up."

"But . . ." Elliot looked like he wanted to argue, but the sharp look from Newton took the fight right out of him. "I'll go get some water."

Newton helped me to the bed and kissed my forehead. "Where's that tea she gave you?"

I pulled it out of my pocket and placed the bundle in his hands.

"Do you think you could hold any of it down?"

My stomach made an irritated noise in response.

"Food?"

I shook my head.

Newton sighed. "I'll make you a sandwich. If you feel you can eat any of it, please do. Just go slow." He patted my leg and disappeared down the stairs.

Before my head could hit the pillow, Elliot returned with his bucket of water. "Get changed and give me my clothes back before you fall asleep." No longer was he full of gratitude that I was alive and well. The bitterness in his voice was unmistakable.

I groaned and forced myself back to sitting. "Shouldn't you be more worried?" I mumbled.

"Shouldn't you have stayed home?" he shot back. "Now, give me back my clothes. That was a good shirt."

I narrowed my eyes at him and yanked on the rope around my waist. As if by magic, the hostility disappeared, only to be replaced by a sort of panic. He whirled to face the wall, hands fidgeting behind his back.

The state of the borrowed clothing made me gag. If this Elizabeth had a good reputation, I certainly put a good-size ding in it. Being rescued by men while covered in vomit couldn't be a positive.

My fingers fumbled with every button. I had to lean against the wall a few times to get more stability. After an eternity, I finally managed to squirm out of everything except my underwear. They weren't in the best shape either.

I cursed under my breath, getting a gruff clearing of Elliot's throat in response. As I stuffed my undergarments beneath the dirty pants, I stuck my tongue out in his general direction.

"Why do you have to stay in here, anyway?" I demanded, grabbing a rag and running it over my body. It surprised me how good the cool water felt. Thankfully, he didn't move a muscle in my direction.

"How many times have you fainted?"

I glared at his back. "Fine. But if you have to rescue me like the hero you think you are, put a blanket over me first."

His chuckle fell short. "Why," he began, "on God's green earth would you run off like that?" The underlying growl of anger had returned to his voice, but only slightly.

I didn't respond. What was I supposed to say? That I wanted to go potentially drown myself with a bad cold and go back to the twenty-first century? An insane asylum would be the only thing that got me.

He threw his hands up in the air. "I didn't ask just to be speaking to a wall! Or did you faint on me again?"

I spoke up. "I'm just tired."

He scoffed. "I would imagine so! Have you even eaten today?"

"No," I muttered.

"Hmph." He left without another word, leaving me in shock on the bed with a dirty rag.

I stared at the closed door for a long moment before taking advantage of his absence. I pulled the clean nightgown over my head and yanked it all the way to my knees. I was clean enough.

He knocked before entering at least. He held a sandwich and a glass of water, more than likely the items Newton had been planning to bring up. He set them down on the nightstand.

"Take a bite," he commanded.

Reluctantly, I did as he asked.

My hunger surprised me. The bread nearly melted on my tongue. I stuffed the rest of it in my mouth, my empty stomach grasping at each bite as soon as it landed. I hadn't eaten in such a long time. It probably had something to do with why I had puked, and likely why I'd been so dizzy. Though with all the coughing, a fever was certainly a potential culprit.

"Good," Elliot said when my hands were completely empty. "Pa's too gentle with you to ensure you'd actually eat it. But he'll want to talk to you in the morning, I'm sure." He grumbled something else under his breath as he scooped up his clothes and the bucket of dirty water.

He didn't shut the door completely behind him, most likely so they could hear if I did something stupid.

When his footsteps went silent, the bittersweet smell of pipe tobacco floated up through the floorboards and into the room. As much as I despised smoking, the smell was somehow comforting. I took a single sip of the water, then curled up under the blankets, my body completely giving up to sleep yet again.

CHAPTER SIX

I woke up feeling much better than the night before. Only starving. Downing the rest of the water beside my bed, I carefully got to my feet. No sign of dizziness. Whether that was because I had slept and it simply hadn't crept back up on me yet, or because I actually was getting better, I didn't know. The coughing, of course, hadn't left completely. Instead, it had changed to a persistent tickle I couldn't quite get rid of. Annoying, and would likely get bad again later, but tolerable for the moment.

I wrapped the quilt around my shoulders as a makeshift robe and headed downstairs in search of food.

I could smell each individual part of breakfast. Bacon. Potatoes. Eggs. My stomach growled and nearly dragged me down the stairs on its own.

Newton was there, fully dressed and already a tad bit grubby. He had a spatula in his hand as he tended to the bacon on the stove.

"Wasn't sure if this would rouse you or not," he said without turning around.

"Bacon would wake anyone up," I said, sitting down at the table. I was surprised that he hadn't asked how I was feeling, or posed any questions about the night before. Maybe he had just determined that since I was down there, I was okay. I silently prayed he would let the situation drop.

"Mhm." He threw the bacon on a plate and brought it to the table along with the eggs and potatoes. "Go ring the bell for your brother." When I hesitated, he glanced up suspiciously. "On the *porch*. Go ring the bell."

I got up to go find the dinner bell, unsure if I was going to find one of the beautiful cast-iron ones, or one of the triangles. I was greeted with an iron triangle hanging from the edge of the porch. It had the matching stick hanging from it.

I tapped the edges, but the noise didn't carry. Maybe I hadn't hit it hard enough? I did it again, the stick hitting hard enough it hurt my fingers.

"What in tarnation . . ." Newton pushed past and took the stick from me. He ran it rapidly around the inside. The sound rang out just as it did in the movies—loud and clear.

"Oh," I said, feeling a bit idiotic.

Newton placed his hand on my forehead and shook his head in disapproval before leaving me on the porch again.

Carefully, I picked up the stick and copied him. Elliot hadn't appeared, so perhaps he hadn't heard it? Besides, I wanted to try. The satisfying sound rang throughout the yard, bringing the shape of Elliot into the doorway of the makeshift sod barn.

"Impatient, are you?" he asked, as he stepped onto the porch, pulling his boots off with ease at the front door.

"Maybe, just a bit hungry." My stomach growled for emphasis.

"Better get to eating before Pa gets a hold of you," he muttered under his breath as we went back inside.

"What's that supposed to mean?" A queasy kind of worry seeped in to replace the hunger pangs.

"Chickens are done, and the livestock is fed. Just need to milk Girdy," Elliot announced instead of answering me.

"Good," Newton said, as we all sat down. "Elliot, will you say grace?"

I already had a hand raised to grab some bacon when he said that. Reluctantly, I placed it back in my lap. I could be patient.

Sam's prayer was short and sweet. Surely he was half-starved as well. Especially after working in the barn for who knew how long.

As soon as he said the final words, though, I grabbed at the food. I spent more time shoving food into my mouth than even considering chatting with them. They definitely needed to learn how to season their food better—everything tasted bland. The potatoes had a strange metallic aftertaste, probably from being burned, and the eggs were oversalted. I didn't care—I couldn't shovel it into my mouth fast enough.

I only halfway listened to them. They discussed what fence lines needed checked, the state of the hay, and the hole by the chicken coop. It was only when I heard the name Rose that I decided to participate.

"What'd you say?"

Elliot glanced at Newton, apprehension written all over his face. "Rose . . ." he began, refusing to meet my eyes.

"You found her?"

Newton cleared his throat. "What exactly happened to the two of you?"

"That says nothing about my horse." I crossed my arms stubbornly. It had to be a horse. What else could it be? My heartbeat pounded with apprehension.

The men exchanged looks, staying completely silent for so long, I thought I would have to strangle one of them to get the information.

"The Holmes found her. Last night." There was a note of dismissal in Elliot's voice, as if he wished the topic would just go away.

"What's wrong with her?" I demanded.

"Her leg was broken, Elizabeth. Richard already took care of it." Newton's voice left no room for argument. I knew full well what he meant.

Even though I had never met the horse, my stomach sank. What had happened to both her and their Elizabeth? My heart felt like it would break at the very idea. The girl deserved to be hunted for, not simply replaced.

When both sets of eyes furrowed, I realized they expected some kind of response. "Oh . . ." I said, gnawing on the inside of my cheek as I tried to figure out what to say.

It wasn't an acceptable reaction to finding out that my horse had been shot. But I couldn't figure out anything better. At least nothing that would sound sincere.

"Are you going to tell us what happened?" Newton demanded.

When I didn't say anything, Elliot joined in. "I don't know if she fully *knows* what happened."

"Well, I'm sure as all get out that she's aware of *who* had to do with it all, where they ended up, or why she disappeared for more than a day and a night!"

My mind swirled, desperately grasping for anything that might be an acceptable answer. "I went and camped out by the river," I finally said, shoving the last piece of bacon in my mouth and standing up. "Does that help?" I didn't wait for a response. The fear of being asked more questions scared me more than being rude. I put my plate on the counter, then hurried for the stairs.

"Elizabeth." Newton spoke my name with such finality it sent shivers up my spine. I stopped dead in my tracks.

"Go get dressed. Then we'll talk." He placed his dish on top of mine, then headed outside.

Elliot picked up the speed of his own eating but kept an eye on me with every step I took toward the stairs. "One day you're going to have to tell us what happened." His brows drew together as he spoke.

I sighed. "You're going to be waiting quite a long while."

I set myself to the chore of finding clothes. Anything to keep the panic from overflowing. Corporal punishment was still a thing. I had no intention of experimenting with *that*.

I dug through the chest, choosing a lightly flowered, well-worn dress, an underskirt, and then one of the more worn corsets. I certainly didn't want to wear the girl's "Sunday best" by accident.

The skirts were easy, but the corset was bound to be a learning curve. I wrapped it around my body, expecting to let out the laces before I could put the hooks together. To my surprise, they snapped easily. I didn't have to pull a single lace. Somehow, it was more comfortable than I imagined. Like it was made for me. Snug, sure, but extremely supportive. The sort that made every inch of my spine feel as though it was exactly where it was supposed to be.

I decided to like the corset only until I bent down again to grab the dress. *That* wasn't comfortable. I simply ended up with the bottom of it hitting into my hip bones and lower stomach.

The skirts fit easily, tying on the sides. Or back. I wasn't sure which direction they went. The dress fit perfectly over the corset, finishing the look with ease.

Everything fit.

I stared at myself in the mirror, completely transformed into a nineteenth-century woman. The brown hair that cascaded down my shoulders to land right above the top line of my corset somewhat distorted the put-together look, but otherwise everything matched the way it needed to. I went through the top drawer of the dresser and found the gorgeous, decorated hairbrush, a few surprisingly simple combs, and ribbons right on top. There was what I assumed was acceptable makeup beside it, but I didn't touch it. I highly doubted winged eyeliner would go over very well with the others.

My hair had tangled badly, meaning I had to brush it slowly. Partially because I was afraid of breaking the brush and comb. They both looked like something out of an antique store, hand carved and elegant. They felt sturdy, but I was still terrified.

There were delicate carvings on the back of the brush. A few flowers around the edges and spirals leading to the bottom. It belonged in a museum.

It did its job, spreading the oils and making it look like my hair could manage just another day without a wash. I braided it down my back and tied it with a light blue ribbon.

If I was going to be stuck for a while, I would have to study the other women to figure out how to do my hair. I really missed the internet.

About to close the drawer, a white, circular container caught my eye. Toothpaste.

I let out a relieved breath. "Thank God."

I pried it open, licked my finger, then dipped it inside the abrasive powder to taste.

It was far from minty. It reminded me of how the air tasted whenever a teacher would bang two chalkboard erasers together. Chalk. Pure chalk. I grimaced.

If I was going to be stuck for a while, I couldn't do so with slimy teeth. I scooped up the small, wooden brush beside the poor excuse for toothpaste. It had residue of the powder in the bristles, which meant it could only be one thing: the toothbrush.

Resigned to my fate, I scrunched my eyes shut and went to work, praying I didn't get some sort of horrific sickness from this doppelgänger. The urge to vomit rose in my stomach. I jogged in place, hoping it would keep my brain distracted from the threat of disease. When I was sure my teeth couldn't stand any more abuse, I grabbed the pitcher of water and practically dumped it into my mouth.

I'd never complain about modern toothpaste again.

Anxiety peaked as I stood in the doorway. I doubted Newton would have left before talking to me about why I ran off. It only made sense.

I glanced back at the chest and felt a smug smile creep onto my face.

I would be the top dog of that argument.

I grabbed the veil and ran downstairs.

"Thank you for joining us," Newton said, as I appeared.

My smile disappeared instantly. "Pleasure," I muttered, glancing at both of them. They sat there, arms folded on the table like soldiers planning an invasion. Together. Ready for the interrogation.

I took a shaky breath, then made eye contact. Newton met it without the slightest bit of fear. He was prepared for me.

Or so he thought.

Breaking eye contact for the brief moment it took to sit down across from them was all it took for fear to creep up my spine. They could pretty much do anything to me. Legally. Nervously, I bit my lip.

Newton began, "You're not leaving this table—"

It was now or never. Before I lost every ounce of bravery that remained, I practically threw the veil onto the table. My hand hit the wood so hard, it sent a bang throughout the room and just a tiny bit of pain through my wrist. I ignored it. The action did exactly what I wanted: shut them up.

"Who?" I whispered, staring at my fingers under the delicate lace.

Elliot cleared his throat, shifting in his seat as the uncomfortable feeling encroached upon the room.

Newton accepted the challenge. "Lukas Barnette. His family owns the ranch that backs up to the river."

"When?" I ran my index finger over one of the flowers on the bottom.

"In a month. April fifteenth."

My fingers formed a fist so tight I felt the delicate flowers from the veil leave their mark on my skin. It was silent for a moment while I tried to calm my racing heart. If I let myself think about it, I would hyperventilate.

I fought to keep my voice steady, though I squirmed under their gaze. "N-No."

Newton sighed. "Elizabeth, listen. You can't be unreasonable about this. You've had a head injury—"

"No," I snapped. "A head injury is enough of a reason to call it off. Or at least postpone it! I'm not going."

"Elizabeth . . . you said yes. We can't call it off just because of your accident. Give yourself a few days to heal, and I'm sure you'll remember everything."

"No," I nearly growled, my heart pounding in my ears as I lost complete control. "If I manage to remember who he is, sure. But as of now, I don't know if his hair is purple. Or even if he's human! I don't fully know who either of you are, I don't know where I am, I don't know how I got here. As far as I know, I'm on the moon!" By the time I had finished my miniature tangent, I was yelling with both hands planted on the table. I glared from one man to the other.

"Sit down!" Newton's tone rang full of a final warning. He didn't have to be my actual father to make my body obey instantly. He sat straighter, shoulders and jaw clenched with all the pent-up tension. "You listen, and you listen closely. You have time to heal. You have time to remember everything. You're twenty-four. You can't afford to wait any longer! You have time to finish that veil and get married like the respectable—"

"*No.*" I stayed seated but leaned in his general direction, feeling the anger travel through my body like fire.

Elliot stood up quietly and made his way for the door.

Newton's head snapped in his direction like a viper. "Where do you think you're going?"

Elliot stopped but didn't turn back to us. "I'm going to be in the barn, getting ready to check the cattle. I'd rather not be here to help tan her hide."

I flinched, my mind rapidly backtracking. I had to figure out how to climb out of that potential mess.

"We'll leave shortly," Newton said, turning back to me.

Elliot left me alone then, closing the door with a purposeful softness. I felt numb from my toes to my head. Just like that, the fight was done.

"We'll discuss your marriage to Lukas later. When you can talk about it like a *lady*. In the meantime, I want you to think very carefully about what you actually want to know. If you can't keep calm, Elliot is right. That"—he nodded in the direction of a dark leather strap hanging on the wall—"will meet with you."

I glared at him, fighting every urge I had to yell. Fingernails pressed firmly into my palms, I forced myself to speak calmly. "I already know what I want to ask."

"All right." He sat down, folding his arms back in front of himself on the table. "Go ahead."

"Where am I? Other than home." I didn't dare look at his face. The scraggly gray beard didn't do anything to soften the hard, angry expression underneath.

"Woodward."

"In?" I held my breath, anticipating the answer.

"Oklahoma Territory."

I visibly flinched as the numbing chills soared down my arms to escape off my fingertips. Territory. Oklahoma didn't become a state until 1907. We were some time before that.

I took a long moment to steady myself. "When did we move here?"

"A year ago." The strain in his voice was becoming obvious as the anger trickled away.

"Land run?"

"Yes."

"Okay, thank you," I said, trying to make it sound like I meant it. It didn't completely answer my real question, but I couldn't exactly ask what year it was. At least I didn't think so. The first land run in Oklahoma was 1889. Every student in the state knew that. Those before were known as Sooners. In this part of Oklahoma, they had their run in 1893.

I wanted to puke.

CHAPTER SEVEN

After the men left, I didn't do much. Everything was still numb from the interrogation.

It was 1890-something.

That other Elizabeth was to be married in a month.

An uncomfortable gurgle in the depths of my stomach interrupted my thoughts.

It was time.

I strode outside to the ominous wooden structure with the telltale half-moon cut into the door.

The outhouse.

It was just far enough from the house to make the trek annoying. I couldn't decide what I missed the most from back home: the plumbing, allergy medication, or air-conditioning. In my garage apartment, I could practically sleepwalk to the bathroom. Easy.

The chamberpot in the cabin was simple enough to use. The day before, I had held it for as long as I could possibly manage before I gave in and pulled it from under the bed. But some jobs don't belong in heavily decorated ceramic pots.

"Here goes nothing," I whispered. I pulled up the wooden latch and . . . The door caught on a loose board. I danced in place like an anxious chicken while I finagled it open, the gurgle in my stomach growing louder by the second. The last thing I wanted to do would be to break the door in my haste. But I had already waited too long.

The outhouses in the museums I'd been to growing up looked like they were glorified splinter traps. I always imagined someone using them and coming back with permanent slivers in their thighs and rear.

Or worse.

The seat area in this little privy was well sanded and worn from heaven knew how many butts. Honestly, it was somewhat comfortable. For a gaping wooden hole.

The toilet paper, on the other hand, was not. It was a farmer's almanac, hung through a hole in the center on a rusty nail.

Groaning, I ripped a sheet off. It got the job done, but I'd dread our next meeting. On the bright side, it was much better than the corncobs I'd read about.

Though the space was dark and rather warm, they tried to keep it comfortable. There wasn't a sign of a single spider or any other unsavory bug. Someone—the other "me" I assumed—had even hung a scrap of fabric on the wall with a cabin embroidered in the center. The words WELCOME HOME were scrawled around the delicate building in little x's of mahogany thread.

I touched the ragged edge and sighed, torn between hoping that she was okay and hoping that she wouldn't pop up before I could get back to my own time.

"This is your life, not mine," I whispered. I could never even imagine doing such intricate work with a needle and thread.

The earlier anxiety rose to form a lump in my throat. I dropped the almanac page into the depths with a sickening plop and scurried into the fresh air.

The next meeting with the outhouse, though inevitable, would come far too soon.

To avoid panic, I worked on washing the dishes with water Elliot had brought in that morning. Household chores were the requirement of a woman in that era, after all. There wasn't much of a chance of them letting all the chores slide for very long. Dishes were simple enough without a machine.

I'd likely have to figure out dinner later, which sounded next to impossible.

Satisfied with my work, I carried the water back outside and dumped it beside the porch. It had sat there before Elliot brought it in, so that was where I left it.

Beside the barn, a milk cow roamed in a large fenced-in area along with an elderly bay horse. I headed that way, ready for my animal fix. I leaned against the rail and reached my hand out to the mare.

"Here, girl," I called. She looked at me skeptically. "Do you think I'm her too?"

She made a sort of noise that was so similar to a scoff, it startled me. Apparently, she either didn't like me, or she was smarter than they were.

"Come say hi anyway?" I wiggled my fingers at her. "Come on." I reached out farther, wishing she would come closer. Just so I could touch that velvety nose. I didn't know much about horses, but I knew they practically had magical powers. If anyone would take pity on my situation and make me feel less lost, it would be a horse.

"She's mad at you," the light voice said from behind me. I nearly jumped out of my skin as I whirled around to face this person. Young, but still a few years older than me. Likely upper twenties. Blond, well-trimmed hair, green eyes, and some second-day beard stubble doing its best to make a statement on his hard jaw. He was tall, right on the edge of being lanky, but with enough muscles to counteract it. I imagined he would have belonged on the high school football team.

"Why?" I demanded, keeping my back pressed against the fence, ready to bolt at the very moment I needed to. Some animal instinct told me to be careful, to keep an eye out for this stranger.

"Because she spent an entire day hunting for you."

I glanced back at the old horse, feeling a bit bad. I didn't think she was one that was meant to be rode hard in search of a missing daughter.

"Do you know what happened?" I asked, weighing the risks. He'd either think me insane, or already know I couldn't remember anything.

He stayed silent for a moment and studied me with suspicious eyes. "They told me you had memory loss, but I had hoped they were exaggerating."

I crossed my arms and glared at him. "No. I have no idea who you are. I'm assuming Lukas. But for all I know, you're my long-lost uncle."

He held up his hands halfway and took an exaggerated step back. "Calm down, my dear," he said. "Don't gotta be so defensive. I'm Luke."

"Good." I didn't relax. I just continued looking him up and down. I was to marry this man. Or rather, she was. "I'm not marrying you," I said suddenly, making yet another mental note about thinking my words through *before* they came spilling off my tongue.

His surprise wasn't as extreme as I had expected. "Why not?" he asked calmly. Almost hesitantly, but I could have imagined that.

"Because. I need some answers."

"You need your memory back first?" He took a few steps toward me, and I held up a hand to make him stop.

"Sure," I snapped. "I don't know you. I don't know anyone here. Whether you believe me or not. Don't come close to me."

His hand absently moved to rub a spot on his upper arm. He cleared his throat before he spoke again. "Are you sure you don't remember anything?"

"Positive," I said. "You get to date . . . er . . . court me all over again." I studied his every move as he stopped massaging his arm, almost as if he realized I was watching.

He let his hand fall to his side and eyed me levelly. He was practically probing my brain with that look. "Just wait to call it off completely. The entire town is looking forward to it. You might change your mind."

"Might," I said. I needed to find this doppelgänger of mine. Soon. For her lover's sake. For *my* sake.

"Are you at least feeling any better than before? Is *anything* coming back to you?" he asked.

I set my jaw and narrowed my eyes. "Like I told you, I don't remember anything."

"I see . . ." he said. The staring contest continued. More and more awkward with each passing second. It was only interrupted by a rider coming down the drive.

We both turned to see who it was.

It wasn't any of my people. Unfortunately. Luke gave me a strange feeling in the pit of my stomach that I certainly didn't like. Perhaps it was just the fact he was my "betrothed." Or maybe it was my senses telling me something I couldn't fully grasp.

Though I didn't really know Elliot and Newton, I trusted them enough to keep me safe. They were kind to me. Or at least tried to be. I wished it was them, coming to save me from the increasingly awkward encounter with this man.

Recognition sparked for me when the sunlight hit his red, shaggy hair. Sam. A smile played at the edges of my lips. I trusted him at least.

He didn't stop until he was right near us, his brows furrowed with suspicion as he got close enough to see. He could probably feel the tension flowing through the air.

"Fighting again?" he asked. I expected one of them to laugh or smirk, but they both remained stone-cold. Expressionless.

As he dismounted and tied his horse to the fence, I noticed he was a lot shorter than Luke, who was most definitely at least six feet. The two of them together reminded me so much of a buff football player and a grown version of the boy that he would shove into the lockers.

"None of your business, Sam." Luke spat his name.

"Well, I think it is," he said, purposely stepping between Luke and me. Both of their bodies were completely stiff. "After all, we don't know what happened to her the other night. Last person who saw her was *you*."

Luke bristled. "What'd you say?" He took a step toward Sam. "Just like I told everyone who asked, I will tell you. I dropped her right off at the property line. She knows the way. Anything happened after that was her doing. Not mine."

I narrowed my eyes in his direction, and he caught my gaze. A sprig of panic flittered through the contact. Though, I could have been imagining it. Maybe I was just grasping for any detail I could.

"Such a gentleman." Sam rolled his eyes. "I have to talk to her. Get out of here."

"We're engaged to marry. As you well know. I can stay and talk as long as I want." He shoved Sam out of the way and cleared the distance between us, ending his pursuit only a few inches from me.

I backed up the half step until my back hit the fence. "Get closer, and I will kick you."

Luke threw his hands up in the air. "The queen has spoken then! I'll be back tomorrow to check on you." And he walked off in the direction that I assumed was his home.

Sam rushed toward me as soon as Luke was out of earshot. "Are you okay?" His face was scrunched with worry as he looked me up and down. "Did he touch you? What happened? You can tell me. I'll take care of it."

I let him get close. I couldn't describe it to myself. Why did Sam feel so safe, but Luke like a cougar on the prowl? The way he stood was less looming, more of a warrior ready to protect instead of someone ready to pummel another.

I shook my head to dislodge the mixed-up thoughts. "I'm fine. He didn't touch me."

"The other night," Sam clarified. "If he did anything to you, I'll kill him. You know that."

I stared at him, wishing I knew who this man was to the other Elizabeth. The worry was real on his face. Similar to that of Newton's, but more frantic.

"No," I said. "I mean, I don't know. I don't remember anything."

He drew back a bit with the shock. "Nothing?" He put a hand over his eyes for a moment and sighed. "So, what they were saying in town was true."

I shrugged. "I guess so?"

"People? Do you remember people?"

A sigh escaped my lips. "No. No one. Nothing. I remember—" I cut myself off. Why on earth did I want to keep talking about it to him? *No, Ellie. No.*

"You remember?" he prodded, moving to lean against the fence beside me. He was mindful of my discomfort, leaving a few feet between us.

"Nothing. I remember nothing."

"Hmm," he said, unbelieving. "You can tell me, you know."

I nodded dismissively. "Why did you come?"

"To check on you. I was on my way into town when I saw your brother working with some of the wandering cattle. I figured I'd check and make sure *Lukas* hadn't shown his face." He stared straight ahead, teeth grinding as though the very idea of my betrothed made him consider murder.

"What is your big problem with him, anyway?" I watched his face closely for any change in expression. There wasn't one.

His lips formed a straight line as he considered what he wanted to share. "There were just some rumors on his treatment and . . . intentions." He rapidly shook his head to dislodge whatever he was talking about before they ate away at his mood.

That info. I needed *that*. I turned to face him completely and crossed my arms. "What do you mean?"

He sighed. "I just mean, you're a girl. Er . . . woman now." He stared at his boot as he dug a hole with his toe. "There is a shortage, I guess you can say."

I took a slow breath, reminding myself that it wasn't an insult to be in demand. I turned away from him to watch the lone horse mimicking Sam's nervous digging.

"Ellie." He hesitated, gnawing on the inside of his cheek.

Ice shot up my back.

My nickname.

I swallowed hard to try to force myself to make an acceptable noise in response. "Hmm?" I didn't turn around. I was sure the encroaching panic was written all over my face.

"What do you remember?" he demanded.

"I don't remember anything that everyone thinks I should," I just said.

"What does that mean?" He pulled himself up to sit on the edge of the fence. He had gradually moved close enough so his leg touched my forearm. "I can't help you if you don't tell me."

I wrenched my eyes shut against the tears that threatened to spill over, sprung to action by that name. It wasn't a common nickname to go with Elizabeth. Lizzie or Beth, sure. Ellie? I'd never met another one.

Before the logical part of my brain trying to keep me in check could chime in, I decided to trust this Sam.

"I remember everything," I admitted. "But not any of this." I turned my head slowly until my eyes met his, hoping the pleading showed through. He needed to understand I didn't have the answers he really wanted.

"Well . . ." he said slowly, taking a big breath and looking up at the clouds as though they held all the answers. "What is your version of everything?"

I opened my mouth to tell him when I heard more horses coming toward us. I whirled, my heart racing. Maybe my betrothed had come back. Heaven forbid.

It was just Elliot and Newton.

Sam leaned in to whisper in my ear, "Do you remember them?"

"Now. But only because they told me who they were. My brother died a year ago. My parents died before him."

The pure confusion that hit Sam was tangible. I glanced back at him to make sure he hadn't given up all hope on me. His eyebrows furrowed, then relaxed, then furrowed yet again.

"I know it doesn't make sense," I whispered.

"You owe me an explanation later," he said back, hopping off the fence to go greet the men. "Mr. Hersley!" A smile spread across his face as he shook hands with Newton, then Elliot. "Beautiful day today! How's everything with you?"

"Ah, all good here! Just grateful we have Elizabeth back safely."

The nearly rehearsed niceties were almost sickening. They continued on, asking how Sam's position at the Holmes ranch was, getting a few basic answers before Sam began to say his goodbyes. He reached out and squeezed my hand. "Meet me at the tree." He said it so only I could hear.

"Where?"

He gave me a one-armed hug. "Go south from here. Straight. You'll know it. Eleven."

I nodded, trying to figure out how I'd escape without anyone hearing. Why was I even considering meeting with him? I was in a relatively safe position with Elliot and Newton—why go and mess it up by meeting with some pre-statehood man?

"Thank you for stopping by, Samuel." Newton stepped forward, the fatherly protective streak in full force. He nearly stepped between us. He gave me a disapproving look down his nose, then gave a similar one to Sam. "Tell the Holmes family hello for us."

"I will. I'm glad you're back safely, Elizabeth!" Sam waved at us before hopping on his horse and heading back down the road without a single glance back.

Newton didn't wait long to start in on me. "Elizabeth." His voice sent shivers up my spine. "You know better than that. Unchaperoned. Not just that, you're betrothed. Accident or not, you can't play around like some silly schoolgirl."

I let my eyes flutter shut in order to keep calm and avoid telling him what-for. "Both he and Luke came by to check on me. That's all." I clenched my fist, my nails threatening to break the skin. The goal was that the pain would keep me from speaking my mind. "You don't have to worry. He was just glad I was okay."

Elliot swooped in to save me. "Feelings run high after something like that. I'm sure Sam didn't mean to overstep."

"Hmm," Newton said, before completely changing the subject. "Is there supper?"

It took me a good minute to figure out he meant lunch. I *knew* I hadn't been standing outside *that* long.

"Oh. Uh . . ." I turned back to the cabin, shoulders sagging. "I didn't get to that?"

Elliot handed his father the reins as he hopped to the ground. "I'll help her. Visitors always make things more difficult."

CHAPTER EIGHT

The nerves overtook me as soon as Elliot's door shut behind him. They'd been up for what seemed like forever, talking about one thing or another. I had taken a nap while they were gone for the afternoon, but it certainly wasn't holding up to a late-night meeting.

Why did I even plan on going? What would even happen if I told Sam the truth? I was some twenty-first-century girl who was used to wearing shorts and T-shirts and had been considering getting bangs. Oh, and I might have died in a car accident.

It likely wouldn't matter. He probably wouldn't believe me anyway. Especially if I started telling him I wasn't the Ellie he wanted to be talking to.

I needed to find out what happened to her. Before I somehow got stuck in her life forever.

I waited until the clock downstairs chimed on the half hour. My tensed body practically exploded into action. I lit the lantern and hurried out of the room. I wasn't very quiet, my leather shoes squeaking like a mischievous mouse with each step. But the boys seemed to be heavy sleepers, as there was no sign of them moving around.

As soon as I entered the dark, night air, a creeping sense of solitude took over me. A coyote howled in the distance, shortly followed by a few others.

They're not stalking you. They don't even know you're here. It was nearly impossible to shake the feeling of something terrifying hiding in the grass.

As I gained distance from the house, something rustled in the grass nearby. Gasping, I stopped any movement. My breathing slowed to almost nothing. That was, until I figured out it wasn't going to murder me. What was it? There was no telling. The grass was tall, effectively hiding anything I might have interrupted.

Fear seeped through my brain with every step I took. I couldn't see a thing. At least not clearly. Everything shadow had a life of its own. Every owl, a mission to destroy life. Every rustle in the grass made me sure one of the shadows would turn into a werewolf, ready to tear me to shreds.

When a cow mooed nearby, I screamed and nearly ran away. When I could see the lone cow belonged to an entire herd, my body relaxed. There was safety in numbers, after all.

There was no way I was going to make it to the meeting on time. When I could finally see the lone tree in the distance, a lantern flickered at the base. I picked up speed, going as fast as my skirts and occasional coughing allowed me.

The oak tree was huge. It had to have been some kind of miracle, out in absolute nowhere with plenty of stories to share. It was forked in the middle, creating the perfect spot for someone to sit, propping their bodies up by leaning against the other half of the tree.

"I was about to come lookin' for you," Sam said, reaching down for my lantern and hanging it on one of the shorter branches. He grabbed my arm and helped hoist me up to the safe nook in the tree.

"It's dark. I couldn't see where I was going."

"Mhm," he said, disbelieving. "Or you just wanted to make me worry." The smirk was obvious in his voice. He leaned against the opposite trunk, his arms crossed over his chest as though he could simply take a nap. The red in his hair shone like fire in the lantern light.

"Nah," I said.

His eyes slowly moved to meet mine, a question written plainly. "Anything yet?"

I didn't have to ask what he meant. My memories. "No."

He stared at me for a long moment, probably waiting for me to tell him everything first. Instead, I squared my shoulders and stared him right back.

"You went to see Luke that night." He watched my every move with the attention of a hunter.

I snapped my jaw shut again, but I knew very well he hadn't missed the shock that took over. My voice wavered as I spoke. "You know something then?"

"As do you." Absently, he laced his fingers together and pressed them forward in a stretch. "You first."

"I-I can't tell you!" I blurted, tapping on my chest to try to slow my rapid breathing. *Good job, self! There's no way he'll let you leave without telling it all now.*

"Your brother and Pa are distracted enough as it is right now. That's the only reason they're not all over ya for the information." He reached his boot forward and nudged my toe. "You said you remembered something, just not what you were meant to?"

I let out a sharp breath, and my head fell back to hit the tree trunk. "You'll think I'm crazy."

He shrugged. "I've known you since you got here. What makes you think I'd count you as crazy so easily?"

I raised one eyebrow. "You *say* that." An irritated sigh escaped me, and I kicked at a loose stick. "You won't let me leave without an answer, will you?"

"Well . . ." He smirked. "If I keep you until sunrise, we're both going to be in more trouble than we know how to deal with."

I glued my eyes shut as if he, and all my other problems, would disappear. The lantern light managed to dance on the inside of my lids, increasing the fairy effect of the night.

Did I really have a choice? Probably, but I wasn't going to make it home alone. "I don't remember everything the way I should," I finally said.

"Yes, you said that," he said, frustration threatening to take over his voice.

Well, there went the option of recycling my earlier answer. I pressed the base of my palms into my eyes and blurted, "I'm from the twenty-first century." My words came so fast, even I could hardly hear the space between them.

His smile faltered. "Pardon?"

"I remember a different life. A life where I was a college student, a barista, could drive a car. Where my brother killed himself a year ago, and where I lived in an apartment above an old woman's garage."

Complete and total silence met me. I stared at his face for a long while, watching every confused emotion in the book wipe across it. He never tensed to leave, which was a plus.

"See? You think I'm crazy."

"No . . ." he said, though it felt forced. As though the word was stuck in the back of his throat. "Not crazy."

"Then what?" I demanded.

He hesitated, looking everywhere except my face as he thought up an acceptable answer. "When people are unconscious, sometimes they dream up all kinds of things. I read about it once."

My shoulders sagged. So much for that. I went back to my only defense, pretending he was right. "A possible dream or not, it's what I remember."

"You have to remember some things, though," he said. "Your ma? No one could forget something like that. The trip here?"

"Nope," I said, letting my lips pop on the P. "Your turn. What did she go to see Luke about?"

Sam hesitated, eyes locked on my every fidgeting movement. "You . . . she . . . went to break it off with him."

I felt my eyes grow wide in shock. "She did?"

An owl interrupted us, the rich hoot shattering any chance I had of an answer.

"You should be getting back." Sam scooped the lantern from its hanging place and hopped to the ground without waiting for a response. "Do you want me to walk you?"

I took the hand he held out to me and jumped to the dusty ground. It wasn't as dark as it could have been. The stars and moon shone as bright as streetlamps now that my eyes had adjusted. Only they were somehow better, making it where I could see the faint outline of everything in the distance.

"No," I finally said. "Home is straight that way, right?" I pointed.

"Yes." He visibly relaxed. "Please stay safe. Don't be afraid to holler if you get lost. Someone will find you quickly."

I shot him a look, though I doubted he could see it clearly in the flickering light. "Just because I got lost once doesn't mean I'll do it again. It's at the bottom of that hill."

I was about to saunter off when an idea hit me. It could probably be considered manipulation, but I couldn't manage it on my own. I needed to get to the river successfully and safely, and I officially had someone who just might be kind enough to take me.

"Sam, will you help me with something tomorrow?" The nerves creeped into my voice, making it sound as though I was a child trying to get a candy bar.

"Maybe? What do you need help with?"

I fidgeted with the sides of my skirt. "I want to go back to the river. Um . . . to try to see if I can remember something."

Sam turned to face me, slowly, deliberately. He surely could see every panicked thought that passed over my face. His eyes traced down from mine to where my fingers had pulled an anxious wad of fabric into a fist.

"And you can't ask Elliot?"

I looked up to the stars, mainly because I needed something other than him to stare at while I tried to figure out a good answer. "I don't want to disappoint him if I don't end up remembering."

He didn't miss a moment. "Liar."

"Am not!"

He grinned and scooped my lantern from its spot and held it out. "Liar or not, I'll pick you up after my chores are done in the morning. Be ready."

"Thank you!" I practically squealed, dancing in place as I toyed with the idea of hugging him or not. We ended up in an awkward, one-armed sort of embrace. "I'll be ready."

He laughed, a lighthearted noise that took over his whole body with its vibrations. "Don't rush too much. It won't be too early. I've got enough to do to keep Mr. Holmes from missing me for a few hours. Now go, before someone goes to check on you."

I rolled my eyes. "You're being a worrywart."

"Then don't get caught and prove me wrong." He shoved my shoulder. "Go, now!"

"You're not supposed to be out here either, are you?" I said, a laugh escaping my own body. Laughter that wasn't forced, a smile that was real. "You're just as afraid to get yourself caught."

"Fine, you got me." He held up his watch to the lantern light. "Just go!"

"Before I turn into a pumpkin?" I was pushing it, and I knew it. The teasing was too much to pass up.

Thoughts whizzed past his face as he thought about his response. With a somewhat defeated sigh, he walked behind me, put both hands on my shoulders, and eased me in the direction of the house. "I'll see you tomorrow, okay?"

"Deal." I had the overwhelming wish to hug him again. Really hug him. Perhaps it was from being so tired, or maybe it was from being truly happy for the first time since the night of the accident.

CHAPTER NINE

Apparently, my cough had subsided enough to warrant some chores. They handed me a to-do list before they left in the morning.

A to-do list!

A few of the things were easy enough: feeding the chickens, sweeping the floor. The one scribbled farther down on the note in blocky handwriting was a different story.

Laundry.

I had no doubt who'd added that one on. Elliot. Most likely to ensure *I* had the pleasure of cleaning his shirt.

By the time I got to it, the sun was high in the sky and I had begun to wish for enough time for a nap. What time would Sam appear, anyway?

I threw a shirt into the bucket of soapy water and got to scrubbing, humming an unidentified pop song as I did so. I had no clue what to do, but I scrubbed it the best I could, then tossed it into a rinse bucket. With the imaginary beat in my head, I threw a pair of pants into the soapy water and went after them next.

"Your voice is pretty."

I gasped, whirling around to see Sam coming my way, horse in tow.

He wrapped the reins skillfully around a post on the porch. "Who's winning?"

"Huh?" I scrunched my nose up and looked back at the laundry mess.

"You or the clothes—who's winning that battle?"

I glanced at the clothesline hanging a few feet away. I needed to have a whole row of clothes up there, but it remained empty. "The jeans are winning," I finally decided.

He made an only slightly accusing look in my direction at the word choice, but otherwise ignored it. "Scoot." He knelt beside me, nudging me out of the way with his hips.

Against my will, a blush crossed my face. I bent down to focus on removing all the soap from the shirt, hoping my cascade of hair would hide my blush.

"What else do you have to do after this?" He scrubbed the pants on the washboard like a pro.

"Nothing, I finished everything else on the list." I risked a glance in his direction. He had already rolled up his sleeves in order to go to town on the next piece of clothing.

Sam laughed, mercifully oblivious to the way I watched him. "He left you a *list?*"

"Shush." I poked him in the side with my toe. "I have memory issues, remember?"

He handed me a finished shirt to hang up. "Ah, yes. The memory problems . . ." He trailed off, and a troubled expression replaced the teasing one.

"I can't help it," I muttered, slipping the clothespins into place.

"Hmm," he said, attacking one of my—or her—dresses. "Speaking of which, did you even heat the water up first?"

I froze. "Wait, what?"

Sam laughed, his whole body shaking.

"What? Stop it! I'm supposed to do that?" I pushed him with my foot again. It only made him laugh harder. I shoved his shoulder as hard as I could, losing my balance in the process. Like a child's ill-formed card tower, I fell. He stretched his arm out automatically, only causing me to fall on top of him instead of the hard ground.

We were both laughing by that point. Until we weren't. Like some romance novel, we had ended up face-to-face in the dirt. I scrambled off his chest with the same urgency he used to push me off.

"Sorry, uh . . . um . . ." he stammered. "The mud. Didn't want you to fall in it." As if I needed clarification, he pointed to the mud puddle by the washbasins.

"No, uh, thank you." I nodded in some kind of awkward bow attempt.

We stood there, smothered in the complete awkwardness. It was worse than high school. Some guy meant to help me, and I had to practically fall on his face.

Sam cleared his throat. "We'd better finish this up so we can get going." He knelt back down to work on the rest of the laundry. There wasn't much, thanks to the art of re-wearing clothes for nearly a week. I had never realized I would truly appreciate such a thing.

We, or rather he, worked in silence for the rest of it. Whenever he'd finish an article of clothing, he'd pass it up for me to hang on the line. Easy. By the time we were completely finished, the sun was high in the sky, trying to burn us into the ground. I was momentarily grateful for the cooler weather in March. With any luck, I'd be home before it got to be over a hundred degrees when the sun got this high. I was pretty sure I would die without my air-conditioning.

When we were finally finished, he dumped the dirty water out for me, wiped his hands on his pants, then held out his hand. "Ready to go find those memories?"

The smirk on his lips sent butterflies skittering through my stomach. "Ready." I took his hand and let him help me onto the back of his horse. I scooted as far back as possible as he swung up with ease.

With great difficulty, he twisted to face me. "What part of the river are we wanting to go to?"

I made a face as I tried to come up with something. It made sense to try to be as close as possible to the car accident. "The bridge?" I doubted the bridge would move very far over the next hundred years or so.

"Okay . . ." he said slowly. To my dismay, he didn't turn back to face the front. "What do you honestly remember?"

"I already told you." I put both hands on his shoulders to guide him in the direction we needed to go.

He sighed but didn't press the issue any further. With a cluck of Sam's tongue, the horse began the journey back in the direction of town.

We were silent for a few minutes as we headed in the general direction of town. I couldn't stand it. My fingers fidgeted with my dress, quite possibly wrinkling that section for the foreseeable future. My toes curled and uncurled again with every other thud of the hooves.

The closer we got, the more apprehensive I became. Like an idiot, I planned on jumping into the water. I'd do whatever it took. If nearly drowning was the way I ended up in this predicament, it made sense that the same thing would send me back. Right?

The idea made my skin crawl. What if it killed me this time? What if it just simply didn't work? What if there truly was no other way home?

The ride took longer than I anticipated. It could have been thirty minutes or a full hour. It felt like at least two.

He remained perfectly silent the entire time, the questions radiating off his back. He certainly didn't believe me and was probably hunting for a logical explanation for my insanity.

The sound of the rushing water reached us before I caught sight of the trees. My heartbeat increased with the sound, and I bit my lip. Each time I shut my eyes, images flashed through my mind. The water, swirling all around, the screams, the impact of unidentified objects.

The certain death.

"Anything yet?" Sam asked, breaking through the line of chaos flowing through my brain.

I shook my head rapidly to dislodge the fear trapped inside. "No, not yet. I need to . . ." I glanced around, looking for any sign of hope. Perhaps I'd be able to see through the portal and glimpse some of the crashed car, or even the modern bridge placed across the water. Instead, I only saw the murky river dance along its way, not sure whether it wanted to be a stormy gray or a sickening green. The wooden bridge stretched across where the modern one would one day be, looking like it could easily collapse with the next windstorm.

"You need to—" Sam started, but I was way ahead of him.

"I need to walk beside it," I said, swinging my leg over and sliding to the ground. He followed, staying a protective distance behind me.

My mind swam with the problems of the situation, trying desperately to create a seven-step plan of some sort. Or even a three-step variant.

Step one: Get rid of Sam.

Step two: Jump in water.

Step three: Go to the hospital in the twenty-first century.

The plan was foolproof.

Not.

When I made it to the river's edge, everything seemed much less probable. The water was much calmer than it had sounded from afar. It would take an incredible amount of effort to drown myself with the water flowing along as though it was on a Sunday afternoon stroll.

Maybe it wouldn't be necessary to *drown*. Maybe whatever sci-fi portal hid in there would just swallow me up and put me back home if I stepped in.

It was worth a shot.

Before I could think anything through anymore, I took a giant step forward.

My foot never touched water. Sam's fingers had grabbed my forearm and yanked me back.

"What in tarnation are you doing?" He turned me to face him and stared straight into my eyes. His blue ones searched my face for any sign of remaining sanity. Apparently finding none, he didn't release his vice grip.

"Let me go!" I snapped, struggling to free myself and get back to the water. I had to go. The old lady who owned the house I stayed at would be worried. My work would be worried. There would be police involvement. I needed to get home!

And Trish . . . I had to know if she was all right.

He held on, not hard enough to leave any sort of mark, but enough to get control of the squirming creature I had become. "Stop!"

"I have to go back!" My voice was as strained as my body, leaning for the water. "I have to go back!"

"You're *insane! Stop!*" he shouted, giving my body a good shake. When I paused to make eye contact, he relaxed only slightly. "You said you were here to remember things. None of that involves going for a swim fully clothed."

"Well then." I smirked and reached behind me to yank on the ties of my dress. If he wanted it that way . . .

With a startled intake of breath, he grabbed my hand with almost as much panic as he had before. "*No*," he said, eyes boring into mine.

"What are you worried about, anyway? I can swim." He didn't need to know that swimming was the last thing on my to-do list.

"I . . ." He paused to think that through. "I'm worried about *you*. You'll catch your death. You already have a cough. You don't need to add water!"

"How do you know I don't need to feel the water on my legs to remember?"

"I'm here to walk you on the bank. No swimming. Got it?" He glared at me until I nodded. "Thank you."

"You think you're all high and mighty," I muttered under my breath. He heard me but apparently not well enough to understand. Thankfully, he didn't comment.

We walked away from the bridge slowly, his hand holding on to my wrist like handcuffs, ready to strike at any moment. I didn't look at him. He'd be fine if I disappeared. He'd get over it. I wasn't the real Elizabeth, anyway. No one knew he was here, so they wouldn't get him for murder either. I hoped.

I made a mental note to check for murders in the land run era when I got home, just in case.

He never tried to restart a conversation. Neither did I. I didn't know this man well enough to trick him into letting me go. I considered just doing a sort of jump-and-wiggle move to pull my hand out, but that wouldn't work either. His hands were large, and my wrists were small for my size. He had his hand comfortably around it, fingers touching each other. There was no squirming out.

To my surprise, I got an opportunity a short time later when his hand dropped to his side and his entire body went stiff. In hindsight, I should have paid attention to his body language a little more. Instead, I jumped for it.

I practically fell into the water, every inch of my body becoming soaked within seconds. It was a frantic sort of movement, ducking my head underneath the water every two seconds like a psychopathic baptism. But I never left.

There was a delay in how long it took Sam to grab me. Another thing I hadn't realized until later. He grabbed my arm, much harder this time, and outright dragged me to the shore. I had no choice but to follow.

"It didn't work." I barely breathed the words, my heart thudding out of my chest. My voice didn't remain soft. "It didn't work. Dammit! Let me go!" I kicked at his legs and shoved at his hand. "Let me go! I have to go!"

He was deathly silent as he forced me to walk in front of him. He pushed me so close to the water's edge, the water teased my boots. Before I could say anything, he pointed straight ahead.

"What is going on?" he demanded.

All the fight drained out of me with an icy finality. Stuck on the debris of a tree in the middle of the river was a woman. Her light blue dress disheveled, crumpled up in various locations to show her extremely pale legs as the water lapped around her. They had a sickening gray tone to them, as did every inch of her exposed skin. Flies buzzed everywhere, making the most of what they could with the water in their way. It was hard to discern her features with how the bloat contorted her. The flies were most interested with the large wound on her forehead, cleaned well from the flowing river. Her brown hair had come out of the once-neat bun and trailed behind her like a mermaid. Her gray eyes stared blankly in our direction.

It was like staring into a sick, twisted circus mirror.

It was me.

"I need to know who you are." Sam's voice was a forced calm.

"You know who I am—" I didn't finish. Everything came together in my frazzled mind. *That*, the bloody mess of a bloated woman in front of me, was Elizabeth. *Their* Elizabeth.

A shiver traveled up my body as I realized how much she would have looked like me before she met her fate. Exactly like me.

Sam jumped to action as though someone had stung him. He pulled on the knot of his rope belt. Before I could figure out why he would do such a thing, he grabbed my wrists.

"Don't you fucking dare!" I shouted, pulling with all my might.

He didn't respond. He just tied my wrists together snuggly, as though I wasn't squirming like a wild animal. With the tail of the rope, he tied my wrists above my head to one of the young trees.

It might have nearly been a sapling, but it wasn't young enough to be knocked over. It would have still created damage to a car if one dared cross it.

"Dammit! *Sam!*" I kicked at him as he walked to the edge of the water again. He didn't even bother to turn around. With much concentration, he waded toward her.

I couldn't see him, or the body from where I was tied. There was too much brush in my way. I pulled so hard my shoulders ached. The fear had graduated to a kind of fight-or-die. I needed to get home. I needed to get home immediately.

The mystery of what had happened to the original Elizabeth had been solved. Unfortunately, it didn't sound like it would help me out. Perhaps some sort of sci-fi portal thing had happened, only it needed payment. A life? Or more likely, was I taking her place?

I forced myself to go silent and listen, to calm my breathing to something that wouldn't eventually cause me to pass out. I could hear him talking to the girl on the ledge, but not well enough to make out words. With each ebb and flow of his voice, his grief punched me in the gut.

What on earth was I thinking, stressing out over my own predicament? There was an actual life that was lost. I had to remember that. People would be grieving.

That poor girl . . .

Then it hit me. If everyone knew she had died, what would happen to me?

Heart rate increasing yet again, I concentrated on slithering my wrists out of the restraints. They didn't budge.

"He must be the one in charge of hog-tying calves," I muttered. With a sigh, I slumped against the tree trunk to wait. There was no escaping him.

The sun was getting close to setting by the time he climbed back up, dirty tears streaking his pale face.

I opened my mouth to tell him I was sorry, when a horse came up on us.

"What are you two doing here?"

Sam cursed and yanked neatly on my rope again, freeing me from the tree, but not actually letting me go. He held my hands so I was forced to stand behind him.

"Don't you dare say a word," Sam whispered. Without skipping a beat, he changed to his normal, friendly self. "Mr. Barnette, how are you this afternoon?"

The older man on the bay horse didn't look remotely friendly. He scrunched his eyes as if against the bright sun, but his hat was pulled down low, making sun sensitivity improbable. He was heavily tanned from all his work outside. Every inch of his stiff body showed exactly how much hard labor he did every day. Back pain was likely in his day-to-day life.

"I'd be doing a might better if you'd tell me what you and my soon-to-be daughter-in-law were doing here. *Together*," he growled. He rode right up to us, staring straight down his nose at Sam.

Chills traveled up my spine. Officially, I had a hard time determining who I disliked more: Luke, or his father. I fought the urge to glance at where the body would be hiding. I could only hope her hiding place would be effective enough. I didn't want to know what would happen if this man discovered I didn't belong.

"We were working on her memories," Sam said calmly. "We were hoping coming back would help."

The man raised an eyebrow. "And why you and not my son?"

"Well . . ." Sam's grip tightened on my wrists as he struggled to come up with an acceptable answer. "I knew Lukas would be caught up with the wheat harvest, so I thought I'd lend a hand."

"Hmph." Mr. Barnette shook his head. "Then you'd best be gettin' out of here. This land doesn't belong to either of you."

Sam went rigid but didn't counter that. "Well, if Ellie marries your son—"

"If?"

Sam shook his head, as though to dislodge the mistake. "I'm sorry, sir. Slip of the tongue. *When* Elizabeth marries your son, she'll have a right to be on the land."

Mr. Barnette stared at the both of us for an agonizing minute. I didn't dare glance toward where the body lay. Sam had hidden her in the brush and undergrowth. I could only hope that the added height of a horse didn't give the man an easier visual.

"Elizabeth," Mr. Barnette practically barked. "Come on, I'll take you home. You don't need to be out here with the likes of *him*."

I opened my mouth several times to speak, but nothing came out.

"I mean her no harm, sir," Sam said defensively.

Mr. Barnette scoffed. "Only to her reputation. That's not something she can lose. Especially so close to her wedding. She'll come home with me."

My voice finally decided to work. "I'd rather stay, please." His piercing eyes turned right to me, turning my anxiety on overdrive. "I want to walk and see if I can remember anything else—"

"No," he snapped. "You're coming with me." His voice was final.

Sam worked at the knot still around my wrist with his one hand, trying desperately to get it to weaken. It wouldn't be fast enough. He might have been an expert at knots, but he hadn't passed the behind-the-back challenge.

"I'll take you to get your hat from the horse then," Sam finally said. The disappointment was plain in his voice.

He turned in place, blocking my hands with his body as he did. I slowly did the same, and we walked back down the hill.

I looked longingly at the water as we reached the horse. It was right there, merely two feet away. Home was so close, but impossible to reach.

Sam practically wrenched the rope off my wrists and shoved it into his pocket.

"Ow!" I rubbed my skin. He hadn't left a mark, at least not that I could see. If there was going to be any damage, it definitely wouldn't be something noticeable to anyone else.

"Shush," he muttered. "Go on, get." He waved his hands toward the imposing man on the top of the hill. "Don't get too happy, mind you. I'm not done with you yet."

"I don't know anything, okay? And I don't want to go with him." The decision was easy. Sam would likely be *much* easier to escape if I needed to.

"Tough." He nudged my back with the palm of his hand. "Go."

"Wait, wait, wait," I said stubbornly. "I didn't bring a hat."

"Yeah, I noticed. As will everyone else. Your freckles are creating a colony of their own on your nose. Just say you forgot it at home."

I glared at him. "Well, if you make me go with him, I'll tell him you had me tied to a tree."

A smile crossed his face. Calm, victorious. "You do that, and I'll tell him that you're actually dead in that river right there."

My frown deepened. "Please don't do that."

"It's not my plan."

"Then what *is* your plan?" I watched him closely. His features had aged a good ten years since that morning. Somehow, I couldn't help but feel slightly responsible for his pain.

"Go," he muttered. "I've got things to take care of."

I hesitated some more, watching the grief begin to take over his face again. There was absolutely nothing I could do. Defeated, I turned around and headed back to the unlikable stranger.

CHAPTER TEN

Mr. Barnette was a downright bastard. In the twenty-first-century version of the word. I didn't give a crap about the original meaning. He could have been the queen's heir for all I cared.

The entire ride back, he lectured me. I listened at first, just in case I was at risk of missing something important. I wasn't.

"Until your wedding is official, I don't trust you, or any of you cotton-pickin' Hersleys on my property. You understand?" was his first point. I had to imagine duct tape securely across my lips to avoid telling him what-for.

"And spending time with that Smith boy. Of all things, you should know better! He'd ruin every ounce of reputation you have. For all we know, he's the one who did this to you. He doesn't even have an acre to his name. Not a dadgum thing."

"Mhm . . ." I muttered at the appropriate place.

"He mighta made something of himself before his pa died, but that man left him nothing. Now, he gets to start from scratch like the rest of us did."

That caught my attention. "How did his pa die?"

"You really should know this already, girl." He looked over his shoulder to give me somewhat of a glare. "Don't you tell me that memory loss of yours is real."

"Humor me." I narrowed my eyes at his back. What was the worst he would do? Knock me off the horse in his frustration? I highly doubted it.

He shook his head in irritation. "He died in an accident at the railroad. Simple as that. When he died, Sam went to work for the Holmes family on their ranch. All that boy's got is the shirt on his back and that horse of his."

He made it sound as though Sam got paid in potatoes or something.

When we reached the top of the hill that looked over the Hersley land, I breathed a sigh of relief. I had managed not to say anything overly frustrating the entire journey. I almost felt like I deserved an award.

The view would have been breathtaking if I wasn't being transported against my will. An oil painting of a sunset strewn across the Western sky, dipping down into the valley with pinks and oranges to meet the two ranchers standing in front of the house.

Even from a distance, their fury was obvious. Every inch of their bodies was stiff. Newton's jaw was so rigid, it was liable to break some teeth. Elliot's shoulders were so straight, it made me hurt.

"F . . . Fudge." Thankfully, I caught it before the word came completely out. Why, why couldn't the damn river have done its job?

"Found something of yours!" Mr. Barnette called as we passed the barn. Immediately, I wished that I could be curled up in the hay somewhere instead. Found wasting the day away with a book, or a simple nap. Newton set his jaw, indicating that would have been more acceptable.

"Levi," Newton called back in greeting. "Thank you for bringing her back safely."

Elliot tapped my thigh to get my attention. He didn't look much more thrilled than Newton did. He pulled me off the horse and mercifully didn't comment when my legs threatened to turn to Jell-O. All the horse riding was beginning to catch up with me.

"Where did you find her?" Newton asked.

Elliot didn't let me listen to Levi tell all about my adventures with Sam. Instead, he steered me into the house.

"At least let me defend myself," I complained, halfheartedly trying to sidestep him and go back outside.

"I don't think you have much to defend at this point," Elliot muttered.

"What exactly did I do that was so bad?" I demanded. Granted, I could come up with plenty of things. But in reality, I hadn't *done* anything improper. I just disappeared. Again.

Elliot confirmed my suspicions, rubbing his brow. "You vanished for over a day and came back with the worst case of memory loss the doctor has ever seen. Then, you tried to run off for no real reason. We have to find you in the fields, still sick enough that you soiled your . . . er . . . *my* shirt."

"You don't have to add that part."

"Oh, I think it's a good point to bring up." His voice had become sharp. "And then, you disappear again today. After doing your chores, of course. Though, let me say you are rotten at keeping a clean house."

"I did the best I could!" I snapped, gesturing wildly at the kitchen. "The floor is a fucking dirt magnet!"

That did it. He loomed over me, his jaw just as immovable as the rest of his body. Since I doubted he would murder me, I held my ground. "That, my dear sister, is a word I would lose. Immediately."

"Or?" Something in my head told me I needed to back off before I ended up in a grave with the other Elizabeth.

Elliot raised an eyebrow. "You're already in enough trouble. I *dare* you to bring your newfound swearing out in front of Pa."

"Careful, I might take you up on that." I pushed past him to grab some of the stew off the stove. The dirty dishes on the counter told me that they had already eaten, so I didn't worry about the potential of being improper. I had to eat too.

The door clicked open, accompanied by a harsh "Eh!" Much like one that would be used to scold a dog. Frozen in place, I turned my head to see if I really was the cause for the offending noise.

I was.

"Put that back and get up to bed," Newton commanded.

"But I—"

"Now." He pointed at the stairs. His entire body was even more rigid than Elliot's. He was breathing with such force, one would think he was in pain.

I set my bowl back down and turned around slowly, my stomach growling as if to prove a point. Sent to bed without dinner. That hadn't been a punishment of mine in so long, I couldn't even remember how old I would have been. It had never really worked, after all. It just made me angry.

Careful to keep a wide berth from the irritated men, I made my way up to my room. They watched every step, making my feet feel all the more heavy. When my door shut, they began talking. Quietly, but with enough force to show exactly how upset they both were.

"Dammit, dammit, dammit." I pressed my ear to the door. It didn't help much. I only heard every few words. Mainly my name with occasional sprinkles of Sam's.

Giving up, I changed out of my damp clothes and into a clean shift before sitting to work on my tangled hair.

The voices downstairs got louder every once in a while, making me flinch. I wondered if I needed to find something to push in front of the door. The vanity chair wouldn't have worked, as it didn't have a back. I certainly couldn't push the vanity itself, or the old chest.

It felt as though I was back in elementary school, awaiting my fate after the one and only time I cheated on a test. Everything I knew about the 1800s told me I might be waiting for the exact same verdict. Only as a twenty-four-year-old.

As a kid, it didn't take very much to make sure I understood when I messed up. I highly doubted anything near as gentle would work as an adult.

With a worried sigh, I put my hairbrush back into the vanity and headed for the bed. If I was asleep, I'd be safe. Hopefully.

The door opened before I even reached it. I whirled around and sat down, nerves flying through every molecule of my body.

Newton stood there, less furious than before, but still on edge. His lips were pressed in a grim line, and his arms were crossed. The strap hung ominously from his right hand.

I backed up until I pressed hard against the wall, eyes focused on the offending object. I crossed my own arms, then let them fall back, unable to get remotely comfortable.

"What in tarnation were you doing at the river again?" he demanded.

I looked from one side of the bed to the other, as though it would tell me the magic thing to say to him. "I, uh . . ." I snapped my lips shut before I could say another word.

Newton stretched his hand out flat on his jeans, taking his time to ensure his voice remained level. It really didn't help. I could still practically feel the anger vibrating from his body.

"I would appreciate an answer."

"I . . ." I fidgeted with the seams of the blanket, focusing on the tiny, perfect stitches. "I was going to be back in time to work on dinner. That really was my plan!"

He eyed me levelly, one eyebrow raised as he waited for me to answer his actual question.

I knew I wouldn't get out of my predicament without calming down at least some. I licked my lips and started my explanation, hands trembling. "I wanted to go to the river again to see if I could remember anything. Since I couldn't find it on my own, I asked Sam if he could take me. And he said yes."

Newton tsked his tongue. "That boy . . ."

"I'm sorry I scared you by running off. I really didn't mean to be gone long." Despite my best efforts, my voice took on a pleading edge.

"And it never crossed your mind that I asked you to stay put? Or even to ask one of us to take you?"

"No," I admitted. *Because I never planned on coming back.*

"Do you have a clue what you've done with this little outing of yours?"

I squirmed under his gaze. "No . . ."

"Levi is questioning whether or not you are fit to marry his son." The words almost seemed painful for him to get out.

The wedding. It was like a shortcut command to igniting the bomb inside my brain. All my well-formed arguments exploded into unrecognizable fragments of information, and I didn't bother putting anything back together before I spoke. "Good! It's not like I wanted to marry him anyway."

"We already discussed that, now, didn't we? It's not up for debate." He paced to the window, staring out of it with such ferocity I wouldn't have been surprised if the glass broke. "I need you to tell me this, and tell me honestly." He shut his eyes as though it would keep the pain of the words from breaking him in two. "Did you and Sam . . . have relations?"

I felt my eyes grow to saucers as I coughed a laugh. For some reason, I hadn't expected that to be something he would be worried about. "What? No! I just asked him to go because he's nice."

"And you didn't think about your reputation at all?"

I almost groaned. "No! Because I *apparently* get married in a month. Does it really matter if I do what I want at this point?" My earlier terror of a looming punishment had morphed into fury. Deep inside, I knew that was a bad sign. But I couldn't stop it.

Newton turned slowly, his harsh eyes focused straight on me, a predator threatening his prey. "It does matter. It matters very much. And you keep that attitude of yours down."

The idiotic decision made, I continued. "It doesn't matter to me. It's my life, is it not? Don't I have a say in what I do with it?"

He blinked slowly, taking a moment to remain calm. "You already had your say. You chose to marry Luke. You had an unfortunate accident. It's not enough to change the decision now that it's already in the works."

I sat taller, refusing to back down from the argument, though I was sure to lose. "Well, I think it is. And you're not exactly the best father if you think otherwise. There's no reason to pawn your daughter off like that!"

He took the low blow well, though his body stiffened. "Elizabeth." He put force on each individual syllable of my name. "We'll discuss your marriage again later. Not now. Or do you want to continue to try my patience and *then* have me tan your hide?"

Like magic, I fell silent, the terror setting up residence yet again.

"Good. Now, tell me. What are you in trouble for?"

I let a long breath out through my teeth. "For running off without telling anyone and putting my fuc—" I caught myself but just barely. His eyebrow raised. "Putting my reputation in jeopardy."

With a sigh, he backed away from the window and touched the edge of the bed. "Come on then."

My stomach flipped. "I'd rather not."

The harsh look he shot me could have controlled an entire army. My body crawled off the bed without my permission, but I certainly didn't get close enough to be caught. Instead, I bolted for the door. The sleeve of my shift rustled slightly as his hand brushed it in his attempt to grab me.

I had no plans on where I would go. Absolutely *anywhere* seemed acceptable enough.

When I reached the top of the stairs, I knew I didn't have a chance. Elliot stood on the lowest step, looking like he'd been yanked from the most important football game of the season for something trivial.

I glanced over the banister, wondering for the slightest moment if it was worth it to jump.

"Let's not do that," Elliot cautioned, taking the steps two at a time and gripping my forearm.

"Come on!" I shouted, pulling roughly. "Just let me go! I'll be out of your hair forever!"

Elliot shoved me back up the stairs, ignoring the times I managed to smack him with my free hand.

"You're insane. Move! He's going to beat me! You're my older brother. You should be protecting me."

Of all things, he laughed. "Spare the rod, spoil the child."

He didn't stop until he had me in the middle of the room. Newton hadn't moved, plainly prepared for his well-trained son to bring me back.

"You lost something." Elliot only let my arm go when Newton had an unyielding grasp of the other one.

I hunted for any way out, panicked tears already leaking onto my cheeks. "This is abuse. *Abuse!* I'm not some disobedient child. And even if I was—"

Newton pulled me toward the bed, ignoring every word that came out of my mouth.

I was pretty sure I knew how to make them listen. "Fuck you. Fuck you all!" I kicked at Newton's shin, flinching as my toes popped on contact.

He sighed heavily, his grip tightening on my forearm.

Elliot laughed again. *Laughed.* "Enjoy that grave you just dug yourself."

I just barely grasped my pillow and chucked it at his head. I missed. My efforts were only rewarded with another laugh. My vision seemed to be clouding over, likely because I couldn't seem to get in a full breath.

I swallowed hard, trying to find some sort of sense in my panicked haze. I needed to breathe. Preferably before I passed out. I choked back the sobs, fighting for just a trace of sanity. The ragged breath I took grated against my lungs. "I'm sorry I ran off," I said as levelly as possible. "I won't do it again."

The snort that came from Elliot showed exactly how little he believed that statement. He slipped out of the door, closing it firmly behind himself.

Newton hauled me to the edge of the bed, using just enough force to get me to move, but not enough to leave bruises.

"It is wrong to hit a woman! Abusive fucking assholes!" I screamed the words, my voice so shrill, it echoed throughout the house.

I knew my fate was sealed, but that didn't mean I would go down without a fight.

CHAPTER ELEVEN

"What is that racket?"

Elliot's voice woke me. I scrambled up to sitting, my rear aching as I did so. Reality. I much preferred my dream world. Reality was painful. I hurt, both from what they seemed to consider a "rightful" punishment, and from fighting him every step of the way.

"What?" I rubbed my eyes as though it would help me see better in the dim light from his candle.

He marched straight to the window, nearly pressing his nose to the glass to see out. "Don't pretend you slept through it. Did you sneak someone in here?" He dropped to his knees to peer under my bed.

I leaned down to push his shoulder as hard as I could. "Go. Away. Why would I bring someone in here when I know what sort of torture awaits them?"

"Hmm." Elliot ignored me, sitting up on his knees when he found nothing.

He *wanted* to find someone? My anger boiled to the point of overflowing. "The only person in here is your sorry ass. Get out." I crawled out of bed, planting my hands on his back and pushing. "Go! You had everything to do with . . . with . . ." I couldn't even finish the sentence. "*Go.*"

He gave the room one final glance before focusing on me. "You know the rules are here for a reason, right?"

He should have left when he had the chance. I kneed him where the sun don't shine. He buckled forward like a wounded doll, a strangled gasp coming from his lips.

"There was no call for that!" He gripped the doorframe as he hauled himself back onto his feet.

I made a poor excuse for a fist and held it up in what I hoped was a threatening manner.

"Okay, okay. I'm leaving." He shook his head, muttering something about headstrong women under his breath. "I'll check outside just to make sure nothing's out there. Call me if you need me."

"Like I did earlier?" I spat. "When you let him beat me? You didn't think—"

And he left, closing the door firmly behind him.

And he left.

Alone again, I relaxed. I fully planned on crying myself back to sleep. But for some reason, all I could think about were his pants. They had been dirt-free and ready for a new day.

Against my better judgment, I flung open the door and leaned out. "What time is it?"

I had caught him right before he made it to the stairs. I had been right. He was completely ready for the day.

"'Bout midnight," he answered shortly.

"Why are you dressed already then?"

He waved his hand absently and hurried down the stairs to check the perimeter.

What was he up to, anyway? It was none of my business, and I really shouldn't have cared. He practically sacrificed me to the strap. The more I stayed out of his business, the better.

"Thinkin' I snuck some guy up here." I pulled the blanket over my head. "If only I could, just to spite you."

His interruption made sleep impossible. My ears were magnetized to every hint of a noise. The rustling as he checked around the wood pile for heaven knows what, the startled squawks as he checked on the chickens. Then, the light plodding of his feet as he came back up to his room, apparently giving up on his phantom bad guy.

When his door closed with the tell-tale click, I expected to fall right back asleep.

Still, nothing.

I waited and waited. I counted sheep, chickens, cows, and only got irritated that I saw too many of them in real life, so I counted cars instead.

Still, nothing.

And then, *tap*.

I sat up like I'd been zapped.

Tap.

Cautiously, I crawled to the end of the bed, craning my neck to see through the window. I didn't see anything in the darkness until something hit the glass right in front of my nose.

Tap.

Startled, I fell back onto the bed to regain myself. When yet another projectile hit the window, I hurried over and opened it. From that angle, I could just barely see the shape of Sam hiding in the shadows of the house.

"What are you doing?" I demanded.

He made a harsh hushing noise and gestured for me to come down.

"Absolute not! Aren't you breaking every single rule of this century? What do you want?" I crossed my arms securely over my chest.

Not like he could have noticed much of anything without any light source other than the moon.

"You're not exactly following the rules either, now, are you?" he shot back.

"Shh!" I poked my head out the window to peer in the direction of Elliot's. Thankfully, he must have fallen back asleep. "They'll hear you!"

"Then get down here! He's gone, anyway."

I blinked in surprise. I could have sworn I heard him return to his room. Unless he had faked it for my benefit. "What do you want?"

"Your help. You owe me that much."

"I owe you nothing!" I spat.

"Get down here before I come up and get you." He took an ominous step in the direction of the front door.

"Dammit." I pushed away from the window and shut it firmly. I rummaged through the pile of dirty clothes and pulled on the cleanest-smelling ensemble I could find before fixing my sloppy braid.

He'd do exactly as he threatened, and I knew it. The last thing I wanted was for him to wake the angry bear of a man downstairs.

My shoes barely on, I hurried down the stairs, pausing only at the bottom to ensure I could still hear the steady snoring from Newton's room.

He met me at the door, horse in tow.

"What makes you think I'm going to help you?" I asked, gesturing roughly in the general direction of town. "Last time I saw you, you tied me to a tree. And then, you sent me off with that . . . that . . . that man!"

"His name is Levi. And don't be so dramatic. It's not like he hurt you."

I glared at him with all my might, hoping my gaze would somehow spear him. Of course, it did nothing. "What do you need my help with?"

"I need your help to bury the body." His tone lacked any emotion as he nodded to the human-shaped bundle thrown over the back of the horse. He moved like a robot, as though if he let any of his feelings out, he would never be able to put them back in.

My heart ached, seeing her there. Her own father slept only a room away while she slowly decomposed.

"Come on," Sam said, beginning to lead the horse away.

I didn't move. "How do I know you're not going to tell anyone about me?"

He took a slow breath but didn't look back at me. "It's obvious something happened. That doesn't mean I should hurt you." Before I could fully relax, he continued. "Just don't give me a reason to think you did it."

I glared at him. "I didn't do it. And you're not giving me much of a reason to go with you. Or at least not a reason to feel *safe* to go with you."

"Come on, you need a little more adventure in your life."

"If you get me in trouble again, I swear . . ." Even as I said the words, my feet hurried to catch up to him. What was I doing? If Newton found out I was gone, I didn't want to imagine how much trouble I'd end up in.

"Me?" He chuckled. "I certainly didn't get you into trouble the first time. The was all your own doing."

I slowed down to walk beside him. "Well, I would've probably made it home earlier if you hadn't sent me off with whatever his name was."

"So, I gather you did get into trouble?" he asked.

I absently picked at the edges of my dress, mainly so I wouldn't rub the affected area. "As if your tying me to a tree wasn't humiliating enough."

One side of his mouth turned up, but he didn't give in to the complete smile as we walked.

The wrapped-up body smelled, though not nearly as bad as I had anticipated. With every step, the stench niggled at my emotions. Sour, rotten, death.

I knew better than to ask where we were going. Sam just led me in the direction of the meeting tree. He didn't say a single word for the entire journey.

The walk was long. Every step mentally painful. The poor girl didn't deserve to be depraved of a proper burial. Instead, she was lessened to being buried in a quilt under a tree.

It's the best we can give her, I told myself. It was true. Unless I came clean to Newton, it was the only option. I prayed none of the ancient beliefs were correct. There were many cultures that thought if a person wasn't buried a certain way, their soul wouldn't be saved.

Depression saturated the air, thick and choking. The silence overpowering, other than the occasional hoot of an owl. We only reached the meeting tree when I wasn't sure if I could survive any longer.

Sam wordlessly pulled the two shovels from the saddle, handing me one of them. He dug a ways out from the tree, not even waiting for me. I followed his lead, digging beside him.

"Are you going to tell me what you really know?" he asked eventually.

I pushed on the shovel with all my might. "I thought I already did."

"You told me something, sure. That doesn't mean it's right."

"It is!" I paused in my work to glare at him. "You're the only damn person I've told the truth to."

He brought up shovelful after shovelful of dirt onto the pile, choosing his words carefully. "You certainly didn't tell me much. You only told me you were from the twenty . . . third—"

"Twenty-first," I corrected.

"Exactly. You said nothing about anyone dying."

I flinched. "Because I didn't know. I was in an accident back home. For all I know, everyone who was with me died. For all I know, *I* died!"

"And what makes you think I'm going to believe you? I'm about to bury my best friend under a tree." His voice broke, shattering what was left of my irritation. "She doesn't even get a funeral. Do you even understand that? The only person that has anything to do with all of this"—he waved his hands in the air—"is *you*."

There wasn't an acceptable response for him. For his pain, for his anger, or even for his confusion. "I don't know what happened," I began, taking my time to choose each and every word. "I was in an accident on the bridge, fell into the water, and woke up somewhere downstream. Only here."

He locked his jaw, showing just how much he didn't believe me. "Get back to work. Otherwise, we'll be here till midday."

I pushed the shovel into the dark ground yet again, all anger gone. I needed to get home by sunrise. If Newton discovered me missing, I didn't want to imagine what would happen. My rear already hurt bad enough. I put everything my tired body had into the digging. I was taking her place. She deserved everything I could give her, after all.

We worked in silence for what felt like hours. The hole was deep enough to stand in, but not quite deep enough to keep a body away from coyotes and other scavengers. Bugs crawled on my legs, despite my picking up my skirt and swatting them away. When I did it the third time, a real, rumbling laugh escaped Sam.

"They don't seem to be bugging you," I complained.

He grinned at me. "They just don't want to go through the trouble of getting through the boots."

I looked closer at his outfit. Instead of the boots I was used to with the seamless decorated leather, he wore a pair that laced up the front. They were still obviously boots, but just not one solid piece. Similar to my own, honestly. He had the top of his pants tucked inside, effectively blocking any of the bugs' heinous attempts at bloodsucking.

"That's not fair." I tossed what dirt was on my spade in his general direction.

He smiled politely but glanced at the quilt-covered body as if to remind himself of the sorrow that was supposed to be overtaking his being.

"Sam . . ." I hesitated. I really didn't know what to say to make him feel any better. "I *am* sorry. I promise you, I didn't see anyone. Not even her. Not even some shadow of a person. When I woke up, there was *nothing*. I'm used to roads, houses, all kinds of things nearby. But there was nothing. I promise."

At first, I thought he was ignoring me, putting a few more loads of soil onto the pile.

"I believe you," he finally said, nearly making my heart stop in relief.

"You do?"

"Yes." He leaned onto the shovel to watch me. "If you were lying, you would have run off as soon as I untied you."

He's not wrong, I thought.

"Also, you're not remotely interested in Luke."

I turned right back to my shoveling at that. "He's a fucking bastard."

"He's many things, but an actual bastard he is not. Hence why you're engaged to him."

"So, what, you're a bastard? That's why it's not you?"

He blinked in surprise, caught off guard by the sudden question.

I changed tactic. "Why *him*? I hate every inch of him, and I've only met him once."

Sam sighed. "Land. Newton's land bumps up to Levi's. Levi swears Newton jumped his claim, and Newton says the same. No one really knows who had which land first. The marriage is a way to make a sort of peace." He shrugged as though it was the most normal thing in the world.

I shook my head, jaw going slack. Who, in their right mind, would even consider such a thing? "And she was *okay* with this?"

"Originally. She hadn't had someone in mind, and she was in her twenties. But she planned to call it off in the end."

I stopped digging.

"I didn't know if she ever got the chance." He plunged the shovel into the ground with as much force as he could muster.

"But . . . why? Why didn't she fight against it?"

The sigh he produced was a little more on the exasperated side than before. "Elizabeth would become a Barnette, bonding the two families. Elliot will take the Hersley farm whenever Newton passes away, but he'll have family as a neighbor. They both would likely be able to work on each other's land."

"I still don't see how that's beneficial for her."

He poked at a large clump of dirt with his shovel. The hole was up to his shoulders. "She'd have a family. A safe family, close to the ones she grew up with. Newton and Elliot are all she had, after all."

The hole was getting deep enough that it was becoming difficult to toss the dirt out. I did my best, but some of it had a habit of falling back down on top of my head.

After a particularly messy avalanche, I took a break. "I can't marry him, Sam." The words sounded much more timid than I had planned.

He didn't respond, just continued with the human-size hole. The feeling in the air morphed from concern to an overwhelming, oppressive sadness.

When the dirt coming back into the hole was more than going out, he finally spoke. "Get back up top, I'll finish up." He made a step out of his hands to boost me out of the near-six-foot chasm.

I sat with my feet dangling over the edge, watching him silently shovel the last bit. When he was satisfied he could do no more, he used the shovel as a kind of ladder and pulled himself out, pulling the trowel out behind him.

"How are we going to . . . do this?" I couldn't make myself say the words "put her in." It seemed too final, too impersonal. All of it was wrong. She deserved a loving funeral, with her family crying over her grave.

"The quilt," he said, his voice cracking. We walked to the body, quite bug-covered and at risk of losing what humanity was left to her. We unwrapped her so that she was lying in the center of the quilt, the two corners on the side for us to hold on to and carefully bring her down.

"I'm so sorry," Sam whispered, kissing his hand and placing it on the cold forehead. The raw emotion in his voice brought tears to my eyes. We sat there for a few solid minutes, just looking at her, wishing things were different, wishing she could have had her full life. Had children. Had a marriage with anyone, even with Luke. Experienced love. The things that made life a full life back then, at least that I thought.

Without a word, we took the corners of the quilt and hoisted her up. The muscles from all the shoveling protested, but I did my best to ignore them.

We walked to our prospective sides of the grave and slowly, painstakingly lowered her down. My tears splashed onto the pile of freshly disrupted soil, and his did as well. By the time she reached the ground, I was on my stomach, arms reaching down with my blanket corner to keep it from being a sudden drop. As if on cue, we both dropped our hold at the same time.

Sam uttered a prayer as he stood up. It didn't take much effort not to listen, as shaking cries tried to escape my lips. The poor girl. She hadn't even had much of a life. And what if it was *me* who caused it all? Some sort of a disruption in the space-time continuum?

At the time, there was no way to do anything other than blame myself for her death. So I cried. I cried for her lack of future, for my predicament, and for the pain ripping Sam to shreds.

When Sam finished with his prayer, he scooped the dirt in. His silent tears had turned into full sobs, shaking his body with every breath. His pain was impossible to ignore. Every ounce of anguish that rolled off his body slammed into me. I knew exactly how he felt. From my parents years ago, and then finally my brother.

The moment before her face disappeared was the most agonizing. His sobbing took on a high-pitched, choking sound as he reverently took one last shovelful and let it slowly fall onto her sickly gray face. He stood there for a long, reverent moment, looking at what could still be seen of her dress, memorizing every ounce of what she had been. Something about seeing a full-grown, strong man cry made it all so much worse.

With an excruciating yell, he shoved a large portion of his dirt pile into the hole. In a much slower fashion, I pushed my own pile in. The hole filled rapidly, erasing the original Elizabeth from the earth.

It took Sam awhile to fully calm himself after the hole was completely filled. Despite an overwhelming need to hug him, I stood there awkwardly. The tears had dried to my own face, but not without dirt sticking to the salty remains.

When he was ready to go, it was as though a switch had been flipped. Perhaps that transformation had to do with the light blue seeping into the eastern sky. He put one arm around my shoulders and led me to the horse without a single word.

I ignored how uncomfortable my rear was as we rode back to the cabin. It didn't matter. We traveled in silence, the sky adopting shades of pink and yellow around the same time we reached the well.

"They'll be waking up now," he said, his voice hoarse and full of exhaustion. It was as though he had aged to ninety years in only a few hours.

Without explanation, he jumped out of the saddle and began to reel up water from the wood-rimmed hole in the ground.

"What are you doing?" I asked, following him down.

"Here." He put the bucket full of water on the edge of the well and dipped his hands inside. Without asking, he wiped the dirt and grime from my cheeks with his fingers.

His cool fingers felt good against my flushed skin, and I closed my eyes, just letting him take care of me. When he stopped, I took over, taking the braid out of my hair and shaking out as much dirt as possible. He helped, picking out anything I missed.

"What about my dress?" I asked. It was equally as dirty. Of course, Sam had an answer for everything. He nodded to the clothesline next to the house. "You didn't put laundry away last night, did you? Go grab from there. Just hurry!" He shoved me in the general direction of the house.

"You need to get out of here before they see you," I warned. Besides, I didn't particularly want him there as I changed.

"I'm leaving," he promised. "I just want to make sure you get in okay."

I paused, not ready to let him leave. "So, you don't hate me anymore?" Immediately, I regretted speaking.

He smirked. "I don't think I ever hated you. Now, go!"

"What will I tell them when I go inside?"

"Go feed the chickens or something. They'll think you're trying to get back on their good side."

"You'd better be right," I muttered.

"Trust me—"

My exhausted brain bristled. "Like I did when you sent me with a stranger to my fate at home? I don't really trust you anymore." The accusation was uncalled for, but my thought process was muddled with sleep deprivation.

Sam visibly deflated. "I'm sorry about that. I should have rode home with the two of you. That way I could make an appropriate excuse for you."

"But instead, you tied me to a fucking tree."

"Yes . . . I did that." He scratched the back of his neck.

"How do I know you won't do it again?" I stood resolutely, arms crossed and hip popped out to the side. The stance likely looked ridiculous in a dress, but it never crossed my mind.

"There's no more surprises like yesterday, right?"

"I certainly hope not."

"Then I won't be tying you to a tree." He pulled himself back onto the mare with ease. "If you get caught dillydallying, it's not my fault," he warned.

Making a face at him, I hurried in the direction of the clothesline.

CHAPTER TWELVE

My heart beat wildly as I stood on the front doorstep. I'd changed in the barn and hid my dirty clothes behind the hay. Then, I'd grabbed all the eggs, placing them carefully in the bowl shape I'd created by holding up my apron.

They had no reason to suspect me of anything.

Except, Elliot—

The door swung open, nearly hitting me in the face. I jumped back, a surprised squeak escaping my lips and an egg making its final leap from my apron to the wooden porch with a definite *splat*.

Tall and certainly opposing, Elliot stood in the doorway, shock covering every inch of his features. "What—"

My mind whirled for something to say. If I just stood and stared at him, he'd know I'd sneaked out. "You made me drop it!" I accused, squatting to the casualty as though it had the slightest chance of being saved.

"I'll get it," Elliot grumbled. "Why didn't you take the basket?"

"I . . . uh . . . didn't think of it." I squeezed between him and the doorframe and into the cozy, nearly too-warm house.

Newton froze in shock, staring a hole through me. "What in heaven's name are you doing up at this hour?" He deliberately folded his newspaper and placed it on the side table.

"I couldn't sleep," I lied, hurrying to the counter to spread the dirty eggs out.

Elliot snorted his disbelief and, without thinking, I shot him a death glare. He knew something. He had to.

Newton watched our silent exchange for a very long, uncomfortable moment. With a sigh, he stood and grabbed the coffee pot off the stove. "Might as well get breakfast going then." He poured himself a cup and sipped it, his angry expression just barely softening.

Bewildered, it was my turn to stare at the stove.

Elliot let out an irritated sigh when I didn't move and pulled a pan from its hiding place in a cabinet. "I'll help her."

"Mmm." Newton nodded, downing the last few gulps of his coffee. Did he even have taste buds left? I could only imagine how hot the coffee would be, fresh off the stove. "I'll be in the barn."

I watched as he left, my feet wanting nothing more than to race after him just to ensure he didn't find my discarded clothes.

"It'll be nice when your brain starts workin' again," Elliot said, placing the pan on one of the burners and snagging one of the fresh eggs.

I forced my eyes from the door and nudged him aside. "I can actually make eggs," I assured him, holding out my hand for the one he had.

He hovered it over my palm for a long second before pulling it back.

"Wha—"

"Where did you go last night?" The edge of his lip twitched into a smirk as he stared me down.

My heart skipped a beat. "Give me that," I demanded, jumping at the egg. I could have just grabbed another one from the counter, but I was too annoyed to take such an easy option.

"Where'd you go?" he repeated, closing his fingers securely around the egg and letting me try to pry them away like a child.

"You disappeared too, don't forget that," I said, letting my hands fall to my side in defeat. "Betcha you weren't supposed to leave, either."

"Ah." He looked away, likely hunting for a comeback.

I had him.

He smoothly cracked the egg into the hot skillet, the whites cracking and sizzling the moment they hit. "You're the one he's more likely to care about disappearing."

"I can just tell him you left too." I grabbed the next egg before he could and cracked it as quickly as possible. My sloppy work rewarded me with bits of shell. I grabbed a fork and worked to chase the irritating speck around the pan.

"Sure, but he won't care about anything you say about me after finding out you left with Sam."

My fork froze.

"Ah, didn't think I knew that part?"

He had me. I couldn't think of a way out. "Please don't tell him!" I begged, turning on him with what I knew was a frantic expression all over my face. I couldn't go through another night like that.

"Don't plan on it. Give me that before you completely destroy that shell you're trying to catch." He took the fork and easily fished out the offending object.

I stood by and watched as he cracked three more eggs into the pan. If he told Newton, I couldn't even fathom what would happen. How far could they go before they crossed the line into what they considered to be abuse?

"Just be careful. A little romance with that boy might be nice and all, but if you're caught—"

"Romance?" I stared, eyes wide. "He's a *friend*."

Elliot raised an eyebrow at me. "My point still stands. Levi is already angry about the two of you being together at the river."

He grabbed a few unidentified herbs and tossed them into the egg mixture.

"I don't give a flying rat's ass what he thinks," I snapped, leaning against the counter and crossing my arms.

"Good Lord, where'd the language come from, anyway?" He sighed. "You should care what Levi thinks. If you don't, he'll take this land easy as can be."

"He can do that?"

Elliot paused with his egg mutilation. "There was a mishap at the land office. Levi says he had this land as part of his claimed property. Pa, of course, says otherwise."

"So, the grand plan to fix everything is marrying me off?" I surprised myself with a shocked laugh. "How barbaric and old-fashioned can y'all be! Is that even still a *thing* now?"

Elliot cocked an eyebrow. "You hadn't chosen anyone. It secures the land. It's a decent match financially. Luke seems to like you, and for a while, you seemed to like him."

"For a while," I echoed, before groaning with more drama than I intended. "What can I do to make it all go away?"

"So you can marry Sam?"

"You're burning the eggs, genius. And no. How 'bout I just get married in my own time?" I pushed past him and took over the job of keeping the eggs from sticking to the bottom of the pan.

"It's a little too late for all that. Even if Pa let you get out of it, Levi wouldn't." Elliot opened the breadbox on the counter and plopped three slices on one of the closed burners. Toast.

Newton walked back into the room then, effectively halting our conversation.

I ate slowly, just waiting for someone to drop a bomb of information that would prove I had been gone, but we made it through without any issue. Newton gave no signs of finding my dress, and Elliot didn't say a single thing about my absence.

The moment they left for their work, I dashed outside and retrieved my dirt-covered outfit and threw it straight into soapy water. I *refused* to get caught.

All day long, my forehead itched. It amazed me how fast head wounds seemed to heal. Before bed, I vowed I would get rid of the itchy bastards. In the meantime, I napped until the men came back home.

Before bed, I gathered the sewing scissors and leaned as close to the mirror as I could, biting my lip as though it would assist me. As I touched the tiny shears to the piece of thread, a voice startled me.

"What are you doing?" Elliot asked.

I whirled to face him, feeling like a guilty child. He stood in the doorway, hands casually in his pockets.

"They itch," I said, giving him the best challenging glare I could manage.

He shook his head, but a grin made it onto his face. "Here, I'll get it." He picked me up easily and set me on the edge of the dresser like a kid. He moved his lantern near my face, studying the wound with enough concentration it made me squirm.

"Are you going to make me wait to go back to that so-called doctor again?"

"No," he said, setting the lantern down beside me and pulling the tiny scissors from my fingers. "It should be fine."

My eyes fluttered closed as he held my face still with one hand and clipped the thread with the other. Each snip made me flinch, but I did my best to stay still.

"Cover for me if I'm not back by sunrise."

He said the words so casually, I hardly noticed them. "What? No! How?"

"I fully plan on being back in time. But if I'm not, tell him I'm in the barn or something." He waved his hand dismissively before pulling one of the stitches out.

"What if he goes in the barn?"

"You'll think of something." He pulled the others out rapidly and dropped them in my lap.

"Where are you going, anyway? You don't seem as tired as I would expect for someone to be running around all hours of the night." I eyed him levelly.

"Where were *you*?"

I kicked at his thigh, hard enough to hurt at least a little.

"That's no way to say thank you for keeping your secret."

I groaned. "You bastard."

"You seem quite awake as well, now, don't you? Slept somewhere during the night?" He smirked at his dirty thought.

"Absolutely not. I took a *nap*. Something I know for a fact you didn't have time for!"

He full out grinned and mimed tipping his hat at me. "Good night, Elizabeth."

I kicked at him again, but he dodged me to head out the door.

Jackass.

I didn't want to be the gatekeeper of his secrets.

CHAPTER THIRTEEN

To my relief, Elliot had returned long before I woke up in the morning. He sneaked out multiple more times over the next week, each time a wordless agreement hanging in the air; if he was late, I was to cover for him. Or else.

To my horror, Luke came by twice during that week. The first time, I managed to hide in the cellar. Thankfully, he didn't hunt long. He had bruises across his jawline and his nose looked swollen, though I couldn't be sure. Whoever he'd been fighting with, I didn't want any of it to come back on me.

Sure, there was always the chance my slimy feeling about him could be completely wrong. Perhaps he was a good guy.

But then, the feeling of unease that followed him around didn't help his case.

The second time he showed up, Newton saw him first. Before I had a chance to hide, he was invited in for the supper I had managed to throw together.

His bruises had already faded to a nasty yellow, and his nose looked fine. Sitting primly in the seat across from me, he looked like a smug asshole.

"Looks like you got into some sort of scuffle," Elliot said, saving us all the trouble of asking.

"Oh, this?" Luke touched one of the fading marks. "Yeah, snuck up on me. Thought to blame me for something I didn't have nothin' to do with." He turned his attention back on me, grasping at whatever he could to get the conversation off him. "You made this?" he asked, looking from my sloppy stew to me, then back to his plate. He didn't put any obvious effort into keeping the scowl of disgust off his face.

"Yep," I said, letting my lips pop on the P.

"Lost some of her cooking skills in the accident, I wager." He laughed, stabbing a piece of beef with his fork.

"I'm sitting right here," I snapped, earning a warning glare from Newton. "There's no need for third person."

His forced, airy laugh continued. "Oh my, we always knew I'd have my hands full with her! Well, it's what happens when a girl doesn't get her mother's guidance during the crucial times in her life."

Even Newton flinched at the low blow.

All I wanted to do was punch him, make the barely visible yellowed bruises into full-fledged battle wounds. I stood up with more force than I originally intended. I didn't plan on dealing with him. "If you'll excuse me, I have to go collect the eggs."

"Oh no, Elizabeth. You don't have to! Elliot and I will take care of it. Spend some time with Luke. The two of you haven't been able to see each other much since the accident, after all." Newton smiled wildly, pulling Elliot to his feet and hurrying out with him.

My stomach dropped as I watched them go. The only thing they left to chaperone were the dirty dishes on the table.

"Ma will be able to help teach you to cook," Luke said resolutely.

I grabbed the dirty plate in front of him and headed to the counters. I didn't care if there was still food left over. He needed to leave.

"So, I'm some project of yours to try to fix, huh?" I held my muscles so tight they ached. I refused to give him the satisfaction of looking at him while I talked.

"Well, a little bit of guidance wouldn't hurt."

"Guidance?" I scraped his leftovers into the slop bucket, grasping the bowl in such a way, it was liable to shatter.

"You have a lot to learn to be an appropriate wife to join my family." He said it so easily, as though he was simply discussing the color of one of the chickens outside the window. "Your pa couldn't even make it to the land office properly. The cooking can't be your only flaw."

I set down the plate just roughly enough to cause a bang, but not enough to break anything. "Well then," I said through clenched teeth, "maybe I shouldn't marry into your family."

That managed to catch him by surprise. "Why would you say that? You know as well as I do your family can't afford *not* to go through with the wedding."

"I really don't think we should go through with the wedding," I said slowly, every ounce of my effort going into maintaining control of my anger.

I heard him stand up, the bench squeaking behind him. "Why?"

"I have my reasons." My body trembled every once in a while, an action that threatened to show off exactly how uncomfortable I was to have my back to him.

"What are those reasons? Be specific." The thud of his boots on the floor brought him a few feet closer.

It was impossible to stay still any longer. I whirled around, heart racing. He was right there, probably only two feet away. Close enough that our breaths mingled as we stared at each other.

"What are the reasons?" he asked again.

I faltered. I had plenty of reasons.

1. I didn't know him.

2. He made me uncomfortable.

3. I certainly didn't love him.

4. The girl he was actually meant to marry was in the ground under the meeting tree.

5. Just no.

However, the words wouldn't form on my tongue.

"You . . . you need to leave, Luke," I managed to say.

"Why?" The smirk on his face made the question seem all the more like it was being asked by a toddler.

I grabbed at the only thing I could think of. "It's not seemly to have you in my house. Especially alone with me."

"Your father and brother are right outside."

"So? It's not right. Please leave." I waved my hand in the direction of the door.

His eyes narrowed to slits. "I have a question for you first. Answer honestly, and I'll leave." He didn't give a moment for me to agree. "What do you remember from that night?"

Shivers traveled throughout my body—as soon as one bout would end, another would begin. What did he know? "Were you there?" I asked, somehow managing to keep my voice from breaking. Sam's words echoed through my head. She had gone to break it off with him.

"You tell me," he said, his relaxed stance returning.

I grabbed on to the counter for stability. "You need to leave—now." He had to have been there. Otherwise, why would he keep asking? The bruises all over the other Elizabeth's body popped into my mind. Over and over, all I could see was her, begging for mercy as someone, in this case him, threw her into the water.

"Oh, come on, darling. Just answer the question first. Your virtue isn't in danger." He reached out to touch my shoulder, and I shied away.

"Don't. Touch. Me," I growled. "And leave. Now."

"Darling," he started, but I cut him off by pointing at the door.

"Go now. Before I throw a plate at you."

He rolled his eyes. "You sent that guard dog of yours after me, didn't you? He's probably who sent you to break off the engagement in the first place, now, isn't he?"

My mouth went slack in shock. "Guard dog?"

"Samuel. Who do you think gave me these?" He pointed to the bruises.

My heart beat loudly in my ears. Sam. "Go away!"

"Betcha you won't see him for a bit, and betcha he won't be nearly as good-lookin' now, either." He laughed. "Mind your manners, girl. Don't want you gettin' hurt. Especially now that you can't remember a darned thing." He tsked his tongue.

I chucked the plate in his direction, watching in horror as it shattered against the far wall. It had passed right by him as though I hadn't been aiming at all.

Luke shook his head slowly. "Manners, *Ellie*. Manners." He took his hat from the hook and pressed it on his head. "Less than three weeks, my dear. Then, all we'll have is time together." He blew a kiss at me before slipping out the door.

An angry scream erupted from my chest. "I won't be marrying you!" I shouted. His laugh was my only reply.

"He left so soon?" Newton said as he came back into the house. "What in heaven's name . . ."

Elliot fell into a heap of laughter, staring at the broken plate beside the door.

"Elliot, stop," Newton snapped. "Grab the broom. It's no laughing matter. What is the meaning of this?"

My eyes had gone dry, as I had stared at the broken pieces for so long. I blinked, partially to bring them back to life, partially to avoid the tears that threatened to escape.

"It slipped out of my hands as I walked him to the door," I lied. My voice sounded strained.

"More like you threw it," Elliot said as he passed me. "There's plenty of shards that made it on the windowsill."

I panicked.

Before anyone could make any sort of decree about my behavior, I raced up the stairs to the safety of my room.

No one came after me, though I heard them arguing in their low voices until nearly midnight.

That night, I had more nightmares than I'd had in a long time. Probably more than I'd ever had. Over and over, her—or rather *my*—face was terrified, bloody, begging for mercy before falling off the edge of a bridge into the rushing water below.

Each fall in the dream was longer than any could be. It went on and on, feeling more like falling through the Grand Canyon before my skin smacked against the water.

Once the sun peeked into the bedroom window and the birds resumed their singing outside, my body mercifully decided it was time to sleep.

I woke to Elliot lightly brushing hair out of my face.

The love on his face was unmistakable. I wondered what he would do if he knew for a fact that I wasn't his sister.

"Hey," he said. "Are you feeling okay?" He pressed his hand to my forehead. Sweet memories of my mother doing the same flooded my head. "You didn't come to breakfast."

"Hmm?" I forced my eyes open for only a second. "I'm fine."

"Didn't sleep well, did ya?" he asked, the smile plain in his voice.

"No," I grumbled, pulling the quilt all the way up to my nose and snuggling down farther into my warm cocoon.

"It's probably the weather comin' in." He patted my shoulder. "I'll leave some food on the table for you when you wake up." He stood to let me go back to my horrific dream land but changed his mind at the last second. "Keep an eye on the sky. Storms are coming today." Then he left, leaving me to wonder how they actually figured that out without a meteorologist.

I fell asleep before I could think too much about it. Probably some old man in town had a special knee ache when storms were a'comin'. It was common enough in my time, why wouldn't it be used as legitimate science in the old days?

When a knock on my door woke me again, it could have easily been noon. My body's attempt to catch up on sleep didn't listen to any rules of time management.

"What do you want?" I muttered groggily.

The voice on the other side of the door jolted me fully awake. "I was wanting to make sure you hadn't died, or caught the plague."

I scrambled out of bed, dragging the quilt with me to wrap it around my shoulders. "I just didn't sleep well," I said, as I opened up the door.

Sam stood there, hair neatly brushed and clothes much cleaner than the last time I'd seen him. Not perfectly clean, but certainly a step in the right direction. He had his fair share of bruises, yellowed marks peeking out under the collar of his shirt, edging his left eye. I could only imagine how swollen he had been directly after his attempt at chivalry.

"You need an alarm clock," he teased.

"Where have you been? I'd started to wonder if you didn't have any interest in seeing me again."

"Well, you could have always come to visit me first," he pointed out.

"Not really. Apparently, it would be 'scandalous.'" I put extra weight on the word as I worked the tangles out of my hair.

"Did they find you were gone?"

I glanced in his direction to catch him leaning against the door-frame, eyes roaming my body. I raised an eyebrow and waited for him to notice. The second he did, he turned away like a scolded child.

"Elliot did, but he didn't tell." I looked at the bruises again. The one under his ear looked too much like a finger to ignore. "Luke came to visit," I said, arms crossed.

He stood straighter. "Yes?"

"He mentioned the two of you were in a fight?"

Sam nearly deflated, head resting against the wall. "I went to ask him about when she went to break off the engagement. He told me I was mistaken, that she never came to do any such thing."

I shivered. "I don't like him."

"You have good reason not to," he agreed. "You weren't at church Sunday."

I welcomed the change in subject, but it still caught me by surprise. "I didn't realize I was supposed to be," I admitted, slightly concerned that I'd be forced to sit in some long-winded service in a few more days. It was the Bible Belt for a reason.

"I figured they wanted you to learn a bit more before being questioned by the masses."

"I guess so," I said. "What brought you here today, anyway? Certainly not the state of my soul."

He paused, the wheels turning behind his eyes as he fought to come up with an acceptable reason. Some part of me wondered if he came simply to see me. That same section of my brain hoped it was right. "I figured I'd help you," he finally said.

"Help me?" It took longer to click in my groggy brain than it should have.

"Help you get home. Though, Newton and Elliot would be devastated to fully lose you . . . well, their Elizabeth. I'm sure you'll be trying to go home again soon." He shrugged. "It's likely safer for me to take you than you go experiment."

Frankly, the thought had been pushed farther back in my mind. I wanted to go home, sure. But I didn't want to drown to do it. Also, every time I thought of the river, I saw her grayed, bruised face.

"But it didn't work last time," I reminded him, stomach churning.

"But if you try again, you won't have any doubts that it won't work."

"That's awfully depressing."

"Well, it would be nice to keep you here. Besides, I have a plan. Hurry, get dressed." He stood abruptly and left the room before I could prod him for answers.

I doubt I looked very put together by the time I finished. I rushed through every step of putting on the outfit. Sure, the thought of trying to head back to my time still made me queasy, but the surprise aspect was enough to have me hooked.

When I made it down the stairs, Sam handed me a sandwich and led the way out the front door.

"Are you going to tell me the plan?" I prodded.

"Not until we get there," he said, swinging into his saddle, then reaching down for my hand. I took his and placed my foot in the stirrup, awkwardly ending up in my designated place.

CHAPTER FOURTEEN

The sunlight flowed across us like a warm blanket, warning about the summer to come as we traveled in the direction of the town and the river.

Summer was never something I looked forward to. It was too hot. I'd been to Nevada before, and the heat was completely different. Even if they were both over 100 degrees.

Nevada felt like what I imagined lying in the sun to bake felt like. Or possibly a tanning bed—though I'd never tried that before. Certainly hot, but not necessarily unbearable.

Oklahoma, on the other hand . . . once it hit above 90 degrees, walking outside meant instant sweat. Always sweat. A choking sort of monster, out to murder each of its inhabitants one at a time.

I hoped I'd make it home before the heat took over. Air-conditioning certainly wasn't an option in the 1800s.

Despite it being the beginning of April, the trees were already losing their buds. Small, green leaves sparked across all the limbs, working hard at taking over their section of the sky. Birds chirped in each of them, sending happy vibes throughout my body.

But the wind couldn't be bothered to show up.

For most places, that was probably a good thing. For springtime Oklahoma, that was sometimes dangerous. The wind was sucked up into the air, replaced with a choking pressure.

The storms Elliot had warned me about. Any Okie knew that oppressive feeling.

"What do you do if there's a tornado?" I asked.

"The cellar?" he said. "You said it happened at the bridge?"

"Yes, the bridge," I said absently.

Even in my time, a cellar was the main option. That, or hide in a bathtub and hope for the best. "How do we know if one is coming?"

Even without him turning around, I could feel his sharp gaze. "You look at the clouds."

"Fair enough," I said, as we entered the tree line that ran next to the river. He had brought me to a different place than my last attempt. This time, we were on the opposite side of the bridge. I didn't blame him for not wanting to go back to where her body had been found.

Hopefully going in closer to where my own body had gone under would do the trick.

"Why are you doing this for me?" I asked as he dismounted and deftly tied the mare to a nearby tree.

"You're not going to stop trying until you're sure you can't go back. So, I'd better be here to make sure you don't drown yourself in the process." He reached up for my hand to help me down.

"Are you sure you're okay with being here?" I asked, glancing upstream. "With how close you two were . . ."

He shrugged, his shirt pulling taut over his shoulders as he stiffened. "I don't have much of a choice, do I?"

"You could have let me try all this on my own."

"I don't trust you not to kill yourself. Until you're convinced you can't go back, I'll go with you."

I wasn't sure if he was trying to be chivalrous with that, or trying to stab me in the gut. My body felt a little of both. "You don't think I can go back, do you?"

He stayed silent, watching his feet as we walked to the water's edge. "I don't have an answer for that," he finally managed.

It made perfect sense that he wouldn't believe me. For all he knew, I was some sorceress who had stolen his best friend's body and left her to die. Or just a witch of some kind. "I promise I'm not lying."

He sighed and leaned against one of the young trees. "I know you're not—I saw her body. But I don't think the river is some kind of door you can walk back and forth through."

Looking at the water in front of me, the doubt continued to creep through my body. He was right. Unless I managed to create the same conditions as before, essentially killing myself, I wouldn't know if it was possible to go back home or not.

The river flowed along as though nothing remotely bad could happen. I wouldn't be able to drown in that.

"Come on. Give it one more try." As I looked toward him, he pulled his shirt over his head and let it drop to the ground. My breath caught somewhere in my chest as I stared at him. Why did I have to notice now? Sure, a perk of the nineteenth century had to be how fit everyone seemed to be. Didn't mean I wanted to be caught gawking.

"Come on," he prodded, turning around to give me some privacy to remove my top layers.

I hesitated, eyes glued to the muscles of his back.

Done waiting, Sam trudged into the water. By the way he froze once he got far enough that it hit his upper thighs, I assumed it was rather chilly.

I shook my head wildly to get it back into gear. If I didn't give in and try one more time, I would always wonder. I tugged my dress over my head and stripped to the shift. Taking that off would cross every boundary, I was sure.

Besides, I *certainly* wouldn't have an admirable muscle structure to gaze at.

Slipping off my shoes and socks, I waded in after him.

The water was freezing. At least in comparison to the warm air. It simply had not caught up from the random freezes Oklahoma liked to send its way. But I powered on, tensing each time the water hit sensitive areas. The water only came to the top of my hips. Once I reached the middle, I forced myself to kneel and cover all the way to my chin.

I had to do it right.

"I have rules," Sam said. He stood right in front of me, so close I was sure he could feel my breath on the skin of his arm. The thought sent involuntary shivers up my spine.

"What are your rules?" My voice sounded choked.

"You have one shot. If I think you've been under there too long, I'll bring you back up."

"What if I actually have to drown to make it back, though?"

He narrowed his eyes at me. "Then I guess this is your new home. It's not worth dying."

Some part of me wanted to argue with him. Some deep-down, sick part of me. But he was right. I would rather be alive, figuring out a new life with these people than becoming another body for Sam to bury in the dark.

"What would Newton and Elliot do if they lost me?" I said, not expecting an answer.

"I don't think they would know what to do. It's been years since your, well, her mother died. They haven't been able to fully let that go."

"Why not? How long has it been?"

"I don't know the answer to either of those questions." He shook his head. "But I do know you're stalling."

"Am not."

"Am too. Get it over with." He roughly pushed the top of my head so it ducked under the surface.

"Hey!" I squealed, wiping the water off my face before the droplets could make their way into my eyes. "That doesn't count as my one try!"

"Then you'd better get working on it. Or else I'll have to help you." He held his hands up in an ominous fashion and wiggled his fingers.

I backed up a few inches. "No, no, no. I can do it. Just give me a minute."

He nodded but moved to a safe spot slightly behind and to the right of me. Easier to pull me back into the air if he needed to, I assumed.

As I looked down at the water flowing around me, my heart rate increased. I had to fight to keep my breath from following its lead. There was no real reason to begin panicking. Sam wouldn't let me drown, I knew that. But that fact didn't do much to calm my heart's rapid fear dance.

What if the attempt didn't work at all? What if it could never work? It was becoming increasingly probable that I wouldn't be able to go back home. Ever. It would be fine, I'd adapt to wiping my butt with a farmer's almanac. There wasn't a family remaining back home anyway. Just everything I knew and had worked for.

Funny enough, I would miss Sam too. And it broke my heart to imagine what Elliot and Newton would go through when they found out they were alone.

But if I didn't try, I'd never really know.

With a kind of frustrated shriek, I ducked under the water. Staying underneath would have been much easier if it was deep. If that was the case, I could have simply swum all the way down, found something to hold on to, and let the air leave my body. If only it was that easy. Instead, I just tipped my head forward, kept my eyes closed, and hoped for the best.

It's harder to drown yourself on purpose. I counted to keep my mind busy, but I only made it to ten. When that didn't keep the nerves at bay, I focused on what I'd make of my life at home.

Sure, I didn't have parents anymore, and my brother had given up, but I had a career path. Or at least I did if the teachers let me take the final exams.

I'd be a teacher. If they would hire me, I hoped to get on at one of the local colleges. I didn't want to deal with all the kids running around, leaving sticky spots all over the classroom. As cute as they were, they had annoying, protective parents.

And that was as long as I could stay under.

I came back up, lungs burning, gasping for air.

The humidity choked me, the soupy weather and suffocating pressure threatening to kill me itself.

I hadn't gone anywhere.

"Dammit!" The weight of the situation settled hard on my shoulders.

Wisely, Sam didn't say anything. Though the snotty question of "Anything?" was written all over his face.

"I can't do it!" I roughly shoved at the water in front of me.

He put an arm around my shoulders and gave them a reassuring squeeze.

"I can't make myself drown," I muttered.

"I appreciate that."

"And it didn't work."

"I see this," he said, releasing a sigh the second he realized he said it aloud. "Sorry." He gave me another squeeze. "Maybe you were meant to be here."

"Why would that be?" There wasn't much of a reason I could come up with that would require such drastic measures. No force on the earth would want to ship someone from one time to another just for fun. Right?

"I've been thinking a lot about it this past week. What I'm thinking is, Elizabeth wasn't supposed to die yet. She was meant to have a full life, carry on the bloodline. But something happened. Maybe you were brought back here to take her place to fix the missing spot."

I stared at him. Spouting some science fiction novel at me. Not what I expected from him, but it did make sense.

"Why do I look like her?"

He shrugged. "Bloodlines?"

He had a point. "So I might be her great-great-great-something-granddaughter?"

Sam smirked. "Nah. That makes me feel old. How about twins in time?"

I narrowed my eyes at him. "Cheesy, much?"

The wheels visibly turned in his head as he mulled over my word choice, but he didn't miss a beat. "It makes me feel better than the idea of being a few hundred years older than you."

I thought for a moment. "Somewhere around a hundred and fifty? Or forty."

He glared at me. "So I'm long dead. Thanks."

"Not as far as I'm concerned. You look pretty alive to me right now."

His grin returned to its normal spot, and he walked for the shore. "Come on. You deserve a distraction."

"Distraction?" I followed, pulling on the skirt part of the shift to keep it from tripping me.

Before I made it out of the water, Sam glanced at me, then quickly away. He looked like a guilty kid who didn't know what to do to avoid punishment. As I pulled on the wet shift to remove its grip on my middle, it hit me. My shift clung to my body, making every inch of my cold flesh obvious underneath. Self-conscious, I crossed my arms.

Dang cold water. Muscular or not, maybe I gave him a better view than I had thought.

I highly doubted *he* needed much of a distraction from the time travel situation anymore. From how he refused to turn his body so I could see him, I was positive he was preoccupied.

"We . . . uh . . ." He tossed my dress at me but held up his hand before I could put it back on. "We're going back into the water."

"What?" Why on earth did he want to let me back into the river?

He didn't bother answering. He stood still, likely mulling over the outfit problem. Finally, giving up, he led both the horse and me downstream. It wasn't a very long walk. We just reached near where the other end of town would have been.

A sod house could be seen just at the base of the hill, watching the town peacefully. It looked familiar but quiet. No one was home.

"Johnathan's house, right?" I asked, gesturing in its direction. "Have they been here long?"

"They came with the run. Johnathan's father participated. He died in an accident around a year later, though, leaving Johnathan alone with his grandmother."

I stared at the little house. "That's so sad."

"It's a common enough story." Sam shrugged, but the way he stared at the ground looked everything but dismissive.

"What about you? What's your story? Where are you from?"

"Kansas." He said it so simply, as though there was no way the story could be interesting.

"Why did your family decide to move here?"

He hesitated, his entire body pausing mid-step. "Ma died in childbed. Pa decided we needed a fresh start."

"I'm so sorry," I said, reaching out to set my hand on his shoulder.

"As I said, it's not an unusual story here."

"That doesn't make it any less sad."

"You said you lost your brother as well?"

I nodded, focusing on the toe of my boot. "He killed himself about a year ago. I don't think he could handle the loss of our parents anymore."

Sam wrapped an arm around me again, sending warm fuzzy feelings flying through my body. It didn't take the pain away, but it kept me from falling into the emotional rabbit hole.

He gestured to the river, standing taller with his knowledge that he had surprised me with something great.

Immediately, all depressing thoughts evaporated into the humid air, replaced by pure, childish joy.

The river was wider in that spot, and definitely deeper than where we had been before. The bank seemed free of most of its grass, worn down from all the feet that had traveled into the water before us. A long rope hung from one of the sturdier trees, knotted at several points.

"Why do I get the feeling this isn't appropriate behavior?" I asked, working a little too hard to fold up my dress and tuck it in the edge of the saddle, out of harm's way.

Sam reached up to grab the rope, testing the branch with his weight. Whether he did so to show off the muscles that rippled down his torso and arms, or simply to stay safe, I had no idea. "Because it isn't," he said, before letting himself fly out across the river, then he paused and dropped into the water.

A grin covered my face, impossible to hide. "Was that fun?" I called after him.

"Most certainly not! Your turn." He ducked under the water, coming back up like a child, all smiles and messy hair.

"Okay, okay," I said, grabbing the rope. Each time I scooted my feet forward, my heart picked up pace and I panicked. It was nearly impossible to talk myself into making the jump. Turning off my brain was the only way.

I jumped, holding on with all my might. It wasn't quite hard enough, but the rope was stationed close to the water's edge. My body flew over the surface, arms screaming in their effort to keep me up. Way too early, my hands slipped, sending me splashing ungracefully into the dirty river.

As soon as I broke the surface to take a deep breath, Sam's laughter took over.

"Hey!" I complained, wading over to him, squatting to keep my upper half safely covered by the water. I'd worn swimsuits, so a thin, wet dress shouldn't have made me embarrassed. But it somehow managed to make me feel exposed in front of him. "I thought you weren't supposed to be watching?"

Red traced across his face like a curtain. Guilty as charged. "You're covered! I just needed to make sure you weren't about to break your neck."

"Break my neck, huh?" I smirked at him. I had a sneaky suspicion his body would give away every bit of his inner thoughts. "If that's all you wanted, you stand all the way up and walk where I can see *you* clearly."

The shock that covered his face was enough to make me laugh. "What?"

"Go! If you didn't have any ulterior motives, go stand over there and prove it." I pointed in the general direction of the rope.

"You're not suggesting what I think you're suggesting . . . are you?" His eyes were filled with a swirl of bewilderment and arousal.

Some burning instinct inside my chest made it impossible to leave him alone.

"Am I?" I was so close to him, the sleeve of my shift floated to brush the curve of his bicep. Gym memberships certainly didn't exist, but his muscles would make any girl drool. Come to think of it, the doctor was the only person I had seen who had any pudge on him.

He scowled. "You're the one who didn't wear all the proper clothing."

"They didn't tell me to bring a bikini from home."

"I don't reckon I know what that is," he muttered, doing his best to keep his eyes from moving anywhere other than my face.

"Swimwear," I just said. My breathing had taken on a new kind of concentrated effort. His had slowed dramatically, nearly mimicking mine.

"You're supposed to wear something over that."

"I wouldn't keep a corset on to swim," I pointed out.

And the world around us broke with a splitting crack and bang, followed closely by a blinding flash.

CHAPTER FIFTEEN

We jerked apart as though we were slapped.

"Shit," he hissed, hurrying toward the bank with me right behind him.

"Where are we going?"

"The Spencers have a cellar," he said, breathless from both the excursion and the ever-thickening air.

As if broken by the curse, the clouds opened up and rain hammered onto us. Instead of a light, peaceful sort of sprinkle, it was the kind that made it nearly impossible to see more than a few feet ahead. The wind picked up to a terrifying level, making the trees nod and sway like a dancer. The entire sky had turned a dark mix between gray and green, looking like it belonged in some kind of oil painting instead of the real-life sky.

I couldn't see it—the trees were in my way, the wind was in my way, the water was in my way. And the hail . . .

The hail hurt, slapping the water with such force it sent it splashing a good foot out. It hammered our bodies, underlining the danger messages spinning out of control in my mind.

"Sam!" I shrieked as the rumble of what sounded like a distant train became unbearably loud.

"Down!" he shouted, practically tackling me to the bank. His body covered mine, half of us in the water, half on the hard ground.

Catching sight of the mare downstream from us, my heart broke. She was securely attached to one of the larger trees, rearing and screaming at the top of her lungs. Bellowing didn't even seem to be the right word. Her noises were agonizing, pleading with the universe to save her just once.

I couldn't hear my own scream over the extreme wind, breathy rumble of the beast, and the mare's suffering.

A tornado.

I would have given anything to be going through the car accident yet again, if only to get out of the way of the roaring wrath of Mother Nature.

The sheets of rain suddenly became heavier, if that was remotely possible. A few deep, booming sounds echoed through the ground. It sounded like far-off bass music.

Buildings. I'd heard the sounds described so many times, there was no mistaking it. The tornado was destroying everything in its path. Sam's body tensed above me as debris flew about. I didn't dare look. I was positive that if I lifted my head for just a split second, I would only see my imminent death as it roared toward me.

Please, please, God. Please let us get out of this alive! The thought of adding in a clause for being uninjured didn't cross my mind. Alive would be enough.

And then it was all gone.

The air felt like it had been sucked up into the vortex. As though I had shoved my head inside a Ziploc bag. The sky remained a sickening green, but we could see light blue coming our way.

The rain still fell, only in a much calmer fashion. The kind that did its best to wipe away the pain the storm had inflicted upon the land.

Hesitantly, Sam pushed himself off me. I let him help me up, my whole body weak from the shock. I wasn't hurt. Maybe a few bruises, but I'd figure that out later. He looked relatively okay as well, though he was covered in straw that had been dropped on us, and the bruises from the hail were already starting to form on his side and back.

"Are you okay?" My voice sounded loud in the silence around us.

"Yes," he said, lips pursed and eyes fixed on something in the distance. I turned to see, realizing as I did that his mare had gone as silent as the world around her.

I wanted to puke when I saw her. She had fallen where she was, a large branch through her middle. Her body lay completely still, the blood flowing out across the saturated sandy ground beneath.

Sam walked as though in a trance, kneeling beside her head to run his hand over her cheek.

Shouts came from downriver. Over in the direction of the doctor's house. My veins turned to ice.

Sam snatched my dress out of its place under the saddle and threw it at me. "Go," he commanded, his voice cracking.

I ran back the way we had come, struggling into the soaked dress as I went. The fabric clung to me, making it nearly impossible to get the skirt to make it all the way down as it should. I hardly noticed, and frankly, I didn't care.

By the looks of the scene in front of me, no one else would either.

Dr. Spencer's house had been hit.

A direct hit. Even though it didn't appear to have been a very strong tornado, it did its damage. The house was torn to shreds, split down the middle with only a few walls remaining. The beautiful red settee looked like something had shredded it, stuffing strewn everywhere. The wood that had done the deed poked out of the cushions.

A whole herd of people were at the rubble, yanking wood from the pile and throwing it behind them. An older woman stood off to the side, wailing as another one held her close.

It was Mrs. Spencer herself. My first reaction was to be grateful she hadn't been inside. My second was the automatic movement of sinking to my knees.

They pulled the body out slowly, yanking the remaining debris off him as though it would change the reality.

Mrs. Spencer's wail took on a new, more desperate pitch as she fell toward her husband's body. They let her go. She touched his shoulder, his pale, lifeless cheek. Though she refused to look at the shrapnel that had impaled him.

The tornado had not followed any of the rules on what to destroy. Glass protruded from his forehead, legs, torso. No part was left untouched.

There would be no way for me to erase the image of the broken man in front of me. The wail from his wife would be even harder. She could hardly breathe she cried so hard. Her friend came over and hauled her back to let the men finish removing her husband's lifeless body.

One of the men took off his jacket and laid it over Dr. Spencer's body.

I looked around the crowd. The entire town had appeared out of nowhere. Children stood among the adults, shock and curiosity written all over their faces. Even the youngest ones couldn't escape the gravity of the situation. A few of the older ones had tears in their eyes, but otherwise didn't react. They had likely seen more death in their lifetime than I could dream of.

Slowly but surely, the crowd dissipated. Some went to help get the body to its temporary resting place, while others went to help Mrs. Spencer rest at the general store.

Dead inside, I followed the crowd.

Children ran along the riverbank, marveling at the tree branches that hung in unnatural directions. I didn't dare look that way. The pain flowing from every corner of the world hurt too much.

I knew the pain far too well.

Unnoticed, I moved to sit in front of one of the buildings on Main Street. Numb. Everything was numb. No emotions, no thoughts, nothing. I simply sat there, watching the people of the town wandering in a zombielike fashion.

After a while, people resumed their gossip.

"I heard the doctor's house got hit!" one lady said, followed by gasps from the ladies with her. There would be no escaping the news. Everyone would be talking of the doctor's death for weeks to come. Maybe even years, for all I knew.

There would be many tornadoes in Woodward's history. There was no way around it. It was Oklahoma. There would be a very bad one in 1947, effectively wiping out much of the town that I could see from my seat. Over a hundred people would die in Oklahoma alone on that day.

"Elizabeth," came the tender voice of Elliot. He stepped onto the sidewalk carefully, as though any sudden movement would scare me. "Are you okay?"

I looked at him carefully, noting the scrapes on his face and the dirt that covered him nearly from top to bottom. "Were you in it?" I asked.

"No," he assured, giving me a one-armed squeeze before helping me to my feet. "Was helping downstream. The Mallards' barn was hit too, and I heard the Indian boy's livestock took some damage."

I felt my eyes grow wide. We'd been right there, and Sam's horse hadn't made it. Why hadn't I thought to check on them first?

"But they're okay, right?"

Elliot nodded. "Yeah, they'll be fine." He led me to his horse and wordlessly helped me up.

We rode in silence for a while, my body automatically leaning onto his back and my eyes relaxing. There was no way I could actually fall asleep. Every time my mind started to relax enough for such a thing, the images of Mrs. Spencer's grief and the horse took over.

And Sam . . . I felt my cheeks heat up at the thought. If only Elliot knew.

Why hadn't he been with Newton, anyway?

"I thought you were working with Pa?" The word tasted strange on my tongue, but I doubted calling him by name would work.

Like a child caught in the act, Elliot froze for the slightest of moments. "I was close, heard the screams."

I swiveled the best I could to face him, but he placed his hands on my shoulders and turned me back to face the front.

"Liar," I muttered.

"You gonna say what you were up to?"

I didn't say a word.

The road to the house didn't have any damage to speak of. Other than the broken limbs on the solitary trees that had managed to sprout so far from the river's edge.

The sod houses that we passed looked perfectly fine—even the partially completed cabin looked okay.

It blew my mind how tornadoes could be so picky on what they destroyed. I'd seen them wipe out a block of houses just to leave one on the corner without a speck of damage.

As we made it back to the house, the rain resumed. A depressing, chilly rain this time. It flowed down our bodies, wiping away what dirt it could and soaking us to our skin.

Being the gentleman, Elliot helped me back down at the front porch. I eyed him closely, hunting for any signs of his activities. I certainly didn't expect to see any.

But there it was. A red mark right under his collarbone.

I stifled a laugh and touched my own collar. "You might wanna button up your shirt the rest of the way."

"What?" He glanced down, immediately turning bright red.

"What's her name?" I asked, leaning against the porch's railing.

"None of your business, Elizabeth," he snapped, as though the use of my name was enough to silence the entire subject.

"Sure it is, if you don't want me telling."

The door opening was enough to silence both of us. The booming voice that followed made my blood freeze.

"Where have the two of you been?"

"Putting the horse away!" Elliot called, gratefully escaping in the direction of the barn.

I turned slowly, wanting nothing more than to run after Elliot.

Newton stood in the doorway, pipe dangling from the corner of his lips, eyes narrowed. The smell of what I could only assume was soap wafted from the room behind him.

I hunted for the easiest excuse. "We were helping in town."

He eyed me, taking in what I could only assume was a bedraggled appearance.

"Wasn't born yesterday, Elizabeth. I got here *before* the storm started."

I glanced back in the direction of the barn, wishing Elliot would hurry up. He'd likely be taking his sweet time.

"Water's still warm. Get washed up." Newton backed up from the doorway, beckoning to let me into the overly warm room.

The tub sat in the center of the room, steaming and inviting. Even though the water didn't look to be the cleanest, a bath sounded fantastic.

"So, I'm not in trouble?" I wanted to kick myself as soon as the words left.

"Hmph," Newton muttered. "Hurry and get cleaned up, then come get us. Elliot goes next." He shut the door between us, trapping him on the front porch to await his son.

I stood for a long moment, wondering whether I was lucky, or if his wrath still awaited me when I didn't look like a drowned rat.

It didn't particularly matter. The bath looked inviting, I was dirty, and there was only so long before someone tried to come inside the front door again.

Decision made, I raced upstairs to grab clean clothes and a hairbrush. I'd certainly have a hard time detangling my hair.

"Don't take too long, it's chilly out!" Elliot shouted when I came downstairs.

"I'll try!" I called back. If Newton hadn't been out there, Elliot would have been waiting a very long time for his turn.

I tried to hurry, I really did. But the warm water practically melted me to the spot. After an unknown amount of time, the relaxing bath ended with a brisk knock on the front door. "Hold on!" I called.

I crawled out of the tub, satisfied that I was just about as clean as I could be in a pre-used tub. I scrubbed myself dry and pulled on the clothes I had brought down. I wrapped the towel around my shoulders to keep my wet hair off me, as well as keep myself hidden under the thin fabric.

"You're safe!" I called when I was finished.

They came in almost immediately, the rain pounding down behind them. Newton hung his hat on the hook and let out a long breath. He looked older than I'd ever seen him, worn out from the day's events.

They shooed me back upstairs for Elliot to get cleaned up. I expected to be banished there for the rest of the night, but when Newton called my name, the worry sprang up in my chest again.

Obediently, I made my way downstairs. I just knew it was all over for both of us. If I was going down, Elliot would be going down with me.

The tub was gone, probably placed out of the way on the front porch, and both men lounged in their chairs. The argument that had been on the tip of my tongue disappeared. He didn't seem angry.

"Come on." Newton crooked his finger and nodded at the empty chair.

I dragged my feet but obediently made my way to the chair and sat down. Newton watched my every move, making me squirm.

He wordlessly picked up the thick book from beside his chair, flipping it somewhere in the middle. It was a Bible, well worn and full of more family information than I could fathom. I secretly wished Bibles were still used as a track for genealogy. It was such a poetic way to do things.

"'Let not your hearts be troubled.'" Newton's voice rang strong and clear, demanding the reverence the verse deserved. "'Ye believe in God, believe also in me. In my Father's house are many mansions: if it were not so, I would have told you. I go to prepare a place for you. And if I go and prepare a place for you, I will come again, and receive you unto myself; that where I am, there ye may be also. And whither I go ye know, and the way ye know.'"

The old words didn't throw me off as much as I had anticipated. I had heard the verse many times throughout my childhood, and likely had memorized it one time or another for Sunday school.

I'd met many people who didn't believe in God, or really any sole creator of the universe. Though I rarely read the Bible on my own terms, I took comfort in the verses. There was always something that helped with every situation.

That was what Newton was doing. He went back a few hundred pages in the old book, finding another well-known verse.

"'Yea, though I walk through the valley of the shadow of death, I will fear no evil: for thou art with me; thy rod and thy staff they comfort me.'"

"Amen." Elliot barely uttered the word.

As Newton continued to read verse after verse, I stopped listening. I let my mind slip deeper and deeper into the sad reality that the day held. All I could see was that man, broken and gone, lying on the ground with his wife sobbing above him. No family deserved that. He deserved more of a life. He had arguably been one of the more important members of society, being the only doctor.

"Elizabeth," Newton said.

My head shot up. "Hmm?"

"Did you hear me?" His eyes were sharp, looking straight into my soul.

I tensed, unsure how to answer and stay innocent. "No?" I finally managed.

"Always somewhere in your head." Elliot rolled his eyes.

Newton sighed, shoulders sagging in defeat. "I know both of you are lying."

I fidgeted some more, wishing I could become one with the chair.

"But right now, I'm too tired to deal with either of you." He stood up and stretched. "Get up to bed, and I'll deal with both of you in the morning."

Elliot and I exchanged glances but said nothing.

"Oh, and Elizabeth, Helen wants to meet with you tomorrow for a dress fitting. She'll be coming here, so you'd better not leave. Do you understand?" His brown eyes narrowed into daggers.

"Yes . . . but who's Helen?" I asked cautiously. If it wasn't one thing I had to be sad about, it was another. The damn wedding.

"Mrs. Barnette," he said, every inch of his voice dripping with a warning against mischief. Perfect, Luke's mother would be showing up. "Come up with something to feed them as well. I believe they'll be here around midday."

"They?" I couldn't help but ask. *Please don't be Luke. Please don't be Luke . . .*

"Her daughter, Mabel."

My whole body relaxed as I breathed a sigh of relief that earned a sharp glance from Newton.

"You hear me, you'll stay here?"

"Yes," I assured. My mind did its best to convince itself that trying on an ancient wedding dress might actually be fun. It worked, but only for a moment. His mother couldn't be nearly as bad as his father, or even him. Right?

"Good. We'll be in town, working with the others on repairs." He waited for my nod of understanding before he continued. "Now, I'm tired. Both of you get up to bed."

Elliot stood up and held out his hand for mine. "Come on, Baby Blue Eyes, let's go," he said, using what I could only assume was a nickname for his version of me. He held out his hand, and I took it, letting him pull me to my feet.

We left our separate ways, and I collapsed on the bed. As tired as I was, I wasn't entirely sure if it was possible to sleep.

After a long time staring at the ceiling, I went to the chest to pull out the veil. It was so delicate, I was afraid to touch it. Even though it was still unfinished, it must have taken the girl a very long time to create.

With a sigh, I laid it on top of the chest and went to curl up again. I had no choice in the matter. Not really. The only thing I could do was go through the motions.

But what about Sam? More than likely, I wouldn't have been upset if it were *him* I was meant to marry. Especially after the river.

But I hardly knew Luke. Perhaps there was a reason the original Elizabeth chose him, or rather agreed to marry him. I'd heard many times that the relationship for an arranged marriage would form a bond eventually. It made sense—the couple would rely on each other, after all.

But what was I even thinking? I didn't ever want to see that blond, pigheaded asshole again. Let alone marry him.

Sleep didn't visit me that night. At least not enough that I could track. The entire time, I flipped from stressing over the upcoming wedding to wondering if there was a fraction of a chance with Sam.

CHAPTER SIXTEEN

Cursing.

Angry, frantic cursing joined with the raised voices coming from Elliot's room.

I groaned and rolled over, pulling the quilt over my head. The sun wasn't even up yet, so I certainly wasn't going to see what trouble he got himself into. More than likely, he'd been caught sneaking back from what's-her-face's house.

The commotion continued from Elliot's room, but I completely ignored it and let myself fall back asleep.

The next thing I knew, I heard footsteps in my own room, followed by my shock as someone dumped water all over me.

I sat up with a squeal, wiping the cold water out of my eyes. I expected Elliot to be the culprit. "What the ever-lovin'—" I cut myself off just in time to avoid spewing every curse word I knew. Newton stood next to the bed, an empty bucket in his hands and the slightest smirk playing at the edge of his lips.

"You're up. Good. Get dressed and downstairs."

Grinding my teeth, I glanced at the window. Nope, still dark. "What time is it? What's going on?" I pulled the blanket up to my chin for comfort but dropped it back into my lap with a splat. Everything was far too wet.

"Four. Get going, girl. You don't want me to catch you dawdling." He turned without another word and walked into the hallway.

"But . . . why?" My voice cracked from the lack of use. "The sun isn't even awake yet!"

Newton ignored me entirely. "You too, hurry up!" he shouted at Elliot's door.

Grudgingly, I crawled out of bed. I didn't dare go against him and go back to sleep—though he certainly didn't deserve my obedience. I was soaked. Sleep wouldn't have been possible, anyway.

I joined Elliot downstairs a few minutes later, my hair braided down my back to try to control it while it dried again. His tousled brown hair was insane, curly and pointing every which way. Also soaked. He somehow looked more miserable than I felt.

Newton paced before us, hands lightly clasped behind his back. "I know the two of you lied to me yesterday."

I shivered. I highly doubted he had any sort of corporal punishment in mind. Elliot wouldn't stand still for such a thing. That, at least, made me feel somewhat safer.

"I know full well the two of you won't tell me the truth, either. So"—he pulled a bucket off the table and handed it to me—"we have visitors coming today, and we've fallen behind on the household chores. So, guess who gets to get it back in shape?"

I stared into the bucket. A rag.

Newton handed a broom to Elliot.

"But before you get started, put some coffee on. I think I might need a little extra to get through the day." Quite pleased with himself, Newton waltzed over to his chair and plopped down to light his pipe.

"Can't we do this once the sun comes up?" I asked, still frozen to the spot.

"There won't be enough time to get everything done if you wait that long."

Elliot tapped the broom against the floor as though testing its efficiency. "What specifically is it we're supposed to do?"

Newton broke into a full grin, holding on to the pipe with one hand so it wouldn't fall. He'd been waiting for that question. "Now, that's the fun part. You're gonna do everything I tell you to until it's time for us to leave and help in town."

Suddenly the house seemed much larger than it had before.

"Go on, someone get the water. The floor isn't going to clean itself."

A groan escaped my tired lips, and I slumped like an irritated teenager.

"Insolence will not be tolerated. Go, before I decide I need the barn spit shined too." He waved his hand absently at us.

"I'll go get water," Elliot muttered, taking the bucket from me and handing me the broom.

It was going to be a long morning.

By the time Newton let us stop working, we were all ready for a nap. He'd drank an entire pot of coffee by himself, had a decent breakfast, and hadn't needed to lift a single finger. The constant smile on his face was enough proof that the old man was enjoying treating us like his own personal servants.

Eventually, he gave in and told us to eat as well. We plopped down at the table like sacks of flour, not planning on moving again.

The house was clean at least. Probably cleaner than it ever had been. I'd never take a vacuum for granted again.

"Come on, let's go help them with the cleanup," Newton said, grabbing his hat off the hook and placing it solidly on his head.

Elliot looked as though he would pass out on the table, but somehow he avoided groaning. He stood slowly, grabbed his own hat, and trudged out onto the porch.

"Elizabeth," Newton said.

My head shot up. "Hmm?" As soon as he shut the door behind us, I fully planned on taking a nap.

"Stay in this house. I don't want to hear of Helen Barnette hunting all over tarnation for you. Got it?"

I nodded sleepily. I didn't plan on going anywhere except bed.

Apparently satisfied with my promise, he shut the door behind him.

I waited until the sound of horses had nearly faded away before hurrying back up to my bed.

They'd arrive around midmorning. I was sure to have at least a couple hours.

I probably didn't even have that.

Thankfully, the sound of the wagon woke me before they got close enough to discover my laziness. I pushed my hair back into place as well as I could and hurried downstairs, brushing all the wrinkles I could manage out of my skirt as I went.

I watched them come from the window, not sure what was required of polite society. I let out a long sigh as I watched a middle-aged woman crawl off the front seat, her lithe daughter holding on to the reins. They worked together while they unhitched the horses, then grabbed a large bag and started toward the house.

With a grumble to myself, I came onto the front porch and reached to help them with their bags.

"Elizabeth! Hi!" the girl squealed, giving me a hug with her free arm. Mable, I assumed. She was tall and thin, looking like some kind of model, or just a cheerleader. She had long blond hair curled neatly down her back. Her eyes were a startling blue, just like her brother's. Right off the bat, the similarities ended there. She seemed bubbly and friendly.

Maybe the dress trial wouldn't be so bad.

One look at the lady's face made me rethink that. Her lips were pursed, matching the rest of her tense body. If I hadn't met her husband and son, I would have wondered if a bee had stung her where the sun don't shine.

"I haven't seen you in so long!" Mable squeezed my shoulders again. "Everyone said you had an accident. I'm so glad you're okay. I'm very sorry about Rose, though. I know how much you loved that mare. Hopefully your pa can get you a new one soon. If not, I'm sure Luke can help you get one after you're married—"

"*Mable*," her mother scolded. "No one wants to hear you babble incessantly."

"Sorry, Ma," Mable said, much of the energy zapping out of her body as her shoulders slumped.

"Mable, stand up straight. Dear girl! What am I going to do with you?"

Almost as soon as we had stepped inside, she got to work. "Elizabeth, Mable, dear. Go get the veil and corset from upstairs. I want to work here, as we have more room." She carefully unpinned her feather-topped hat and laid it across the back of the rocking chair, then pulled the pure white fabric out of the bag.

I obeyed and headed up to my room, Mable close behind me.

Mable barely waited until we had crossed into my room before speaking again. "Pa said you lost your memories. Is that true?"

"Yes," I said, kneeling to open the chest.

She plopped herself onto the edge of my bed. "So you don't remember nothin'? Not even your mother?"

I shook my head slowly as I handed her the half-finished veil and decorated corset. The special wedding corset had a lot more to it than the one I actively had on my body. It looked more constricting, if that was fully possible. It still had the snaps at the front, but the lace lining the edges and the perfectly stretched fabric across the boning made it look much more like a torture device.

"You okay?" Mable asked, putting the corset in her lap and fiddling with the lace.

I nodded. "Yeah, just tired." I knew I didn't sound very convincing.

"You're not getting cold feet already, are you? Everyone says that's normal."

I couldn't help but smile at the thought. If only it was classic cold feet.

But this wasn't butterflies.

"The accident changed some things," I said, using the foot of the bed to pull myself back to my feet.

"Oh." Mable's smile sagged. "We'll be sisters, though. That'll help." That thought alone was all it took to replace the smile in full force.

"That's true," I couldn't help but say. If I couldn't get away in time, this young girl would likely be the only good part of that relationship.

"I really do envy you, though," she said with a sigh, running her fingers along the edges of the veil.

I raised one eyebrow. "Why on earth would you envy me?"

"You're free to marry the one you love. I'll never be." She slumped again, eyes not leaving the fancy lace.

"First off, no. Second off, no." I sat down beside her. "You have a better chance at marrying for love than I do, don't you?"

She shook her head slowly. "Pa already hates him."

"Already hates him?" I leaned forward so I could get a good look at her miserable face. "How old are you, anyway?" She didn't look a day over fifteen to me.

"Seventeen," she whispered.

"And you already have someone in mind?" Every ounce of her happiness had been thrown out the window and trampled by an entire herd of horses.

She nodded.

"Who?" I asked, wishing she'd go back to her talkative self and tell me everything.

She gave me a look that made me think the other Elizabeth already knew the answer. Even so, she lowered her voice. "Johnathan."

"Oh . . . Oh!" I said, growing louder as soon as all the information clicked. His grandmother had mentioned he had a girl, but I hadn't expected it to be Luke's sister.

"Shh!" She waved her hand wildly as if it could take the words out of the air. "It's a secret. My family *can't* find out. I don't want to know what they would do."

"I won't tell." I ran my fingers over my lips in a sealing gesture. "Promise."

"I know you won't. You're good like that." She gave me a one-armed hug. "I'm worried about him with the storm, though. I think they lost some livestock, but I don't know what else got hit. No one will tell me."

"Maybe you'll see him at the funeral?"

She shrugged. "Only if I can get away. He probably won't be there. You understand how it is."

It took me a few moments to gather exactly what she meant. Johnathan wasn't white. It would probably affect what social things he participated in.

"We have work to get done down here!" Helen shouted, her voice shrill enough that it made me flinch.

Mable laughed. "You'll look great, let's go." She grabbed my hand and pulled me toward the door. "I can't wait to see what it looks like *on* you! Luke's not gonna know *what* to think when he sees you!"

My steps faltered as I made my way downstairs, unbidden thoughts creeping into my head.

Wedding night.

That would be a thing.

It would *not* be happening. I shivered as I imagined his hands pulling at the ties of my dress.

Helen had all kinds of things laid out on the table. A woman on a mission, she didn't wait for anything other than for me to stand still so she could get to work. She expertly undid the old dress and let it drop to the ground.

I knew I was more covered in my ancient-style underwear than even my pajamas at a sleepover, but the air that hit my collarbone still sent a chill up my spine.

I had to get out of this.

There was no possible way I could survive such a marriage.

Switching corsets went better than I had feared. The fancy, tight-laced-looking version still fit like it was made for me. And I guess it sort of was. Every inch of it hugged my body and lifted it into place. It was uncomfortably snug at the small part of my waist, which was only made worse by yanking the laces.

I gasped in surprise and placed my hands on the back of the chair to keep my balance. Helen watched my breathing, and the moment I let it out, she pulled. She was quite happy to take it past the point of being comfortable and to the body manipulation point.

"It's too tight," I choked out as I stood up, my hand running along the front of the corset, feeling each of the precise stitches holding the boning in place. It was amazing to me that the device didn't even look stretched to its limits. It was strong, prepared for my torture.

"No, it's not," Helen chided, as she tucked the spare laces back into the corset. Otherwise, they'd likely drag the ground. "I told you, you needed to be lacing your daily corset tighter. If you had, this wouldn't be at all uncomfortable." She picked up what looked like some strange, thin, double-stacked airplane pillow and tied it around my now tiny waist, settling it onto my rear.

A bustle. The idea that it was created with a funky neck pillow made me want to laugh. Fashion had its quirks. Even in my own time. After all, weren't shoulder pads a thing when I was born? And tights—those blasted leg-hair-destroying monsters.

I let myself fall back into my quiet misery while the girls adjusted petticoats, messed with the butt pillow some more, and then finally picked up the massive white dress.

It contained so much fabric, I could feel the weight on my shoulders before it even touched me. But weren't modern wedding dresses the same? There seemed to be no limit to how much fabric was obscene.

"You're so lucky," Mable breathed, as they slipped it over my head and let it drape to the floor.

The collar was lace-lined, the edge of the sleeves were lace-lined, the waist was lace-lined—pretty much anything that could be lined in lace had been. The train wasn't abnormally long, but it was most certainly decorated. There were what looked like bows attached on the skirt, flowing down into the train. There were so many details it made my head spin.

"Why am I lucky?" I asked, unsure of how to really phrase the question. The dress was gorgeous. High quality, handmade, and definitely expensive.

"To get a dress like this, of course." Helen tsked her tongue. "Don't be so ungrateful."

I shot Mable a questioning look, hoping she'd save me and manage to explain. She didn't disappoint.

"All the ladies of town helped make it," Mable said, reaching out to caress the fabric that flowed from my hips. "I hope I can have a dress like this one day."

Helen scoffed. "You won't. Not unless your father strikes gold somehow, which ain't gonna happen anywhere in this godforsaken place."

"It is very extravagant," I admitted, turning my hips as well as I could to watch the fabric swish from side to side. This earned a sharp tug from Helen as she worked to fasten the back.

"I'll probably just have to wear my Sunday dress." Mable sighed, plopping down in the chair.

"I'll make sure you get more than that," Helen snapped. "No daughter of mine will go without a special dress. However, it has to be practical."

I let my fingers trail over one of the bows. It made sense that they would have to wear dresses that were able to be worn more than once. There was a good chance that Mable would have to wear a new, nice dress that would double as her future Sunday best.

"Maybe you can wear this one," I heard myself saying. Perhaps she could wear it to get married to Johnathan. I certainly didn't plan on using it.

"Hopefully it's still in style by that point." Mable had her arms crossed and a pout on her face. "I'll probably be some old maid by the time I get married." She shot her mother a defiant glare.

"The right man just hasn't come around yet," Helen said. She knelt and began adjusting the hem, pins held securely between her teeth. "Elizabeth, stop squirming."

I held myself rigid, hoping it would be enough. There was so much fabric, it didn't take much to make it move.

"Why do I get such a fancy dress?" I finally asked, feeling a bit idiotic to ask such a simple question. What did it matter if I asked? I had "memory loss," after all.

"Because you don't have a ma," Mable said simply.

"*Mable!*" Helen snapped. "Be polite!"

"Sorry . . ." Mable ducked her head. "But that's really why. They felt sorry that you didn't have anyone to help you with your dress, so everyone helped instead."

A community wedding.

My stomach churned, and I had to close my eyes to keep from falling into mass panic mode.

It didn't take Helen long to determine that all her alterations had been perfect. She immediately got the garb off me. The second the snaps of the corset were released, I felt like the Pillsbury Doughboy. I breathed in and out, letting my body fill with air like a balloon.

Hellen shook her head in disapproval. "Tighten your regular corset, Elizabeth."

"Yes ma'am," I muttered. Only because I knew if I didn't, she would probably do it for me. Getting dressed in my own clothes again was liberating. Even though it still involved a corset, it felt like the perfect amount of support instead of a constricting jail cell.

"I'm afraid we can't stay for tea," Helen said, as she put the dress back in the bag. "We must go assist with the funeral planning in town. You need to get that veil finished. Don't think I didn't notice that you haven't finished the stitching on the bottom. Your mother would be rolling around in her grave if she knew how you were slacking off on your stitching."

Good, I thought. I hadn't made anything for them to eat anyway. "Yes ma'am." Her penetrating gaze made me squirm. I had no plans on touching the veil. I didn't plan on wearing it in the first place, but I certainly didn't know how to add a single, tiny, decorative stitch to the thing.

"Good. Now, we'll see you at church tomorrow!" Helen smiled some kind of overly happy, fake smile and headed out the door.

Mable waved back at me, genuinely beaming. "I'll see you tomorrow!"

There was no way I couldn't wave back at the girl. If her brother had been more like her, I might have let myself consider going through the motions until I escaped. But he certainly didn't have a lick of her charm.

CHAPTER SEVENTEEN

The requirement to go to church didn't seem like much of a big deal, until I had to wake early for it.

Elliot's idea of a polite way to wake me that morning was simply to take my arm and pull. Carefully, sure, but that didn't change the fact that I had been deep asleep.

I woke in a fit, slapping wildly at the offending monster. My mind hadn't been given any chance to catch up. He didn't give my mind time to process. For all I knew, he could have been a monster.

So, I bit him.

It wasn't hard. Well, not really. My teeth certainly left a mark, but not enough to draw blood. That alone had to mean something.

He didn't agree.

His first instinct was to slap me.

The sound struck me before his hand, but the moment the stinging recognition hit me, my earlier surprise was immediately replaced by fury.

"You hit me!" I yelled, hand flying straight to my cheek. "Don't do that!" I punched him in the arm and lay back in bed.

"Well, you bit me!" He rubbed the bite mark hard enough that the friction had to hurt.

The sun wasn't fully up in the sky. Dull light peeked through the window, but not even enough for the birds to begin saying much of anything. One made its own squawking in the distance, but he certainly didn't count.

"You have to get up, dadgummit." He pulled on my arm again, this time hard enough that my whole body moved to the edge of the mattress.

"I'll get up when I'm damn ready to!" I pulled back with all my might and tried to wrap my body in the quilt. He simply yanked on the covers, effectively pulling them completely off my body. Thankfully, I didn't toss and turn much, meaning my nightgown stayed where I wanted it during the night.

"You bastard! Give that back!" I shouted, leaning to the end of the bed to grab the blanket. Before my fingers got close, he scooped me up like a doll. "Let me go! You . . . You . . ." Every bad name I could think of swirled through my head so fast, I couldn't pin one down.

"Elliot! Elizabeth! Stop your bickering immediately and get ready! Don't make me tell you again," Newton shouted from his inevitable spot downstairs.

It worked. Elliot plopped me down, and we both went our separate ways to be grouchy and get dressed in peace. Simple, as though our squabble had never existed. Like siblings.

I missed my own personal vat of coffee that I'd had in my apartment back home. I would easily have downed an entire pot before my eyes had fully opened.

Instead, I was handed a sad sandwich when I got downstairs. I was dressed in a somewhat nice, dark brown dress, my hair pulled back into the best bun attempt I could make. Since no one said anything about my choice of attire, I figured I had done it correctly.

Wordlessly, we all took our depressing breakfast and went to the wagon. While I had taken my sweet time getting ready, as Elliot was sure to point out, they had hitched up the horses and made sure everything was ready to go.

We all sat on the bench seat, Newton driving, Elliot beside him, and me on the edge. I didn't bother holding my hat to my head; it rested on my back, holding on by the ribbon tied around my neck. Elliot mentioned something about hat pins, but I ignored him entirely. Instead, I hunted the landscape for tornado damage.

There wasn't much to be seen, as the touchdown had been on the other side of town. Trees speckled the landscape, many of them with freshly broken limbs hanging precariously. The life of a tree would usually be short in Oklahoma.

The number of wagons lining Main Street was shocking. Everyone must have shown up for the funeral. Even for a small town, they took up most of the street.

The cool wind was no match for the dark mood that filled the air. A few people exchanged hellos and a light hug together, but otherwise there was no noise. Not even a bird could be heard, as though Mother Nature knew a family had been ruined by her hand.

I waited as the men got off the wagon and hitched up the horses. It appeared to be what the other ladies did, so I tried to follow suit. The last thing I wanted to do was cause a scene of some kind at a funeral. Sure enough, as soon as they were finished, Elliot came to my side and helped me down. It certainly was easier, holding his hand and getting to step out instead of hop.

Well, you're less likely to show off those overly sexual ankles. I brushed the wrinkles out of my skirt and looked around. Most people were in black, or darker shades in general. The closest I—or rather, she—had in her chest was the brown, sad dress. So, it was what I wore.

Before we moved on to begin the depressing mingling, Elliot tapped the hat on the back of my neck. With a sigh, I pulled it back on my head, shade instantly covering my face.

At least the pale skin I'd been given wouldn't burn. Though, the unfashionable freckles had already taken over.

Sam stood by one of the newly arrived wagons, talking to some-one just around the corner. I tried to step in his general direction, but Elliot's arm came to rest on my back, effectively pushing me forward.

"You'll see your dear Sam later." His voice was teasing but sent chills up my spine instead.

I strained my neck to see around the corner, catching a glimpse of who I could only imagine was Johnathan.

Before I could turn my eyes forward again, I caught sight of who Elliot had seen. My breathing quickened as I spotted him. He stood by the hitching post while his father assisted his mother and sister in getting out of the wagon. His eyes were focused right on me.

"Come on." Elliot pushed me over the threshold.

As if by magic, a sense of calm came over me the moment I was inside, as though the focus from Luke had been broken, effectively releasing some kind of built-up pressure inside. However, it was more likely related to the depression that had control over the entire town that so drastically affected my mood. Even so, it had me momentarily grateful.

The three of us walked down the center aisle, heading for a spot halfway through that was relatively open. I prayed with everything I had that Luke and his family wouldn't sit by us.

The church had been made as fancy as they could manage. Long in shape with a steeple on top, many windows trailing along the sides, and wooden pews placed evenly all down the room. My blood ran cold as I realized the church still stood back home. I'd likely sat on the same pew.

My stomach did a nauseating flip-flop at the thought. I could still smell the fresh wood as I did with every building I saw. The place couldn't have been more than a few months old.

I let my eyes wander around the architecture, marveling over the fact that it would still stand over a hundred years in the future. Sure, many things had been updated over time, but the very idea was startling. Much of the town had been destroyed by a tornado in the '40s, after all.

"Hey!" a fairylike voice squeaked. My first reaction to it was to smile, but it was immediately replaced by dread. Mable. That would undoubtedly mean her family wouldn't be far behind.

She scooted in the seat beside me. "I was hoping to sit by you," she said, resulting in a sharp shushing sound from her mother.

"Glad to see you too," I echoed, watching very closely as Luke came to sit on the other side of his sister.

"Elizabeth." He nodded his greeting, eyes tracing every inch of my body before they finally landed on my face.

I couldn't help it. I turned my face away to look at the wooden coffin in the front. Couldn't even have the decency to keep his eyes off my body for one moment?

The coffin was simple: a light wood grain, made carefully so that it was as close to seamless as possible. The carpenter must've worked all night on it to make it so perfect. Or he had help. Most likely both.

I hardly noticed Helen scolding her daughter and extracting a promise to be seen and not heard. I just sat perfectly still and watched up front, waiting for everything to begin.

By the time the pastor made it to the pulpit, the seats were full. Children chattered along as quietly as they could while their mortified mothers wanted to melt into the chairs. Everyone else remained completely silent as they gave all their attention to the pastor. He droned on and on about God's love and his promises that we would be together again.

All the people paid attention except me. All I could think about was my escape route for the second he said amen.

To get out, I really only had two options. Trek past the knees of both Newton and Elliot and hope for the best, or venture in the direction of Luke himself.

I preferred the unspoken emergency option. The one where I would slip under the pews and scoot to an open spot, then run. Unfortunately, that one would wind me into an impossible web of trouble.

The service lasted for the longest time. Even my stressed mind dozed. A few of the older gentlemen seemed to have given in to the sleeping option. Their heads leaned back in the pews, a few with their mouths opened slightly. One occasionally let out the smallest of snores.

When the pastor finally said the anticipated word, almost everyone stood up as though they had been stung. The melancholy feeling still existed, of course, but the growling of their stomachs had begun to take over. I practically pressed my body against Elliot's as we filed out that side. Mable was behind me in an instant, but just as quickly, she disappeared. I scanned the crowd for her but only caught a glimpse of her mother.

I didn't bother to wonder where she'd gone; I just pushed through the crowd and into the sliding sunlight. I made a break for it the second there was space for me to move. Only, I didn't get far.

"Oh! Sweet Elizabeth!" came the crackling voice of an elderly woman. She hurried to me, oddly spry despite her voice and age. "You're just the girl I wanted to see." She took my hand and pulled me in the general direction of a group of women.

The group included none other than Helen Barnette. I squeezed my fists, the worry about what they might want flooding my insides.

"I found her!" The old woman beamed, pushing me into the circle.

"Oh, good! She's very good at disappearing the moment she can," another woman said with a laugh.

"I really do hope you're feeling better, doll. You scared everyone there when you went missing," the old lady said.

As if on cue, everyone went silent to wait for my answer.

"I . . . I'm feeling much better. Thank you." I ducked my head awkwardly.

"Oh, good, I'm so glad! Now, we ladies had an idea."

"Oh, yes!" The agreements chorused throughout the crowd. I felt like they had lit the bomb, and all I had to do was wait for it to explode in my face. These *had* to be the ladies who worked on my dress, after all.

It would be impossible to escape the wedding.

"All this terrible funeral business"—the speaker clucked her tongue—"is not what a growing town needs. Not in this day and age! We have to stay positive, after all. Otherwise, we're all liable to simply sink into the ground after them."

I looked from face-to-face, not paying remote attention to what they looked like. All I wanted to know was how to escape. They had me completely enclosed. There would be no escape. Besides, what else would make a crowd of women as excited as a wedding?

Helen joined in on the conversation. "I know the wedding is still a week out, but we were thinking, since the dress is all ready, we can go ahead and go forward with it."

This was all that was needed for the whole group of ladies to start clucking like excited hens.

"Put some joy back into everyone's lives!"

"It's not healthy."

"Yes. Please, please, let's do this!"

"I'll go straight into town in the morning to get the stuff for the cake."

"Oh, good, I'll start on the decorating as soon as I talk to Reverend McAlester."

I felt dizzy as I turned in circles to face each speaking woman as they began to throw everything together for my wedding.

My wedding.

"Excuse me." Before I could hurl, I shoved between them.

And I ran. I ran as fast as all the petticoats would allow. I don't think the women realized I left their little planning party. When I reached the general store and looked back, they were still chattering away in their circle.

I hoped that Newton and Elliot would decide to mingle as well so they wouldn't miss me. From the looks of things, they were doing just that. I didn't see them anywhere near our wagon. Though, it was always possible they were assisting with the actual burial.

With that thought in mind, I slipped down the alleyway beside the general store and hurried back toward the river.

Two people stood a few buildings away, arms wrapped around each other, heads tipped together in a kiss. Mable's blond hair had come loose in one spot, trailing elegantly down her back.

Johnathan's tanned skin was a stark difference, his fingers tangled in that hair.

Boy, they would be in trouble if they were caught. But I was still jealous of their obvious affection.

Not wanting to bother them with my impending panic, I turned and headed to the train tracks. I had almost made it there when Sam caught up with me. He placed his hand on my shoulder to get my attention. Unlike anybody else who might've done that, it didn't terrify me. Somehow, I knew it was him. Surprisingly, I wanted it to be him.

"Are you okay?" he asked, eyes narrowed with concern.

I didn't answer. I just stared up at him, wishing for anything and everything. Wishing I had managed to go home. But then again, I was secretly glad to have met him. But I would have given anything to simply be in control of my own life for once.

"Ellie, they will notice that you ran off. Are you sure you're okay?" He was eyeing me up and down, hunting for any sign of injury.

No matter how hard I blinked, the waterworks started. I fell into him, wrapping my arms securely around his middle and pressing my cheek against his chest. "They want to move the wedding up."

His body stiffened, but he completed the embrace. His arms wrapped around me, one hand absently rubbing my back as he fought for words. "I'm sorry," he whispered.

"I can't do it!" I wailed. The panic came loose deep inside, impossible to control. "I can't! I won't! Why couldn't it be you? Why? You liked her, it was obvious enough, so why didn't *you* propose first?"

He abruptly pushed me to arm's length and stared into my face. "Stop that. She was like a sister to me. There was nothing that made me want to take her home as my wife." His voice was raw, pained.

I crossed my arms and narrowed my eyes at him. "Then what was that at the river?"

He didn't miss a beat. "You're not *her*."

Stunned to silence, I gawked at him. Was I supposed to take that in a romantic sense? As though maybe his heart was thudding in his chest just as much as mine? I opened my mouth to speak several times, but nothing came out.

If he liked me, in any kind of lovey-dovey way, was I allowed to do anything about it? Could I kiss him? It was as though some primal instinct had been activated inside me. My lips tingled at the very thought, and my body leaned toward his without my permission. My feet squirmed, trying to get onto my tiptoes to meet him. He maintained our distance, arms straight and hands on my shoulders.

"You're betrothed," he said sternly.

My body stilled as though I'd been slapped. "Going off your own logic, *she* is betrothed. *I* am not."

He leaned forward, so close that I could feel his breath on my lips. "Then go stop it. Before you get hurt, go stop it."

I huffed and glared at him. "You know I can't."

"Do I?" He raised an eyebrow.

"Yes. You do." I adjusted my skirts so I could sit on one of the tracks. "They think everything is just memory loss. I tried to convince them that I don't want to get married. I already tried! But it's just memory loss. They don't accept it as a real reason."

He sighed and held his hand out for me. "Get out of the dirt, or you'll have to explain how you got your dress dirty."

I took his hand, but instead of standing up, I pulled.

"Hey!" His balance faltered, but he managed to regain it. "As far as I see, you're simply going with the whole wedding idea. No one has remotely noticed your distaste for Lukas Barnette."

The name sent a shiver up my spine. "I don't know what to do." I threw my hands up in the air in exasperation.

"When did they set the date for?"

"I don't know," I admitted, a pout taking over every inch of my face. It was hard to slouch in a corset, so I brought my knees up to my chest and wrapped my arms around them. My skirts flowed happily down the front of my body, turning me into some sort of miserable cupcake. Not something that would remotely be possible in one of my skirts back home.

"Well then, you'd better get that figured out so we know what we're working with." He took my hand and pulled me up, not taking no for an answer.

"We?" I asked, brushing the dust from my rear.

"We," he said. With a shake of his head, he helped me, brushing as much dirt as he could off my skirt without getting dangerously near any of my curves.

"I can't exactly text you to tell you the date," I said.

He blinked slowly, staring at me. "What?"

"I can't text you. I can't call you—"

"Oh! Yes, you can call on me. You know where I live."

I shot him a look. "Not what I meant. And no, I really don't."

His brow furrowed as he worked to picture the location. "The tree we met at—keep going. You'll run into the Holmes farm. To the south of the main house is where the hands sleep. There are three of us, so don't just come bargin' in."

"Then . . . how will you know that I'm there?" I asked. Honestly, I wondered why we couldn't just meet at the tree like we had before.

"I'll keep an eye out for you," he assured me. "You need to get back before they realize you ran off."

"Hold on," I said before he could walk off. "What plan are you thinking of?"

He paused, shifting his weight from foot to foot. "I don't have one right now," he said. "Not enough of anything to help you. But I'll see what I can come up with."

"I'll find out when it is, then. And I'll tell you tonight."

He didn't move from his place on the tracks. "Good."

I turned with a sigh and stalked off, but before I got more than a foot away, his hand caught my wrist.

"Please be careful." With his own sigh of defeat, he pulled me into his arms, pressing his lips against the top of my head.

It wasn't a real kiss, sure. But it made every inch of me tingle.

"I will," I promised, my voice muffled by his chest.

The women planning my wedding had most certainly been looking for me. By the time I got back, that bomb they had lit had long since exploded.

"There she is!" one of the younger ladies said, hurrying toward me, trailed by Mable. She gave me a one-armed hug and pulled me in the direction of the church steps.

"I saw you got to see your boy," I whispered in her ear. She turned the color of a ripe tomato and ducked her head.

"Don't tell?"

I nodded before anyone could try to discern what we were saying.

"Did they decide on a specific date?" I asked. There was no reason to sit there silently and hope someone would magically tell me. All the women had begun to gather around again, cooing about how beautiful this or that would be at the reception. I didn't pay much attention.

"We figured," said one of the younger blondes, "that midweek would be wonderful! No one really wants to wait until the weekend, after all. Especially after all this sad mess! We could always use a celebration."

"Wednesday!" Mabel grasped my hands and hopped around in excitement. Her mother cleared her throat, which only quieted her down a little.

"So soon?" My throat went dry. "Are you guys sure? It's—"

"Oh! Doll, it's perfectly fine!" The oldest woman beamed. "We have almost everything situated already anyway! It won't take nothin' to assemble everything in the church here!"

My eyes fell on the church, tracing every beam, every line in the wood, hoping for some sort of answer.

"You need to be sure to have the veil finished," Helen was saying. "I don't want a daughter-in-law of mine who comes unprepared. It's not ladylike to avoid sewing like that. Don't disappoint me, you hear?"

I swallowed hard and nodded. "Yes, ma'am."

"Good girl."

It took every ounce of effort I had to stand straight. All I wanted to do was sit on the steps and stare into space in hope that some answer would attack me like a dive-bombing pigeon. "What time will the wedding be at?"

"Three!" yet another woman chimed in.

"Oh, yes, late enough that the men can have the chores they insist on being done, and we can have everything all ready!" The older woman clasped her hands, eyes sparkling. She gazed at the church as though it were her own child. Her own pride and joy.

Three in the afternoon on Wednesday.

That was my fate.

"What time do you need me here?" Every word felt like sandpaper across my throat.

"Eight sounds good, don't you think?" Helen asked everyone, receiving instant nods. "Good! Eight it is! Don't be late. And don't forget anything."

"I won't forget," I promised, wiggling my toes absently in my boots to distract myself from the pure panic welling inside my chest.

"Good! Let's go tell everyone our plans!" The elderly woman took my arm and hurried me to one of the nearby wagons. Everyone else followed, Mable being the closest. We climbed onto the back, officially towering over what had to be a large portion of the town.

"Everyone!" the older woman shouted. "May I have your attention!" When, for the most part, everyone continued chatting away and enjoying the downtime, she pressed her fingers to her mouth and let out a long whistle. I flinched at the piercing noise. "Everyone! We have some amazing news! The wedding has been moved up. Lukas Barnette and Elizabeth Hersley will be married *this Wednesday*! Three in the afternoon. Right here! Spread the word!"

Cheers erupted through the crowd. Whether because they got another partial day off, or simply from the idea of a celebration, I had no idea. I only wished I could join in and be happy about any single part of it.

I scanned the crowd, my eyes easily finding Newton and Elliot. Both of them smiled. Newton looked like the perfect, proud father. His face looked strained from all the smiling he had been doing, stretching his skin into a special kind of leather. Elliot didn't smile, but he still managed to look pleased in his own way. I wondered for a brief moment if he would be able to help me out of this situation.

Then, my eyes found Luke.

All my breath escaped from my lungs, as though someone had punched me straight in the chest. He stared directly at me. No smile, no emotion. Simply staring.

I gulped and let my eyes move away from his and down to my feet. What did that look mean? I prayed I would never find out.

There were plenty of congratulations before we could leave, and plenty more along the way home. Newton asked what made me agree to changing the date, and Elliot essentially repeated the question. I didn't answer. In fact, I didn't say a word. There wasn't a real answer for them, after all.

Because I wouldn't be getting married. Not to Luke. Not ever.

I went straight to bed when we got home, refusing the offer of a simple dinner, or even sitting up and reading with the family.

I just muttered something about being tired and hid in the room. I couldn't think of anything better to do.

The veil came out of its hiding place and sat on the foot of the bed, staring right back at me. It was judging me, glaring back as though it could shame me into finding a needle and thread to finish the project. But it couldn't. There was no way it would win.

By the end of everything, I passed out on top of the blankets, fully clothed with the veil laughing at my misfortune.

CHAPTER EIGHTEEN

It was a long night. No matter what I did, I couldn't keep my mind steady. When sunrise came and the men began to fiddle around with breakfast downstairs, I didn't move. I couldn't even consider spending time with them. Especially if all they wanted to do was pawn me off the following day.

I forced myself to take naps throughout the morning. If they could even be called such a thing. They were more like waking nightmares that refused to let up. I tried shoving the pillow on top of my face, screaming into it at one point. Nothing worked.

My mind wandered constantly. To the wedding, to what might have happened to *her*, to why on earth I was stuck in the 1800s.

But what I preferred to focus on was Sam himself.

He'd only pressed his lips into my hair. An unmistakable sign of affection, sure. But not necessarily a romantic one. It was probably just some kind of goodbye, not wanting me to go without feeling cared for in one way or another.

Normal, right?

But then at the river . . .

By the time the sun was high in the sky, I was so riled up about the whole situation, the floor could have split from all my pacing.

I knew one thing: I needed to get to him and see what plan he had come up with.

My heart skipped a beat when I caught sight of a lone rider approaching the house. It had to be Sam, right?

Then I paid more attention. The horse had the same coloring as what Luke had been riding when I'd seen him last. As he got closer, it confirmed my fear. He had short hair that hid in his hat. Not the longer reddish locks of Sam's. He sat tall and invincible, daring anyone to cross him.

With a curse, I threw on my shoes and hurried downstairs.

The last thing I wanted to do was deal with *that* overpowering asshat. Especially alone. I didn't trust him as far as I could throw him, and that certainly wasn't far. Everything about him was simply suspicious.

I slipped out of the front door as he was hitching his horse to the fence that spread from the barn. Before any thoughts could enter my mind, I ran for the opposite side of the house.

I stood there, back pressed to the boards, eyes pressed shut. *Don't hunt for me. Just leave. Please,* I begged.

His boots clipped on the porch before he knocked, slowly, deliberately. I held my breath, hoping I could even calm my heart down so he wouldn't manage to hear that. When no answer came, he knocked again.

He then switched tactics. "Elizabeth!"

The harsh voice sent chills down my spine. He walked over to the window and looked in, then knocked yet again. No, it was more like a bang. A harsh, demanding, horrifying noise.

I flinched. There was absolutely no way he was going to get a chance to see me. If he had a chance before, that pounding certainly took it away.

The door handle rattled, and he stepped inside. I clamped my hand over my mouth, praying he wouldn't hear my breathing. As soon as the door clicked shut, I ran for the barn.

I ran as fast as I could manage, picking up my skirts to my knees to avoid tripping.

I skidded to a stop in the barn, coming face-to-face with a bay horse. He was taller than me, his nose coming to rest on my forehead. With a shaky hand, I reached to touch his snout. "Please help me. Please don't hurt me."

Without a second thought, I made my way into the stall. The horse remained calm, though he watched me carefully as I grabbed his mane and scrambled up the fence. With a huff of effort, I practically jumped onto his back.

He fidgeted and moved out of the open stall, my body slung over the back like a corpse.

"Hold on, hold on! Stop. Stay . . ." I clambered for his mane and pulled my leg over his rump. My efforts were sloppy, and when I had managed to sit up, we were just coming out into the open.

My eyes caught movement at the house just as Luke came back onto the porch.

"Elizabeth!" he shouted, taking off at a run for me.

I held on and kicked at the horse. We had to *go*. He responded as I had hoped, jumping to action and going into a full run, mane flying into my face. Luke met me in the middle of the yard, reaching up to brush my leg. I kicked at him, managing to jerk free and out of his reach in time.

He swore and raced for his own horse.

"Go, go, go!" I shouted at my own mount. "I don't know your name, but please, *please* don't let me down!"

We ran faster than I had ever gone on a horse, pointing in the basic direction of the Holmes ranch. I held on, squeezing my thighs on his back, my body pressed against his with every effort not to fly off.

I had ridden horses before, but not very frequently. Honestly, I hadn't ridden since summer camp in middle school. For that, I'd been required to wear an ugly black helmet and put a saddle on. And a bridle. And a horse blanket. It took forever to get out on the trail.

I also hadn't been allowed to *run*.

But I didn't have a choice at that moment. So, I clung on to him like a monkey.

It didn't take long to disappear into the trees. Hopefully I had escaped far enough ahead of Luke that he wouldn't have an ability to catch up with me.

But then again, I really didn't know what he was capable of.

When the ranch came up on the horizon, my body did the opposite of what I expected. I didn't calm down. Every inch of me became more anxious.

We had almost made it to the nearest long building when he appeared.

Sam raced to me, panic written plainly over his face. He reached out and miraculously grabbed the horse. I have no idea how he managed it, but he did. The horse came to a stop, pawing at the ground and sweating.

"Shh, shh . . ." Sam petted the horse's nose as he led us to the barn. "Ellie." When I didn't release my hold immediately, he tried again. "Ellie, are you okay?"

I picked my head up slowly. "He's after me."

"Who?" He pulled us into the barn and expertly placed a rope around the horse's neck. He tied him to one of the stalls with ease, then peeled me off and set me on the ground. "Ellie, who is after you?"

"Luke—he came to the house." I was hyperventilating, gasping for air and clinging to anything I could. That thing happened to be Sam's arm.

"He came to the house?" His voice was so calm, it felt like some sort of magical drink, coating me with peace.

"Yes, I looked out the window, and he was there. I got out, and he started banging on the door. When I didn't answer, he went inside!" Sobs shook my body between every other word. It was a miracle he understood everything I said.

He pulled me down to sit on the pile of hay in the back of the room. "What did he do inside?"

"I don't know! That's when I ran. I don't want to see him. I don't want to talk to him!" I didn't pause for breath, only making my panicked dizziness all the worse.

He took both his hands and placed them flat on my cheeks, forcing me to look straight at him. "Why, Ellie. *Why?*"

"Because . . ." I didn't have a tangible reason. He was suspicious? He simply was tall and opposing to me? There was no *real* reason why I disliked him.

Sam sighed and walked over to the corner of the barn to grab something. Slight mews echoed around us as he scooped up a tiny kitten.

"You have every reason to be afraid of him. He's likely the last person she saw alive."

Despite his words, my sobbing stopped as if by magic. Sam brought the tiny creature over to me and set it in my hands. He was light gray with dark stripes across his legs, and dark-tipped ears and tail. His meows were raspy and demanding. I held him up to my chest and immediately turned into the classic female, making kissy noises and aahing like an idiot.

Sam smirked and watched from his spot a few feet away. "The barn cat had kittens. That one is the only survivor."

"Aww! Poor baby." I kissed the top of his head before placing him in the straw.

Immediately, the tiny beast took off, hopping at one piece of hay, then another, then suddenly racing back to the safety of his mother's corner.

"How old is he?"

"A month or two." Sam shrugged. "I haven't paid much attention. But I figured he'd cheer you up."

"Is Mr. Holmes keeping him?"

"I'm assuming so. It doesn't hurt to have another barn cat."

The cat raced around his area, everything his playground. He tackled anything that might have ever moved. Straw, a clump of dirt, a chicken feather. Anything he saw was his. His mother sat nearby, watching him closely, only jumping down to herd him back when he got too far away.

"Luke got on a horse to follow me," I said, shattering the tense calm that had engulfed us.

Sam stayed silent for a moment as he wiggled a piece of straw for the kitten to chase. "Do you think he managed to follow you this far?"

"I don't know," I admitted, lying back in the straw.

He sighed and lay back beside me. The kitten mewed and went on to chase something else. "Hopefully he didn't."

I couldn't help it. My body moved without my permission. I rolled onto my side and leaned against him, head resting on his shoulder like the most comfortable pillow.

"What if he comes?"

He shrugged. "I don't know."

"Will he . . . kill anyone?"

Sam turned his head to stare at me. "Kill you? No."

"How do you know? Do you really know the guy?"

He sighed and reached his free arm over to pat my shoulder. "I won't let that happen."

"He went into our house! When he didn't know if anyone was *home*! Do people normally do that?"

Sam hesitated. "No . . ."

"Then, we don't know what his actual plan was."

"He probably just wanted to talk to you about the wedding or something."

The word alone made me shiver. "I don't want to talk about that."

We went silent, both lying there staring up at the ceiling, lost in our own thoughts. The kitten ran around, doing his best to cause an early World War I against the flies that buzzed around.

"I was worried about you last night when you didn't come," Sam finally said.

I winced. "I'm so sorry, I fell asleep."

He squeezed my arm. "You probably needed it. What time did they say the wedding would be at?"

I sighed. We couldn't avoid planning the escape forever, though I really would have preferred if it would simply disappear. "Three."

"What time did they need you to start getting ready?"

"Eight."

He narrowed his eyes at me. "Lots of one-word answers, huh? I need more than that. Are they coming here, or are you meeting them at the church?"

"I have to meet them at the church," I said.

He thought for a long moment, biting the end of his tongue as he made his calculations. "I'll come get you at seven. Be ready to go. Okay?"

I propped myself up on my elbow. I hadn't expected it to be that easy. "What's your plan?"

"I don't really know." He stared straight ahead as though the exposed beams would provide him all the answers. "We'll figure it out as we go."

I wrapped my arms around his waist, pleased to find he didn't pull away from the closeness. Less than twenty-four hours, and I would be free. At least free from Luke.

"Sam?"

"Hmm?"

"Can I ask you something?" A completely different kind of apprehension creeped into my chest. The kind I hadn't felt since high school. And even then, it couldn't be the same. The fear of rejection, but for once, it felt like it truly mattered.

"Yes?"

The English language completely skipped my mind. I stared blankly at the ceiling, panic welling up inside. Memories of rejection against my high school crush. Memories of dreaming about what I should have said, or done, over and over again. For way longer than I should have.

I propped myself up on my elbow again and stared down at him, my hair falling around my face and to his shoulders, locking us in our own little world. Eyes stuck on each other, breath mixing in the space.

I leaned forward, one hand on his chest, the other beside his head. My chest touched his, his heartbeat fluttering obviously, even through the corset. Or maybe it was my own? I hovered directly over his face for a moment, questioning whether it was acceptable behavior or not. But then, did it really matter? None of this would be acceptable behavior.

"Fuck it," I whispered, pressing my lips to his.

They were warm, his stubble brushing my own upper lip. They were on the chapped side, but the rough feeling only spurred me on. His body jerked into action, his hand coming up to cup the back of my head. I adjusted the rest of my body then, propping myself up onto my knees so I had as much leverage as I needed.

His teeth pulled on my upper lip, and I returned the favor, my tongue then tracing his bottom lip. He opened his mouth to capture it, officially engulfing every ounce of me in pure lust.

There was no telling what happened to the kitten after that. As long as he didn't get stepped on by a horse, that was all that mattered, right? Sam flipped me onto my back, straddling me and kissing me. His hands ran down my sides, pulling on the skirts. I let him, ready to let anything happen. Not thinking about any kind of consequence.

When he stopped pulling at my clothes, I reached back to pull on the hooks of my dress, squirming out as well as I could, leaving me in still far too many layers.

He didn't seem to mind. He worked the hooks of the corset like a pro, pulling it off me easily. Absently, I wondered if corsets were somehow easier for the men. Bras usually had a latch on the back, after all.

I pulled on his shirt, yanking it over his head and throwing it to the side. Some part of my mind pulsed with the warning that someone could come in at any moment. But frankly, I didn't care.

Likely, I wouldn't get married if we were caught. Well, at least not to Luke. And I was perfectly okay with that consequence.

But that wasn't my reasoning for any of it. I craved him. Every inch of my body craved him with a fire I'd never experienced before. I pulled him to my body, taking away the chance for him to remove any more clothing. There was no chance I could wait. I needed his touch. I needed him.

He obliged, tracing my body through the thin, remaining fabric and sending shivers through my entire being. I pulled the petticoat off, hearing a slight rip as I ignored the ties on the back. It didn't matter. The fabric belonged in the haphazard pile somewhere in the distance. For all I knew, the kitten was playing with the ties of my clothing.

"This is a bad idea," he whispered to my skin, kissing my collarbone and up to my lips.

"I don't care." I tangled my fingers into his hair and pulled him as close to me as possible, my legs wrapping around him to keep him from moving away.

His body vibrated with a laugh, and his hand slipped back down the thin fabric of my side, down and down, sending jerks and shivers through my body for just a fraction of time.

Until he stopped. He pulled his half-clothed body off me and simply walked off.

"Hey!" I protested, scrambling up to my knees. "Come back! You can't leave me like that."

He ran his fingers through his hair, struggling to get his breathing under control. I got to my feet and made my way to him, reaching out to touch the muscles in his back.

"Stop."

My hand fell back to my side and the erotic joy crashed around me. "What'd I do wrong?" I hardly heard my own voice.

"It's not you."

"It's not you, it's me," I snapped. "I've heard that too many times before."

"That's not what I'm saying." He sighed and turned around, taking a long moment before he opened his eyes. "You're betrothed, Ellie." He stared straight at me, pain coursing through his eyes.

"No, Elizabeth is. Or . . . was. Not me. *I'm* not going to marry him!" I protested. "I don't want to even see him. Let alone, touch him!"

"It's not seemly." He scooped up one piece of clothing at a time, organizing them by who they belonged to on his arms.

"None of this situation is seemly. I'm from the future. None of this is *seemly*."

He held my clothing out to me. "We'll wait."

"Ugh." I snatched them from him and fought to put everything back on. Redressing myself was much harder in a hurry than taking them off. My fingers slipped on the eyelets of the corset. When he had pulled his own shirt over his head, he came over to try to help me with the tiny details.

"No," I snapped, turning away from him like an angry child. "You caused enough torture."

"Really?" He shook his head slowly and went to scoop up the kitten and return him to his mother's protection before he could get stepped on by the cow. "You can be mad if you want. It's not gonna change my mind."

Deep down, I knew there really wasn't a reason to be angry with him. It made sense that he wouldn't want to spoil me one way or another. Especially with my being "taken." Only, I most certainly wasn't taken. And I wanted my "virtue" to be ruined. Rather badly. Everything throbbed with the need. Every inch of my body felt swollen. I craved the release more than anything. Craved his touch.

"After tomorrow I won't be engaged, right?" I asked when I finally got the last eyelet latched on the corset and got the petticoat in its required location.

"I reckon so."

"Then, when you pick me up in the morning, can we . . . you know . . ." I felt my body swish side to side like an awkward teenager.

He smirked and walked right up to me, just far enough away that our bodies didn't touch, but his body heat mingled with mine. "We oughta get everything settled first."

"Can we just run away and never come back?"

"No." He leaned down to barely brush my lips with his. "We'll stay here."

"Then how will I be no longer engaged?" I turned so he could tie the back of my dress into place. "Newton will simply set a new date, won't he?"

Sam let out a long breath. "Perhaps so, perhaps not. You'll just have to break it off."

"How? I tried! I tried to explain to Newton that I didn't want to do it already."

"You'll have to end the engagement yourself. With Luke." His voice held no room for argument, but his eyes flittered all around my body, as though he was afraid I might shoot the messenger.

It felt as though I'd been told I had to undergo some horrifying medical procedure. I stammered, trying to find the correct words. "I can't."

"Can't can't do anything," he said, quoting the phrase he'd likely heard from his mother since birth. I'd also heard it one too many times.

"I don't know if he'll let me break it off, either."

"There's only one way to find out." Sam went to a very quiet, old horse in the corner and started the process of saddling her.

"I don't know what to say."

"You have to say something. You can't just leave the man at the altar tomorrow and not give him any kind of an explanation."

"And if he hurts me?"

Sam paused for a long moment. "Don't do it alone. Take Elliot. Newton. Just don't go alone, and nothing will have a chance to happen. He won't be happy, but he'll get over it."

"Then who do you think killed Elizabeth?"

His entire body froze, saddle hoisted above the horse's back. "She probably tripped."

"Tripped? Really. You believe that just about as much as I do. She wouldn't have been that bruised up if she just tripped."

"Talk to him tomorrow evening. I'll come by and make sure everything is okay."

I let him hoist me into the saddle. "I don't want to talk to him."

"You have to live in town, so you might as well avoid making too many enemies." He swung into the saddle and took off, bringing me and the other horse back home.

CHAPTER NINETEEN

I lay awake staring at the ceiling, stressing out over everything that could go wrong in the morning.

Luke could force me to elope with him before the wedding. That was a thing, right?

He could simply run off and rape me when he found out my plans.

I could be handcuffed to a chair and forced through the ceremony at gunpoint.

Though the options weren't particularly probable, the midnight air had some kind of magical power that made everything feel inevitable.

I managed to be fully dressed, my hair brushed and braided into some kind of crown on my head by the time the sun started to show its face. Extensive for candlelight pampering, but it *was* my wedding day. Technically. Besides, I needed something to do to keep my mind somewhat occupied. Fighting my long brown hair into its own headband did just that.

But when finished, the clock still sat at 5:45 or so.

Before I could even sit down on the bed and waste more time, a terse knock sounded on the door. Almost immediately, Elliot walked inside.

"Oh! You're up!" He looked me up and down. "And ready?" He, on the other hand, was certainly not. Dressed in the long socially accepted nightgown, complete with bare, bony feet. "Why did you wake up so early?"

"I couldn't sleep," I admitted with a shrug.

"Guess I'd better hurry and get ready to take you to the church, then." He ran his hand through his hair as he stretched.

I practically vaulted to my feet. "No, you don't have to rush," I blurted. "I don't have to be there for a while."

He didn't notice the frantic edge to my voice. "Arriving early never hurts." He only disappeared back into the hallway.

I desperately glanced at the clock. Six. It was still only six.

"No, no, no, no . . ." I whispered to myself, hurrying down the stairs to see if I could find a way to push back the departure time.

Newton blinked in surprise when he saw me. He was already dressed and ready to go, a newspaper spread across his lap and pipe in his lips. The shock of my spiffy appearance made him go perfectly still. "You're awake."

"Yes," I said, coming to sit down at the kitchen table. "Nerves, I guess."

"On my wedding day," Newton began, the air of nostalgia filling his voice. He held his pipe away from his mouth, staring up at the ceiling as he thought. "I had a chest full'a woodpeckers that mornin'. Thought there was no way your ma would show. When I heard she was already at the church waitin' for me, I wondered if I would even make a good husband. Or father, one day."

"You seem to have done well," I said. He did, after all. He was harsh, but his tactics worked. Elliot was a stand-up man, though one with some secret nightlife, and I'd learned early not to cross a direct order. The other Elizabeth had likely been a very well-behaved young lady.

"Thank you," he said, a smile playing under his mustache. "Well then, since you're all ready, we oughta get you to the church. The ladies are bound to be there extra early to make you prettier than a—"

"We don't have to go early!"

His eyes narrowed only slightly. "Why is that?"

"I . . ." I looked around the room, hunting for a good reason. "I was hoping to get some food first."

"Mrs. Holmes said she'd be bringin' something for everyone helpin' out this morning. We don't have to worry about that. Don't worry." He tapped his pipe on the edge of the fireplace, expelling the ashes into their rightful place. "Elliot! You about ready?"

"Coming!" Elliot's voice was followed shortly by his footsteps on the stairs. "We headin' out?"

"Yep, just gotta get the horses hitched up."

Elliot nodded his approval of the plan and hurried off to the barn.

"Now, you go hurry and get the things you need for today. We'll be ready to go in just a few." Newton then followed him, leaving me to wonder how to escape, with more than thirty minutes left to kill before Sam arrived.

I took my time going upstairs to get the veil, corset, and what looked to be the nicest shoes. What else was I to do? I couldn't escape out of the window. Especially not alone. Besides, there wasn't really anywhere to hide outside. From Luke, maybe. But from these two, I was sure I'd be found in no time at all.

Frustrated, I brought the clothing downstairs to wait.

The men were skilled at hitching up the horses. We only had half an hour left until my impending escape rendezvous when Elliot came back inside to get me.

"We really don't need to leave so early," I protested, as he helped me into the wagon. "I'm perfectly fine with being fashionably late."

"No Hersley will be late to her own wedding," Newton vowed, as we started off toward town.

The whole bumpy ride, I scanned every structure, every tree for a sign of Sam. I never saw a thing. He'd be stuck at the house, waiting for me to show my face to escape with him. Alone, bored, and likely a bit on the angry side. Hopefully, he'd be worried instead.

Right then, I felt as alone as I had the first day I'd arrived. I had no one to help me out of my situation. No one.

One of the sod houses we passed along the road had three young children out front. They were busy doing morning chores, likely before breakfast. The younger two were still in their nightgowns. It didn't stop them from running after the wagon and waving excitedly until the older of the three caught up and dragged them back home.

I was a celebrity for a day. All the children were so excited, especially the girls. As we came into town, more children showed up, grins plastered onto their faces. It was like my own personal parade to death.

Once we reached town, it took everything I had to get my body to move. Each step toward the church's front door felt more and more final. When I stood on the top step, another wagon made its way into the street.

Of course, it was none other than Helen. My dress was in a bag in the back, along with multiple other bags. The only thing I wanted to see with her, but was definitely nowhere close, was Mable.

"Oh, good. You're not late," Helen said. She hopped out of the wagon and handed the reins to Newton. "Help me with the bags, dear. We have much to do." She grabbed one of the smaller bags and gestured for me to do the same.

Newton shot me an encouraging half smile as he kept the horse still. I couldn't help but give him a half glare in return as I grabbed two of the other bags. One of them, the long, makeshift garment bag that held the dress.

There was no way to escape.

"Hurry, Elizabeth, we don't have time to dawdle." To my surprise, she didn't head into the church. Instead, she went straight into the building across the street. The general store.

My sour expression turned to pure confusion as I looked at Newton for help. He didn't offer any. Instead, he just nodded in her direction so I would follow.

With a huff that would be the envy of any teenager, I followed the woman. It took more effort than I would have ever thought not to let the dress drag in the dirt. As if I needed something heavy to drag my mood down further.

With a last, futile look around for some miraculous help, I stepped into the store.

It didn't disappoint. Trinkets for sale here and there, candy at the front counter, some flour and other food items in shelves against the wall, and a mannequin with a gorgeous pale blue dress in the window. The dress looked so fancy, I couldn't help but run my fingers over one of the ruffles on the rear. Or bustle. Most of the women I had seen in town hadn't bothered to wear such a thing. It just wasn't practical. Except maybe the doctor's wife. With how intricate her house had been, I envisioned the dress would have been right up her alley.

"Come on, come on," a blond woman said brightly, coming around the counter to take the dress from me, all the while herding me in the direction of a door in the back. I recognized her as one of the women from the crowd at the funeral.

I let her usher me into the parlor of her house, resisting the extreme urge to grab one of the licorice pieces from the bowl on the front counter. It felt like *ages* since I'd had an extreme amount of sugar.

"C-Can . . ." I stammered, my eyes fixated on the candy like an addict.

"Lordy, girl! Why must you always take so long?" Helen snapped me back to reality. It would have been much easier to deal with if I had some sugar in my mouth. "Come on, come on. Let's get you cleaned up before the other ladies arrive."

The blond woman removed the other bag from me and placed it on the settee against the wall. Before I could stop the flow of my sugar-deprived brain long enough to ask any sort of question, they dragged me into the kitchen. The large metal tub sat in the middle of the room, steam rising from it like a hot tub.

"Fun," I muttered sarcastically. They didn't seem to notice. Or care. Without asking any sort of permission, they worked on removing my clothing. I let them. What else could I do? They had such urgency to their movements, such excitement. I would have thought I was getting married in an hour with how much they were trying to hurry.

My body kicked into gear when I was down to my underwear. The second the blonde touched the ties for the glorified shorts, I stepped back.

"Come on, Elizabeth. We don't have time for this modesty," Helen chided.

"I can bathe myself, please." My voice came out softer than I originally intended. I'd never been one to change in front of others. School locker rooms were torture, and I'd perfected the art of covert changing. I didn't care if I saw someone else's business, but no one was seeing mine.

Except Sam. The extreme *need* to have him that close to me was unreal. But that wasn't anything close to what I was supposed to be thinking of at the time.

"We're here to help you," the blond woman said. She had a tender, mothering tone. Despite her urgency, she didn't seem so bad.

"I'd like some time to myself, if I can." I looked desperately from one woman to the next. "There's a lot of changes, after all. Can't I have just a few minutes to . . . um . . . reflect?"

They exchanged glances, wordlessly discussing. Then, with a shrug, the blond woman turned around and headed out into the sitting room.

"Be sure to scrub every inch. And wash that hair too. We want you cleaner than you've ever been," Helen commanded. "Where is that veil of yours? I want to inspect your stitching while you bathe."

I bit my lip almost instantly.

She gasped. "You didn't finish! Heavens to Betsy! Rachel, go get your sewing kit. We have work to do." She hurried into the other room after shooting me a glare, the mission suddenly the most important thing in the universe.

I waited for the door to swing shut behind her. Their staccato steps faded off as soon as they had the veil and set to work. Only then did I pull the chemise over my head and pull the underwear off. The chilly air that kissed my body sent me into action almost immediately. I hopped into the water, nearly burning myself as I did so.

It was certainly not a cold bath. Sweat popped up on my forehead as my muscles relaxed. If anything was going to get rid of all the toxins in my body, that bath would.

I trained my ears to listen for any approaching human, as I simply lay back and shut my eyes. The women were certainly unhappy about the state the veil was in. They sounded like some angry birds with juicy gossip. Only, it sent butterflies through my stomach knowing it was *me* they were upset with.

I didn't want to actually finish the bath. The idea of just relaxing was heaven. Perhaps with a bath bomb if someone would be able to come up with one. Of course, there was no such thing, and of course, I wouldn't have time to relax as I wanted.

I was to be married in just a few hours. The unfinished veil might have been a distraction, but it wasn't a long-term solution by any means. Especially considering the angry chattering had slowed and they seemed to be getting things done rapidly.

I looked around the room, trying to spark a new escape plan. A window sat above the kitchen sink, but it didn't look like it opened. A door stood on the opposite side of the room, but it didn't appear to go anywhere other than a bedroom. Besides, if I was to get out, where would I actually go?

Defeat settled onto my shoulders, the weight trying to drown me little by little. I gave in and started to wash my body. Everything felt hopeless. Unless there was some miracle, I would be stuck in my own personal horror story of an arranged marriage.

I still took my time running the soap through my hair and swishing it clean under the water, enjoying the sensation of the soft strands tickling my back and shoulders. But it couldn't last. My peace would never last.

When there was no further way to procrastinate, and the water was getting uncomfortably cool, I got out.

I didn't bother with getting completely dressed. What was the point, anyway? They were about to shove me in all kinds of white lace. It didn't make sense to put on more than the undergarments.

"I'm out," I called through the door. My voice sounded hollow, far away. Like a child hiding on the stairs, afraid of the monster under her bed.

"Good, good." Helen set down her sewing supplies and hurried over to me. "We'll get that veil done in no time. The other ladies should be here any minute, after all. And then everything will fly by exactly as we hope." She sounded strained, as though she had to force the happiness to come out of her mouth.

"Good morning, ladies," another voice came from the entryway. Another one of the women from the planning circle hurried in, a toddler holding her hand.

I watched the kiddo, a smile playing on the edge of my lips. Nothing could match an innocent child's ability to make things just a little bit better.

He looked around the room in wonder, as though he'd never seen anything so grand. In reality, he probably hadn't. He likely lived in a sod house with minimal furniture. Even though this place was small, it held gorgeous, plush, colorful items inside. A child's dream.

"Oh, perfect timing, Alice!" Helen clasped her hands with the immense pleasure her presence brought her. Her forced smile faltered only slightly when she noticed the kid. Certainly not the stress relief she'd been hoping for. "Richard couldn't keep an eye on Junior?"

"No, a coyote got some of our cows last night. He can't take care of them with Junior getting into everything." Alice got down to one knee, looking her son in the eye. "You listen to me good," she said, her childlike face as stern as she could make it. The blue eyes contained too much laughter to really be commanding, but she did her absolute best. "Don't touch *anything*."

"Actually . . ." Rachel laid the veil down on the settee and headed to the steep staircase in the corner. "The girls might be able to keep an eye on him for you." She disappeared into the second story, daintily holding the front of her dress just above her feet as she traversed the steps.

The relief washed over Alice's face. "Oh, that would be wonderful!"

"It's already half past nine," Helen pointed out. "We need to get busy. Otherwise, we'll never get her out there in time."

Nine thirty? Already? My heart sank a few more inches into my stomach, the acid threatening to snuff out any comfort that remained.

"Oh, right!" Alice gave one last stern look to her son before fluttering over to stand in front of me. Her startling blue eyes searched my face, then down my body, then finally back to my face and hair. "You're going to look so beautiful." Her voice was an admiring breath, as though she were looking at a world-famous painting.

Or rather, she liked what she might be able to turn me into. There was no way she was in awe with my drowned-rat appearance. At her insistence, I sat down on one of the dining room chairs that Helen had dragged in.

She got right to work, fingering the strands of my hair as she determined exactly what to do. Her hands were gentle, almost massage-like as she worked the comb and oil through the tangles. I let my eyes close and forced my mind to concentrate only on being pampered. Not on the need to escape.

If they only left me alone in the room for even a minute, I would be gone. Whether it was through the window or exploring the other room. That was the vow I came up with. But considering I was the center of all their attention, it didn't look like that would be an option.

I could request a visit to the bathroom before we put on the dress. That would be completely understandable. Likely, they wouldn't want to go with me. Unless the need to create a bathroom party like modern times was more than a fad.

There weren't many trees to hide in, even if I did escape. There was so much space between the buildings and the river. There were the tracks, sure, but the station would certainly be closer. But it was almost always crawling with busy men.

The more I thought about it, the stiffer my body became, and the more uncomfortable Alice's tugging got. My anxiety increased tenfold as two other ladies entered—the elderly one and another one I didn't recognize.

"I-I uh . . ." I stammered, eyes darting all over the place.

"Yes, dear?" Alice asked sweetly. Her voice gave no sign of her noticing my stress level increasing.

"I need to . . ." How was I supposed to ask for it, anyway? Bathroom? Restroom? Neither of those terms were really used, were they? "Can I make a quick trip to the outhouse?" I finally asked.

"Oh!" Her eyes went wide, and she glanced around. "Let me get you to a stopping point first. If I let you go right now, these braids might as well fall right out." She laughed at her own joke and went right back to work.

I sighed and shut my eyes, working hard to keep myself from losing it. The braids were tight on my head, crisscrossing their way intricately into some kind of an updo. When she released me, I didn't bother to look at it in the mirror.

Permission was granted, a dressing gown was placed around my shoulders, and I hurried off to the outhouse. Somehow, alone. I walked casually, terrified that all eyes were still on me. When I was just a few feet away from the outhouse's door, I changed directions and hid behind the tiny building.

I pressed my back against the wood, eyes closing as I listened for any sound of discovery. Birds sang here or there, and sounds from the workmen at the train station filled the air, but otherwise it was silent. Perfect calm.

Steeling myself for the race to the tree line, I took one final look around. Nothing moved. At least nothing that wasn't supposed to.

There were a few rabbits out by the corner of the building, nibbling at all the green grass they could get their ever-growing teeth on.

So, I ran. It took effort not to look behind me or watch for any strange movement. But any pauses to check behind every shadow would slow me down. At least, that was my logic.

Then, he stepped out of the shadows.

I'd only made it to the tracks. But he'd been waiting. For how long? Had he really been expecting me to run?

Luke stepped out from behind a boxcar, arms crossed over his chest, face full of anger. I skidded to a stop, only a few feet from him, dust flying around me.

"What are you doing?" he asked. No, *asked* wasn't quite it. It came out more like a growl.

"I'm going on a walk." There was no way he would believe that. I was *running* in a dressing gown, after all. Nothing screamed suspicious like a jog in a fur-lined robe.

"You couldn't have been more creative with your excuses?" He took a step toward me, and I skittered back. "What's wrong?" He did the classic head tilt, sending me right back to reality.

"You're not supposed to see the bride before the wedding." My voice came out hoarse. I turned my feet to the side, ready to bolt.

"You're not supposed to leave the mercantile, now, are you?" He took a large step in my direction, and I ran for the distant trees. His long arm shot out like a snake, easily grabbing my forearm. There was no degree of gentleness to his grip. I could feel the future bruising throbbing underneath my skin.

"What do you know?" he demanded, taking my chin with his other hand and turning my head so we were face-to-face.

"What do you not want me to know?" The squeaky tone of my voice wouldn't leave. The obvious signs of my distress only made my fear worse, triggering the trembling of my knees.

"You can't be that dumb." He narrowed his eyes at me, searching for any sign of the truth. "You have to know something."

My fear didn't do anything to keep my mouth silent. "I know that you had something to do with it," I snapped, trying to pull my chin away from his grip. He only held on tighter, his fingers grinding on my jawbone.

"Go on," he growled. "What do you know?"

I locked my jaw, glaring right back at him. He jerked my head roughly, shaking my body. He didn't actively hurt me, just popped my neck and scared every ounce of stubbornness away.

"That's all," I somehow said. My words were slurred, hardly understandable. He would kill me. This man would kill me if he got the chance. I was suddenly sure of it.

"Now, you march yourself right back into the mercantile. Get that dress on, make yourself pretty, and show up to your wedding promptly at three o'clock." He let go of my jaw and pushed me toward the back door.

"You bruised my chin. They're going to notice." I tried to yank free one more time, getting absolutely nowhere.

We were standing nearly outside the building by then, so close they would have heard me if I screamed. They would have helped me. But if I dared make a sound, what would he do then?

He looked my face over, eyes narrowed as he rethought his decisions.

Good, I thought, *maybe he'll regret what he did already.*

No such luck.

"You shouldn't a' been so clumsy then." Without the simplest glance for a warning, he shoved me face-first toward the back step.

I squawked before I hit the step, fear-induced sobs immediately taking over every inch of my body. Warm blood trickled down my cheek, making me fear the absolute worst.

When the door swung open above me, Luke was long gone. Hands fluttered all over me, hoisting me back on my feet and checking the wound on my head. In the distance, I caught sight of Mable, frozen and staring at the scene in front of her.

Had she been there the entire time? Before I could think much on it, she had disappeared around the corner.

Rachel cooed at me like I was a broken doll. Alice had run back inside to do something. Whether it was to grab rags to clean me up, or get the settee ready, I had no idea. Either way, Helen helped get me to the long, couch-like chair and Alice showed up with a damp rag.

"What happened?" Helen demanded.

"Poor dear, and on your wedding day!" Rachel took the rag and dabbed at my face, getting all the dirt off first, and then working on the slight stream of blood on my chin.

Trying to catch my bearings, I noticed that Mable had joined us. She stood in the entryway, face empty of all emotion. Her eyes were wide but dead inside. She looked exactly like she knew what had happened, and it killed her.

I fought to gain eye contact, to find out what she knew, or if she would defend me if it came to it. But there was nothing. Absolutely nothing. Until Helen spoke up.

"What are you doing here? You're supposed to be at the church working on the decorations!"

Mable blinked, a pleasant mask replacing whatever dull emotion had been there before. "I was just out back to use the outhouse," she explained, flitting her eyes over me as though I didn't exist. As though if she really paid attention, she'd spill it all. "I just wanted to see if Elizabeth was ready yet."

"Goodness gracious, girl. We've got time yet! We'll be there in time, you rest assured of that!" Helen fluttered her hands in Mable's direction. "Shoo, shoo!"

With one forced, pleading sort of glance back at me, Mable hurried out the front door of the mercantile.

She had to have seen everything. She had to know. But why didn't she say anything? Had he hurt her before too?

"What happened, dear?" The elderly woman knelt beside the couch to examine the bruises on my chin.

My response was instant, the decision made. "I tripped." The fight inside of me broke in two at the very words. Why didn't I simply tell them what happened? If I did, they wouldn't make me go through the blasted wedding. Would they?

I looked from woman to woman, bile rising in my stomach. Fighting for the rights of a woman wasn't a thing yet. Not really. Wasn't it still legal for a husband to beat his wife, as long as it was with something thinner than his thumb? There was no way they would help me.

Marrying me off was their duty.

They worked hard on my appearance, cleaning me up and assuring that the cut would hardly be noticeable. They paid extra attention to that area of my face with their makeup, though. The bruising probably showed through.

It was as though I was in some bad dream, drifting along while everyone worked on me like a doll. No one said a word about the bruises on my forearm as they yanked the laces tight on the fancy corset. Neither did I, despite the tears stinging my eyes from the emotion that threatened to spill over.

"Oh, sweetheart, don't worry. No one can see the little scratch," the older woman said. She'd said similar things throughout the entire process. Her attempts at comfort never stopped. When they helped me into all the padding and finally the dress, it somehow got stronger. She must have seen the hopelessness creep into my face.

"Oh, sweetheart." She gave me a big hug. "Everyone is nervous on their wedding day. Let me tell you, I certainly was."

Every single one of the other women chorused their agreement.

"I thought I would pass out the second I got to the altar," Rachel said.

"I was sure Richard wouldn't even show to my wedding," Alice said, shaking her head sadly. "He told me later he was afraid of the same thing."

"Smile, dear," the old lady said. "It's all going to be okay. You look gorgeous, and we had word Luke is there. You will be getting married in . . ." She glanced at the watch hanging from her neck. "Less than an hour. Don't you worry about that!"

My knees gave out, and I plopped onto the couch again. The dress felt hot and clingy, like a foreshadowing of the mess I was about to be permanently stuck in. "I don't want to do this," I said.

"Oh, dear." Rachel sat down beside me and wrapped her arm around my shoulders, rubbing my arm right above the bruising. "It'll all be worth it. It always is."

I swallowed hard. "But what if he's not the man everyone thinks he is?"

"No man ever is," Alice chimed in. "Everyone has their faults. We all learn to live with them."

She couldn't know her council didn't work with my situation, but it still sent chills up my spine. Learn to live with it. The man had already hurt so much. It wasn't something I could just learn to live with.

"Everyone's ready," came the tender voice from the mercantile. It was immediately recognizable. Mabel. She looked as queasy as I felt, fiddling with the front of her dress as though it alone could fix her problems.

"Come on." Rachel helped me to my feet, and the others got to work, making sure every inch of fabric was where it was meant to be.

And we started to walk to my fate.

CHAPTER TWENTY

"Can I talk to you first?" Mable said as we all clustered around the opposing wood doors of the church.

"We don't have time for this—they're all waiting inside," Helen argued. "Tell her afterward."

"Please? I just want to wish her luck." She had the most innocent expression on her face, full of big blue eyes and slightly pouty lips. Somehow, it worked.

"Fine, hurry up," Helen said. "I'll go grab her father."

She squeezed inside, the cluster of women filing in after her.

"Did he hurt you very bad?" Mable's voice was so light that my foggy brain hardly registered it.

"Huh?" I blinked, my vision suddenly becoming sharp. "Who?" Though I knew who. I knew exactly what she was talking about.

"Luke. I saw what happened. Are you sure you're okay?" Mable reached out and cautiously brushed my bruised arm. I winced, giving her the exact answer she was looking for.

"Run," she said suddenly.

"What?" I stared at her, mouth open in shock.

"Go!" She shoved at me, careful not to actually press on anything that might hurt. "Johnathan's over at the stables waiting for you." She blushed as she said his name.

I felt like a fish, unable to do anything except stare at her. Why? Why would she do something so reckless? The potential for her to get caught was high. Right? Why would Johnathan be the one trying to help? Where was Sam?

"Go, dadgummit!" She full-on shoved me toward the steps. "I'm going to start screaming after you! You'd better get going so you have a head start." When I still couldn't grasp what she was saying, she added, "Before your pa gets out here!"

So, I ran for it, skirts lifted nearly to my knees as I raced through the dusty street for the stables. There were so many horses along the street, so many wagons. Everyone had to be inside of the church, ready to watch my freedom be snuffed out.

Not if I could help it.

As promised, Mable shouted after me when I was almost to the safety of the building. She had to protect herself, and it was the best way to do it.

I'll never be able to repay her, I thought, as I rounded the corner into the stables. Each stall was filled with a horse that looked straight at me, wondering if I'd take them on an adventure. Horse thievery wasn't exactly on my agenda. Besides, it would be just my luck that I would grab the wildest of the bunch and end up with a few broken bones for my efforts.

I hurried for the back entry, momentarily wondering if Mable had lied to me. After all, there was no real reason for her to take care of me in such a way. Maybe Luke had told her to trick me into running off. He'd likely be laughing his ass off at the front of the church while everyone rushed after me.

"Over here," came the lullaby voice. The tall frame of Johnathan emerged from the shadows, and he held his hand out for me. "Sam asked for my help."

I didn't question it. I just followed him to a paint horse in the back of the stables. He helped me up like the gentleman he was, then swung up in front as though it was some kind of dance move. There was no saddle to hold on to. Just him.

I wrapped my arms around his middle and held on. I likely looked the perfect picture of a runaway bride, skirts flowing out behind me, veil doing the same. As elegant as it must have been, none of it was comfortable. The corset was tight and pressed into my hip bones as I sat, and the entire dress was more snug than I wanted. It felt as though the stitches would begin popping if I moved much.

We headed straight for the shelter of the trees and the riverbank.

It was a miracle no other horse popped up behind us. I could hear the faint shouting from the town, but nothing more. Maybe we would actually make it.

When we reached the riverbank where we had gone swimming before, Johnathan slowed the horse to a walk. I breathed a sigh of relief. We were safe.

Sam came out of the shadows, a grave expression written across his face. He rode a paint horse I hadn't seen before. She was either young, or simply high spirited. I couldn't really tell which. She pranced in place, sick of waiting.

"Where'd you get her?" I asked, slipping to the ground.

"Mr. Holmes let me borrow her until I'm able to get a new one." Sam reached down to help pull me into my place behind him. It was a wild scramble, but I made it.

"Thank you for coming to get me," I said, looking back at Johnathan.

He smiled quietly and ducked his head.

"Did they see you?" Sam asked.

"I don't think so."

I narrowed my eyes at Johnathan. "If they saw you, wouldn't they . . . wouldn't it be bad?" I wasn't entirely sure what they would actually do. Especially since I wasn't getting out of town like I wanted. But if they blamed a Native American, it couldn't be a good thing.

Johnathan shrugged. "They'd put the blame on us, anyway."

"We need to go, before they manage to catch up," Sam said. His voice was strained from all the potential problems that could still pop out of nowhere.

"Thank you again," I said back to Johnathan as we started off again. He simply nodded, then rode off down the riverbank.

Sam waited until we came out of the trees before picking up speed, the urgency certainly not lost. The young horse ran, mane flying into our faces. My dress flowed out behind me as though I was in a fairy tale. Like Cinderella, my time had run out. I could only hope my story had the happily-ever-after ending.

I secured my arms around Sam's body and pressed my cheek against his back. My veil tugged on my hair as it flew out behind me, ruining the façade for just a moment until I reached back to pull the comb out of its place in the braids. The thin, lacy fabric floated into the air like an angel, flying off to land wherever it wished. My freedom felt official.

Sam really pulled through. He, Mable, and Johnathan. I would be safe. At least temporarily. I hoped beyond anything he would change his mind and we could run off. That I would never have to worry about Luke again.

"I don't want to go back to the house," I said, as we came into the yard.

"We can't leave town, you know that," Sam said with a sigh. "Your family is here. Everything you have is here."

"*Elizabeth's* family. Not mine."

He raised one eyebrow. "You don't think they've become your family too?"

I did my best to ignore the fluttery feeling that sprang up in my stomach. He might have been right, but I certainly wasn't going to admit it. "We can make a new start somewhere!" I protested. "If I stay here, they'll just make sure I have the wedding again."

Sam touched the tip of my chin with his index finger, anger flaring in his eyes. "Get the makeup off your face, and I don't think they will."

Vanity struck me, and my hand flew up to cover the bruises. "You can see them? The other girls promised the makeup covered them well enough."

"They were right," he assured, a smile sneaking onto his lips, but it didn't reach his eyes. "But I can still tell."

"How?" I asked. "Did Mable tell you?"

"Not really. She just told me that Luke wouldn't be kind to you, that I needed to do something. But you keep moving your jaw funny. And it's a tad bit swollen." He held his fingers up about half an inch apart. "But I don't think anyone would have noticed unless they were this close to you."

"Can you just tell them what happened?"

"No." He didn't try to sugarcoat it. It was a simple fact to him. "They won't listen to me. Besides, I don't know the full story. Now, do I?"

"I guess not." I sighed and leaned against his back again. "I don't want to do this."

"I know." He pushed me back up and slid off the horse. "You'll never get anywhere in life if you don't keep moving forward." He reached up to help me down.

"I'd rather ride off into the sunset," I muttered.

"I'm sure you would." He gave me a big hug, pulling me into his warm embrace like a protective shield. "Go get cleaned up before they come to find you." He tried to pull away, but I held on.

"Sam?"

"Hmm?"

"Thank you." I looked up at him, catching the venerable worry that etched every mark on his skin, every line.

He first tensed one muscle in his cheek, then another as he warred with the emotions inside him. It didn't take long for him to give in, lean down, and press his lips to mine.

I melted. If I was to be kissed in a wedding dress, I wanted the kiss to be just so. Warm and comforting, making the rest of the world disappear for as long as it lasted. Like some kind of princess movie from childhood.

As it had to, it ended too soon. He traced my jawline with his index finger and frowned. "He'll pay for this," he promised.

Though the vow made me feel all the more warm fuzzies throughout my body, it also sent a stab of fear through my spine. "I don't want him to hurt you."

A genuine smile made its way onto Sam's face, finally. "He won't hurt me," he assured. "He won't know what's coming."

"He's not getting married. Wouldn't that be punishment enough?" All I could envision was a standoff in the middle of town, both men standing a set distance apart, ready to grab at their guns the moment someone gave the cue.

It wasn't my luck that Sam would be the victor.

"Nope. Go get changed and cleaned up. I don't want to be here when your pa gets home."

I let him walk me to the door, then watched every step he took as he left. The horse nearly pranced, ready to ride off in an instant. Full of energy.

By the time Newton and Elliot showed up, I had changed into another dress from the trunk. My hair loose and flowing down my shoulders, and every ounce of makeup scrubbed off my body. For once, I felt like myself. Even if I was in someone else's clothing.

"Elizabeth!" Newton bellowed from downstairs.

His furious tone didn't spark the amount of fear it should have. "Have courage, courage!" I said into the mirror, making a fist halfway into the air, as though the movement itself would give me all the strength I needed to face the bear of a man downstairs.

I took my time, working hard to keep from overthinking anything as I did so. I had a script in my head, which I repeated over and over with each step I took on the stairs.

"I cannot believe . . ." Newton said the moment my feet hit the floor. He shook his head slowly, trying to align his own thoughts. "I am *so* ashamed of you. The disgrace this brings to every one of us! What makes you think that boy will marry you now? After this stunt?" He held the crumpled veil in his fist, moving it up and down with each word, giving the impression of conducting a band.

Elliot stood off to the side, arms crossed as he took in his surroundings, including me. I felt his gaze travel up my legs, torso, then finally face. They burned into my skin as he caught sight of the blue coloring that was still forming under the skin.

"Pa," he said, his voice hardly audible.

"We relied on this! *You* needed this! You're twenty-four for Pete's sake! You can't keep running around like a—"

"Pa!" Elliot snapped, getting all the furious gazes turned onto him. "Look at her." His eyes narrowed in a sort of challenge, an unspoken argument from the past reminding his father of what he was supposed to do when raising children: listen, observe.

Newton turned his gaze back onto me, his entire body stiffening as he finally *saw* me.

The dress I had chosen to wear had much shorter sleeves than the others. Even so, the sleeves went to my elbows. I assumed because of this, as well as how good the condition was, it was the Sunday best sort of attire.

Positive I had their undivided attention, I rolled up one sleeve to expose the purple-and-blue fingerprints on my arm. Elliot sucked in a breath, and Newton's jaw clicked shut with such force, I wondered if he needed emergency dental care.

I had their attention, and I had to be sure they understood everything. Even though there had been a script in place to explain, the dramatic approach seemed more powerful. I walked straight to Newton, took the veil from his hand, and threw it into the fireplace.

He jumped to action, reaching for it right as I dropped the match inside.

The lacy garment caught quickly, shriveling into nothing in a matter of seconds. We all watched, no one saying a word until it was ash in the bottom of the fireplace.

Newton was the first to speak. "Luke did this?" His jaw was clenched so tightly, the startling-blue vein popped on the side of his neck.

"Yes," I said.

He turned on his heel and reached for the shotgun. "I'm gonna kill him."

"No!" I shrieked, rushing to block the doorway. "Please don't do that. I don't want him to hurt you instead."

He laughed, a sick, rattling sort of sound. "Hurt me? He won't get a chance."

His threat was so much more real than Sam's. So much more violent. "No, because you're not going to go down for murder for me." I pointed at the rack for the shotgun until he put it back. I'd have to watch him closely. He certainly would march out after Luke the second I wasn't looking.

"Why didn't you tell us he did this to you before?" Newton asked. Any ounce of calm he had was forced. His hands balled into fists, every joint in his body stiffened to that of a statue.

I shrugged, unsure how to answer. Elliot wrapped me into a wordless hug, joined soon after by Newton, his arms holding both of us close to him.

To my astonishment, it felt right. Like family. Not the one I lost, but something.

No one was home the next morning. There were leftover grits on the counter, but nothing else. Considering they likely hadn't gotten much done the day before, it made perfect sense they'd be out early to work the cattle.

I pretended everything was normal. I went about my daily chores, washing up things inside the house and taking care of my dear chickens.

I knew when Sam rode up to the house. Not because of the specific sounds of his horse, as he was still borrowing from his boss, but because of how the air changed.

It didn't make any sense, even to me. But I knew it had to be him. It couldn't be anyone else.

Thankfully, I was right. I raced to greet him, jumping to give him the biggest hug I could manage the second he had his horse tied up.

"It worked!" I squealed, giddiness overflowing from my body.

"I told you it would." He grinned.

"Yes! They didn't ask any questions. They believed *everything*!" I squeezed him tighter.

He laughed. "Well, why wouldn't they? You certainly aren't lying."

"True." I sighed and leaned my head against his chest. "Thank you again for helping me out of this."

"I had help," he said with a shrug. "I'm just glad it worked."

I made a mental note to thank Mable when I saw her next. Johnathan too, if I could ever find him. Without another thought, I grabbed his hand and tugged him toward the house. He scrunched his brows together in an unspoken question, but followed.

After pulling him into the main room of the house, I shoved the door shut with my foot and stood on tiptoes to give him a teasing kiss. "Please?" I asked, tracing random designs on the ground with my toe.

He did his best to hide the deflation in his mood, but I felt it anyway. He wrapped his arms around me and picked me up. My legs did their best to wrap around his torso. It wasn't nearly as romantic as the movies, but I did my best. He pressed his lips against mine as he walked me to the couch.

So it would be in the living room. The thrill of someone potentially walking in on us only furthered my excitement. Until he unceremoniously set me down and backed up a few steps.

"No," he said firmly.

My frown was instant. "What? But why?" There was no denying the childish whine that coated my words.

He leaned against the hearth a few feet away, arms crossed as he watched me for any movement. When he took too long to say anything, I did just that. I hopped out of my seat with the intention of closing that distance between us. He sidestepped me easily and didn't return to his comfortable place until I sat back down.

"You're still engaged."

The words sliced. "I'm not! And it doesn't fucking matter! I'm not marrying him." My blood boiled, despite my attempts at calming it down. The audacity of it all! At that very moment, I wanted nothing more than to share happiness and love with *him*. Sam, him. Not Luke. Never Luke. And yet, the bastard was still managing to be the ultimate cock block.

Sam winced slightly at my word choice but carried on. "Where you come from—"

I tried to stand again to feel his warmth close to me, make it seem less like a flaring argument.

He held up his hand like a stop sign, effectively halting me. "Listen, please. Where you come from, what is acceptable behavior for an unmarried woman—"

"Don't you dare start that bullshit." I crossed my arms and glared at him.

He narrowed his eyes right back at me. "Shh. Don't think I wouldn't love to do everything you want. But in this current world you live in, you're unmarried and *not* engaged to me. That simply means, you're not mine to take."

I let out an annoyed sigh. "I'm not engaged to anyone else."

"Well, the rumors around town are that you were taken by an Indian."

I stopped short. "What?" Automatically, fear filled every inch of me. "Did they see him?"

"All they saw was you riding off with someone on a strange horse. They made up whatever story they wanted. That means, you're still engaged. Just kidnapped."

So, Johnathan was technically safe. For the time being. "But Newton and Elliot know! They're on my side!" I let my gaze fall to the ground as I tried to come up with a way to rectify the situation. "They aren't going after any of the Indians, are they?"

"No, Elliot figured it out fast enough to tell everyone you made it home. His excuse was that you just needed some more time after your accident."

"But I told him. He saw the bruises!" Panic replaced every emotion that had been fighting for space in my body. "He knows!"

"He made the excuse for you *before* he knew," Sam pointed out. "I don't think he'll let you get married to Luke now."

The panic faded as fast as it had begun, going straight back to irritation. "Then how am I engaged?"

Sam shook his head, the frustration plain on his face. "I'll make a deal with you. I will sleep with you as soon as there's no way you'll have a bastard child."

I gnawed on my cheek, the tingling throughout my body only egging on the anger. "So, never."

"I didn't say that."

"Well, I don't exactly have ten suitors lined up asking for my hand, now, do I?" I stood up in a huff. "And I don't exactly see you standing there with a ring in your hand, either."

He shifted his weight from one foot to the other anxiously. "No," he admitted.

"Then what is this?" I pointed wildly between us.

"I had hoped something more than lust."

His sting made me pause, embarrassment hiding in the back corners of my mind. He had a really good point. A relationship wasn't just sex. If it was, it was likely destined to fail. The need I felt to see him, the obsession I had with wondering what he was up to, or putting him into my daydreams as I fell asleep—wasn't it all more than simple sex?

"It's not fair," I muttered. "You can't tell me you haven't done it before."

Stunned, he opened his mouth twice before he finally spoke. "Life ain't fair."

"So, I have to be a good, nineteenth-century girl," I said bitterly, deciding to dwell on the fact that he had managed to have some other chick later.

He smirked. "Prob'ly a good idea." He managed to leave the "a" out of the center of the word, bringing his accent out just a tad bit more than before.

"I don't want to wait."

He finally closed the distance between us, coming to sit beside me on the couch. "If it helps, I don't wanna either."

"Then, can we just give in?" I turned my head up to his, hoping the pleading had all been channeled into my eyes.

He grinned at my attempt of a puppy face. "That doesn't work on me, dear." He kissed my forehead and hopped to his feet before I could grab him. "If you were to . . ." He gestured wildly at my torso. "Your reputation would be ruined."

"You could marry me if that happened," I pointed out.

He sighed. "I have nothing to my name. I don't even have a horse anymore. I'm the worst person to consider as a father, or even a husband."

"Who said I cared about that?"

"No, Ellie," he said sternly. "I'm not going to marry you." He was at the door, hand on the knob. When I didn't respond, or even react, he opened it, the fresh breeze sneaking inside. "I have to get back to work. I'm supposed to be checking on the herd with the others." He waited for me to say something, but I didn't so much as look up. "Please be safe."

"I will." The words had to be choked out, as they hid far behind a wall of emotion.

"I'll come check on you when I can," he promised, hovering in the doorway to watch me. Eventually, he gave up and slipped outside, leaving me to fall apart as my heart began to break.

CHAPTER TWENTY-ONE

D id I just propose?

Sure, desperation might have had something to do with it. It could have easily been the spark for the entire ordeal. But the overwhelming depression that brought tears streaming down my face wasn't because I needed him as a crutch. I'd be fine without him. I had a new family that would help keep me safe.

Instead, it was because of what he said: "I'm not going to marry you." The finality of his words swirled around and around in my brain.

Friend-zoned.

Despite that probability, the glimpses of a redheaded baby toddling up to our front door with arms outstretched for us wouldn't stop interrupting my self-deprecation. Why did I even care about something like that? I had plenty more that I should have worried about instead, but his rejection was as good as a stab in the back.

I sat in front of the extinguished fire, trapped in some kind of trance. There was no way of knowing how long I obsessed over Sam's single sentence. The only thing that finally broke my hypnotism was more hoofbeats in the yard.

Almost instantly, I was on my feet and at the window to push aside the curtain. Somehow, I hoped it would be Sam again. Back to apologize for worrying me with what he said, convince me that anything was still possible with such a feeling inside. I was completely trapped in the schoolgirl mental torment.

The sight of a bay horse made my blood run cold. Certainly not Sam. To make matters worse, the incoming rider had learned from his previous visit. Instead of tying his horse up at the barn, Luke rode right up to the house. There was no escape.

Something clicked in my mind, and I rushed to the counters, rummaging around in the drawers until I found a knife. It was one that I assumed was used for wild game, but I couldn't be sure. It just looked more ornate. Plus, it had a leather sheath.

Why? Why? A knife shouldn't be necessary, I thought. The bruises floating under my pale skin said otherwise. *Better safe than sorry.* As the door swung open, I shoved the whole thing in my boot and whirled to face my intruder.

"Good afternoon, Elizabeth," Luke said. His voice was more polite than I'd ever heard. The hollow sound of it sent panic flowing throughout my veins.

"What do you want?" I crossed my arms, hoping to look at least a little opposing. Everything felt as though it was a dream. Just a simple nightmare. My heart racing high in my chest broke that fantasy. "I don't have time for a visit."

He raised an eyebrow. "You don't? Well then, I'm sure you'll have time to spare for your *betrothed.*"

"Nope." I let my lips pop in the middle of the word.

"It's not an invitation." He closed the distance between us and grabbed my forearm, right on top of the bruising.

Automatically, I tried to pry his fingers off. "Let me go, please," I said through my teeth. His fingertips were white with how tightly he held on. "Let me go!" He didn't adjust by even a fraction of an inch, so I pounded at his knuckles to get him to release me. I might as well have been a pesky mosquito for how much good I did.

He pulled me out the door and toward his horse. I yanked back with every bit of my body weight, sending pain through my shoulder and a sickening sensation of something similar to rope burn on my arm. When I was almost sitting on the ground with my effort, he'd had enough. He picked me up easily and threw me over his shoulder, securing my legs so I couldn't kick his nose.

That certainly didn't keep me from trying. I kicked and pounded my fists against his back. "You damn motherfucking bastard!" I shouted, hitting his lower back as hard as I could. He flinched when I hit his spine, but he somehow powered through.

Silently, he practically dropped me back onto the ground by his horse, immediately dropping down to straddle me. He produced a rope from his saddle and tied my arms and legs with ease.

Being tied up would officially never be a turn-on for me. I spat at him, my own anger only increasing when it completely missed his face. "Let me go! I'm not marrying you, you understand? Last I checked, you spoke English! Use your damn words!"

As though he didn't hear a single word I said, he reached back to my ankles and gingerly pulled the blade out of its hiding place. With care, he turned it over in his hands, examining each notch in the handle, every decorative stain on the sheath.

"What was this for?" he asked levelly.

"Gardening." As soon as the word left my lips, I scrunched up my nose. It had to be the most ridiculous answer I had ever come up with, and I was sure of it.

He raised an eyebrow. "Gardening? Well then. I don't want you getting hurt with it hidden down there in your sock." He tsked his tongue as he got up, leaving me to turn into a worm on the ground. My squirming got me nowhere. He slipped the blade between the saddle and blanket, then came right back to me.

"Let me go! If you don't let me go right now, I can make sure everyone will know about this!" I jerked hard to the side as he picked me up again, accomplishing nothing.

"I can make sure you won't." He placed me over his horse, swinging into the saddle behind. The saddle horn rubbed uncomfortably against my stomach, and the horsehair scratched against the underside of my arms.

"Come on!" I tried to do a wormlike movement again, only to get boxed in the side.

"Stay still. You don't want to fall off and get trampled, now, do you?" And he took off.

Despite my every wish, I obeyed and stayed still. Tears stung my eyes from the intense fear that threatened to break me.

The realization that no one would be coming to save me any time soon dropped into my gut like a stone. Sam had just left, and he likely wouldn't be back to see me for at least another day. Maybe even two. Elliot and Newton had left to . . . to do what? They'd never actually told me. Regardless, they wouldn't be back until nearly sunset.

I felt sick as we rode, my body straining to avoid the legs of his horse. My nose was far too close to the shoulder for my comfort. Though, nothing in the situation was remotely close to comfortable.

What if he simply wanted to talk with me? There was always that chance. But then, why did he have to tie me up? Why did he even have to take me elsewhere?

Nothing made my stomach stop churning. There was no way in which everything would work out well. No way at all. No one would tie up someone else just to talk to them. Not unless it was an interrogation. A simple conversation could have happened at home.

He wouldn't take me so far off if he hadn't intended something heinous. Even worse, he probably didn't believe I'd stay silent once he let me free.

My mind, body, mood, everything broke. Sobs shook my body. The least glamorous kind. The kind where snot poured down my face along with the tears. Though, hanging upside down, nose to shoulder with a large animal made it worse.

"Quit your damn blubbering," he snapped, as he reined in his horse. He didn't bother to move me until he had her tied securely to a tree.

We were at the river.

Not only that, we were on the exact ridge that we had found her body.

As he dragged me off the horse, the realization hit me. My crying halted. This was what had happened to the other Elizabeth. I was suddenly sure of it.

He untied my ankles first, tucking the rope into his pocket. He grabbed my forearm yet again before he untied my hands.

Immediately, I slapped him. Why I chose a slap instead of a punch to the nose, I had no idea. Slapping just felt more natural somehow.

"You bastard."

"That, I assure you, I am not." He smiled, sending bile spinning through my stomach. "Now, my dear, why did you leave our wedding yesterday? So many people worked very hard on every minute detail. You broke my ma's heart."

He stared down at me. His eyes sad, nearly showing a broken heart inside, but there was something else. A knife hiding in the depths.

"I told you I wouldn't marry you," I said, standing a smidge taller as if it would help my dwindling bravery.

Elizabeth died here.

He killed her.

"That was just the memory loss speaking, now, wasn't it?" He made that noise with his tongue again as he shook his head. "Now that we are here, won't that help you remember? What *do* you remember?" He pulled me to the edge of the river. I looked down, stomach churning more than the river ever thought of. It was calm down there, flowing along as though it had nowhere to be anytime soon.

"If I remember correctly, Pa said he saw you out here with that boy. Hmm, what was his name? Samuel. Yes! Him!" He smiled at his own devious train of thought. "Now, from what I remember of that fateful event yesterday, I also saw you with him. Didn't I?"

I couldn't speak. I could hardly even breathe. It didn't matter that he couldn't have seen us together. Not unless he hopped on a horse to take chase. Even so, he somehow knew.

The longer I looked at the river, the faster it seemed to flow. The more ominous it felt. I could swim. It wasn't flowing nearly fast enough to drown me. But if he held me underneath, he could easily end it all.

Or maybe I would go back home. Finally.

But I didn't particularly want to go home. Not at such a high cost.

I had a family here. A father, a brother, and someone who I honestly wanted to see all the time. Would Sam be heartbroken if I disappeared?

There was no doubt in my mind that Sam would be devastated. Everyone would be. Everyone I knew I cared about. Really and truly cared about.

"Did you hear me, brat?" He shook me roughly, causing me to gasp as I came back to reality.

"You don't want to do this, Luke."

He let out a booming laugh. The sound made me feel as though I was already drowning. It was true, uninterrupted happiness. Bliss.

"What do you think I'm going to do?"

My eyes betrayed me, darting to the water.

"Oh, no, no, no, sweet darling girl. You'll just have to wait and see what I have in store for you." He wrapped one arm around my shoulders and began pacing. A few steps to his horse, then a few steps back to the water's edge, all the while dragging me along. "First, let's discuss this Samuel Smith."

"He has nothing to do with any of this."

"Really?" He brought his face down to stare into my eyes, reminding me of a python coming in for a kill. "Then why was he your savior yesterday?"

I set my jaw and glared back at him. There was no way I was going to implicate Sam in any of this. Especially with the sinking feeling growing in my stomach. He had to be the one who hurt Elizabeth. No, murdered her.

"You're gonna go quiet for once?" He grinned. "That tells me all I need to know." He switched his grip to the back of my neck, yanking my hair as he continued his pacing. "Your pa and brother came over to our house earlier."

My steps faltered only slightly as I feared the worst. Did he kill them? Were they ever coming home? Would they ever find my body if he killed me?

"Oh, don't fret." He shoved me harder in the direction he wanted me to go. "Your pa just wanted to talk to mine. Tell him how I wasn't *fit* to marry his daughter." His laugh echoed through the trees. "Well, as you would imagine, my pa didn't take kindly to that. Especially when he went on to say how my own ma was covering for her own mistreatment! You know, he got a good beatin' after that!"

I gasped. "You beat him?"

"*I* didn't beat him." His chest rumbled with laughter. "My pa certainly did, though. I got the pleasure of holdin' back your big brother. Ain't as strong as he thinks he is."

I shut my eyes, doing my absolute best to push the images of Elliot being thrown around like a rag doll. Or worse, Newton being beat for something he didn't deserve. My heart ached for them. "Are they okay?" I was almost too afraid to ask.

"Oh, of course." He waved a hand dismissively in the air. "They oughta be headin' back home again soon. I'm afraid they won't quite like what they find."

My feet quit moving, toes digging into the ground to try to remain still. "What will they be finding?"

"Well." He paced in front of me, like a cat sizing up its prey. "You said you won't marry me, correct?"

"Yes." I watched his every move. Even the way he moved his hands was mesmerizing.

"Well, I made a decision a long while ago. And if you remembered anything from before, you'd know this." He took a dramatic breath. "I ain't lettin' you go. You're *mine*. And that's as good as it gets. You don't get a say."

My stomach fell to the floor. There was no escaping. Not with the daggers on full display in his eyes. The sparkle that remained was only from the sick, twisted joy he found in envisioning his plan.

"Just let me go, Lucas," I said, as firmly as I could. The tremor that threatened to overtake my body managed to seep into my voice anyway. I took a step back, and he let me. Only, like a sick and twisted dance, he took the exact same step.

"I didn't mean to let you go last time. What makes you think this time will be any different?"

Another step back, then another. Again, he matched both. "Get away from me," I warned, holding my hands out in front of me like a shield.

"I never break my word. I said I'd never let you go, and I meant it." He grabbed my wrist.

"This is a bad idea." My voice hopped an octave spontaneously.

"No, it's a very good idea. We all know that memory loss of yours was never real." He brought me back to the starting location, right near the horse.

"I can promise you this: I don't remember a single damn thing from whatever you're talking about."

"Really? That's a lie." He brought his leg behind mine, hitting the back of my knees with ease. I fell flat, the air flying out of me in a gush. "Now," he said, coming back to straddle me. That was when I saw it: the knife he had tucked into his waistband. The same blade I'd had in my shoe.

"Oh my God, no!" I shouted, my voice jumping a full octave. I squirmed this way and that, not caring if I injured myself with my thrashing. I whacked at every available inch of him, hoping to turn into some kind of Tasmanian devil and break free.

"You're supposed to be mine . . ." he said, his voice coated in sugar.

"Are you wanting me to say I'll marry you? 'Cause I will! Just please don't hurt me." I couldn't fully believe the words coming out of my mouth. But I knew it was true. If I could avoid pain, suffering, and even death, I would probably marry anybody.

He grinned and leaned down slowly, so slowly I could feel every muscle activate. He positioned himself so his chest barely brushed mine, his lips hovering right out of reach. There was nothing sensual about it. Nothing exciting.

"Get off me," I growled.

"How much fire are you gonna give me?" he asked with a grin. He didn't wait for a response. Without any warning, he pressed his lips to mine, forcing them open with his tongue and roughly tracing an outline on the edges of my clenched teeth.

His tongue felt like something crossed between a snake and an eel—unwelcome and frightening. I turned my head away, but he held it still, kissing me until he had his fill.

"I will be the only one you ever have," he promised, yanking at the fabric of my bodice so the skin above the line of the corset was visible. I felt faint, like every bit of my blood ran away to my feet.

But his plan wasn't what I anticipated.

He pulled the knife out of the sheath and traced my collarbone. The touch was unnervingly delicate, sending terrifying shivers throughout my body, whimpers flowing along behind.

"Oh, no more fight left in ya?" The grin was sickening. His laugh was sickening. He added a touch more pressure to the knife, slicing a thin, shallow line under my collarbone.

The second he lifted it to admire his work, I turned my head and retched all over the grass. The smile fell from his face for only an instant as he witnessed my lowest of lows.

The smile didn't stay gone for long. It reappeared shortly after, with the same menacing laugh. He hurried lower, ruffling my skirts up over the rest of my body.

I didn't stay still then. I couldn't. There was no way he would be allowed to touch me without a fight. Especially with a knife in his hands. I kicked him as hard as I could, aiming straight for his nose. It made purchase, sending a satisfying crack through the quiet air.

The happiness evaporated from him, followed only by a cool acceptance of what he had to do. I scrambled to my feet, taking on the closest stance I could come up with to fight him, one foot slightly in front of the other, fists raised.

He smirked, blood flowing over his thin lips and dropping onto his shirt. Unfazed, he waltzed over to me, grabbing at my arm with more confidence than I'd seen yet.

I kneed him, satisfied when he doubled over. When I repeated the same movement, he crumpled forward, arms wrapping around my body as he went for the ground. I gasped as he pulled me down with him, gaining the upper hand again.

He sliced at my chest, tearing the fabric open in an easy stroke, smiling at the result. Momentarily, I was grateful that bikinis were normal in my time. An exposed corset was not a big deal.

I tried kneeing him again, but he was on top of me, legs intertwined with mine to keep them still as he traced the upper edge of the corset with the blade again.

"What was all that for?" he cooed. The sick, twisted happiness in his eyes had slowly changed to straight, angry daggers. He held the knife up to my throat. "I *will* have what I want. You learn that good. Even if it's the last thing you ever learn."

When he released the pressure on the blade, I thought I was safe for a moment more. Until he brought it up and sliced into my arm.

A scream echoed along the riverbank, loud and shrill, pained and desperate. My scream. I followed it with cries for help, all of which were drowned out by his hand over my mouth.

"Oh, shut it," he snapped. "We have business to attend to. Best not invite anyone else."

He shimmied back down to wrestle with the skirts, arms pressed on either side of me like a brick wall.

I turned into a squirming monster. I pushed off his legs with my own, shimmying backward as fast as I could. A sharp pain hit my thigh, but I did my best to ignore it. I went for that knife. I reached desperately for it, turning on my side and continuing my kicking pattern as I did. I must have made contact with his still bleeding nose, as he staggered back, hands going straight for his face. The knife was still in his hand, but loose. I grabbed it, cutting a gaping line into the palm of my hand as I did.

The pain didn't mean anything. As if in slow motion, the handle slid from his own hand. His eyes went wide, and I lunged. No thoughts, no planning. I shoved the knife hard toward him, the blade sinking into his chest.

He gasped in a mixture of pain and realization as he fell to his side, the fight seeping out of him instead.

I backed up as fast as I could, the knife still in my hands. The blood that flowed freely from my own cuts didn't remotely compare to the blood gushing from his chest.

Already, he lay in a pool. His body twitched and he groaned, clawing at his chest. His breathing was raspy, strained. Like an asthma attack. But it wasn't that. It was so far from that.

"Help," he begged. Or mouthed. I couldn't be sure if there was sound even coming from his lips. It didn't fully matter—I knew exactly what he said. He reached for me desperately, eyes full of a kind of dull panic.

I backed up a few steps, my body shaking harder than it ever had.

I was dizzy. So dizzy. My head was fuzzy and light. I could hardly stand, I could hardly focus on his strained face as he gasped for breath.

I tried to fight it, I tried to move toward the horse, to make my way home. But my body had other plans. It wasn't invincible. It wouldn't move forward just because I wanted it to.

This is how Elizabeth died.

So, I fell to the ground into the nightmare-filled world of my dreams.

CHAPTER TWENTY-TWO

"Elizabeth! Elizabeth!"

Someone shook me.

The air was filled with a foreboding sense of panic, and it smelled like death and human waste. I didn't want to join that world. I wanted to go back to the blackness I'd hidden inside. My safe corner where I could simply exist.

But fate had other plans.

"Elizabeth, please, wake up!" The man continued shaking me. Desperately.

It felt like sprinkles were hitting my face, but I remembered it being the perfect, sunshiny day before.

Had it really been long enough for the weather to change?

My eyes jerked open the second I remembered everything. Elliot crouched over me, holding me in his arms like an overgrown infant, tears flowing down his cheeks.

"Oh, thank God," he whispered, pulling me up and pressing me against his chest. "You're alive."

I didn't pull back. I was too weak, too stunned to do much of anything. "He killed her." My voice failed me, cracking into a sob.

"Killed who?" Elliot asked, pushing me to arm's length to stare straight at my face.

"Elizabeth. He killed Elizabeth."

"Oh, no." He pulled me close again. "You're okay. You're right here. We'll get you taken care of in just a moment."

"No . . ." I protested, feebly pushing away from him. Something was wrapped around my thigh, tightly enough that it throbbed. A bandage? A boa constrictor? One of those. "The other Elizabeth."

Confusion crossed his face for a split second, but he let it pass when he glanced down at my body. Worry replaced everything then. "That's of no concern right now. We need to get you home." He scooped me up and set me on a horse, never once letting me go so I could fall over as he swung up behind me.

I may have muttered a few other things at him. I remember him making vague sounds of agreement as we raced for home. As for what I said, it's likely even he didn't have a clue.

We rode faster than I ever had. My eyes would flutter shut, then open up again, putting us a long way down the road. My leg throbbed painfully, pins and needles prickling at my toes. I welcomed the blackouts each time they came around, hoping they would keep me until I could function again.

From the time we pulled up to the house to the time Elliot helped me to bed, I blanked out. It was disorienting, going from riding on a horse at what felt like breakneck speeds, to lying on my own bed, needle pricks making me squirm.

"Stop." I reached down aimlessly at Elliot.

He moved my hand away. "Shh, just go back to sleep." His voice was like a lullaby, rocking me back and forth in my delirium as the needle poked in and out of my thigh, then later my palm.

My body didn't fight it. I felt it, sure, but not the same as I normally would have. It was like my mind filed the sensation in a completely different box. One that didn't matter but was opened every third or fourth stick of the needle to ensure I made a squeak noise and jerked.

The next thing I knew, someone was stroking my hair and singing to me in a low voice. Tobacco laced his breath, the intense, woodsy kind that felt like a warm hug.

Newton had arrived at some point, and I was glad. His fingers in my hair brought me right back to childhood. Sent me straight into restless sleep, then back out again.

Eventually, when I fully awoke, I was alone. They had dressed me in a clean shift, and for once I didn't care. My whole body ached and felt like it'd been torn apart. I could feel the bruises without moving an inch of my body. I could feel the tug from where the stitches had been placed on my inner thigh and then hand.

When I shoved back the blankets to get out of the bed, the world swam around me. I hadn't lifted my head more than an inch off the pillow, but the dizziness still took over. I let my body go still on the mattress, a fear sneaking its way into my disorganized mind.

Was I going to be okay?

"Elliot?" My voice was hardly more than a whisper. "Newton?"

Nothing.

"Elliot? Pa!" My voice cracked in each of the words, but it was loud enough to be heard. Even if not fully understandable.

Within a matter of seconds, the door flew open and both men rushed in, panic written on every inch of their bodies.

"Are you okay?" Newton asked, rushing to my side, his eyes looking wildly for any signs of more blood.

"What happened?" Elliot was doing the same from the foot of the bed.

My words abandoned me then, making me wonder why I actually wanted them there in the first place. I wasn't bleeding, so I wasn't dying. Right?

But he had . . . he'd looked so frail, wasting away in his own blood. He'd asked for help, and I had backed away. But would

I have been found if I had helped him in the first place? Or rather, would he have let me have a chance to survive?

No.

He had killed Elizabeth.

And Newton needed to know.

I took a sore, shaky breath before forcing the words out. "I lied to you."

Newton furrowed his brow, reaching over to carefully push a stray hair out of my eyes.

"I doubt that," Elliot said, though unmasked concern covered his face.

"No, I did." I closed my own eyes to block out the worry, to block out any disappointed reaction. They would hate me. They would kick me out. That was, if they actually believed me. "I'm not Elizabeth."

Silence was all I got. Complete, utter confusion mixed with concern. Nothing close to what I had expected. But then, after I had first arrived, I may very well have said the same words. They certainly didn't believe me then.

"He killed her," I continued, concentrating hard on every breath I took. "Luke did. Sam and I found her when I was trying to go back home."

Newton grabbed for the bedpost as his legs faltered. Elliot took one large step to stand close to him, ready to catch the older man if he went down.

"What are you talking about?" Elliot demanded. Each breath was audible and fast, but his voice was strong, like he was scolding a child.

"I'm not Elizabeth." I looked between both of them, hoping for some form of recognition. Something. My mind had cleared for the slightest of moments, making it easier to communicate what I wanted. "And I'm not crazy. I promise. My friends and I were in a bad accident. I guess, like a wagon accident? I'm sure that happens somewhere." Their narrowed eyes proved they were listening but not necessarily understanding. "I fell in the water and drowned. But I woke up here. I remember everything. My mom, my dad, my big brother." Tears pricked at the back of my eyes, but I blinked them away. "They all died a few years ago."

Elliot sat down on the edge of the bed and patted my unwounded shoulder. "I reckon you've just had too much going through that mind of yours. It'll all come back—"

"No," I snapped, slapping his hand away. "I wear pants. I had a cell phone. You use them to call people all over the world. And cars! I guess for a while they called them horseless buggies? I don't know! It doesn't matter. You just have to believe me! We were in the twenty-first century. Way over a hundred years in the future."

Newton really faltered that time, Elliot grabbing him to keep him steady. He pulled him over to take his own spot on the edge of the bed.

"You're telling the truth." Newton's voice wavered. He was nearly shaking, but he was doing his best to keep himself steady. "That explains your behavior, the language, everything."

"Yes," I said. It would have been so much easier to continue to lie to them. But they didn't deserve that. I couldn't pretend to know how to be a nineteenth-century housewife forever.

Elliot started to pace, jaw slack with amazement. "What were you wearing when I found you? Those pants were so tight, they showed the world . . ." he trailed off, shaking his head wildly. "And those couldn't have been acceptable undergarments. There wasn't enough fabric anywhere!"

I smirked, crooking an eyebrow at him. "You were looking at my underwear?"

Newton roughly cleared his throat. "Let the girl explain."

"I do think I'm related to you—it's just been a while." I fidgeted with the edge of the blanket. "I'm sorry."

"What did you do with—" Newton paused, fighting with the word somewhere deep inside. "Her?"

I gnawed on my lower lip, tears pricking at the corners of my eyes. I couldn't lose it. Not yet. "We buried her, Sam and I. Over by that tree." I gestured vaguely, hoping he'd understand the one I meant. There weren't very many to choose from, after all.

Newton closed his eyes and didn't reopen them for a long time. "Excuse me," he finally said, his voice cracking. He roughly pulled from Elliot's support and headed downstairs.

The stab of loss hit me hard. His daughter was dead. And he believed it. The tears sprang over the edges of my lids, threatening to overtake me.

Elliot pulled me to a sitting position and wrapped me in a huge hug. The kind of hug I hadn't been in since Travis had been alive. It'd been a long year since I'd felt such a thing. The kind of hug only a big brother could give.

"I'm so sorry." I sobbed into his shoulder. He held tighter, unyielding. His own body shook with emotion, and his tears dropped onto me.

"None of it is your fault." He said it as though he was reminding himself of that fact. "It's not your fault."

"It's not yours, either."

He said nothing, but his body stiffened. With a caring pat on my back that only a brother could provide, he left the room, leaving me alone for the emotions to crash over me. The worry of being kicked out on the street, the worry of being shoved back into my own time. The worry of facing all of it.

The worry of how I'd killed a man.

I'd killed a man.

I'd killed Luke.

And the dam broke, releasing the tears yet again.

Hours passed before I decided to get out of bed. It had been completely silent downstairs. There was no evidence of Newton ever coming home, and Elliot was likely outside. Either that, or he decided to take a forbidden nap.

Everything hurt as I got up. The bruises were beginning to show all across my arms and my legs. I felt like I'd been through some sort of massive car accident. Or rather, I'd been hit by a train.

There was no sign of anyone downstairs. No leftover food out, nothing.

My stomach didn't care that I didn't particularly have the energy to cook. It still growled.

I pulled myself onto the counter to rummage through the cabinets, hoping to find some kind of dried fruit. Something sweet. Anything sweet.

When my fingers hit something soft, I got excited. A ridiculous idea or not, I envisioned some elderly woman had wrapped some sort of gourmet sweets inside a handkerchief to keep it safe from pests.

The second I had the simple napkin in my hand, I knew it wasn't edible. Whatever was inside was familiar and hard. Slowly, carefully, I unwrapped it.

Inside sat exactly what I didn't want to see again.

The knife.

Its sheath was long gone, but the blood still remained, staining across the entire thing. It dried in the decorative etches of the handle, solidified in random clumps.

Certainly not the comfort food I had desired.

My breath caught in my throat and all the feelings returned in a rush, along with the throbbing, unrelenting pain in my muscles.

I killed him.

I had.

It wasn't some story I had simply read about, or even a dream. I had killed him. Me, and only me.

Sure, he would've killed me if given half a chance. He had killed Elizabeth, after all. That didn't change the fact that his blood had been over my hands.

Suddenly the door swung open so hard it hit the wall. I jumped and whirled around, automatically tucking the blade behind my back.

As if he lived there, a burly man walked into the house. He looked so comfortable, so at home. He had on the classic pants of the era, dark-colored shirt, and light vest with a star pinned on it. I didn't even need to read the letters marked on it to know he was the sheriff.

My fingers tightened along the blade, as if he would sense its presence. It wouldn't have surprised me if he could smell the dried blood.

After all, why else would he have shown up? He had to have known about the body. Newton must have told him.

Elliot came in next, a grave expression written all over his face. He was so pale, it looked as though he'd been sick. Right behind him came Newton. In contrast, he looked resigned. To what, there was no telling. My fate?

My senses on high alert, I noticed everything. I could plainly see the bruises covering Newton's face. Elliot had plenty as well, but none of them looked more than that of a bar fight. Newton looked as though he had been trampled. The wrinkles in his face showed all the more in every place where the blood pooled under the skin.

Luke and his father had done a number on him for sure.

"Ah!" The sheriff looked me up and down, more sizing up my condition than any kind of romantic interest. "Elizabeth, it's good to see you. How are you holding up?"

He might as well have asked me about the weather. It didn't matter if it was an innocent question—it still felt like I was being interrogated. I squirmed, positive he would see straight through everything, anything. Clearly, he knew everything I had done. He knew exactly who I was.

Who I wasn't.

"Erik had some questions to ask you," Elliot said. His voice was strained, choked.

"Questions to ask me?" My voice squeaked despite my best attempts at keeping it stable.

"Oh, yes!" Erik did a good job of acting like it had simply slipped his mind. He waved his hand and cleared his throat. "I just want to see if you could tell me about some . . ." He paused, hunting for the right word. "Whereabouts."

I looked from Newton to Elliot, then back to Newton again. Their faces gave away nothing. Were they turning me in? All the times that Newton had been upset at me during the past few weeks came crashing down upon me. Made sense that he would want to get rid of me. This way they wouldn't have much of a mess on their hands. If I was pegged as a murderer, I was no longer their problem.

Erik didn't wait for me to ask him for specific questions. He grabbed one of the chairs by the table and turned it to face me before plopping down happily. "Where were we? First, I must ask you if you know anything about what has transpired throughout today?"

I squirmed. "Today?" My skin crawled, and my empty stomach felt as though I had some trapped rabbit inside, hopping every which way to try to escape.

"Yes, when your pa went to the Barnette ranch next door to talk about your wedding."

I took a steadying breath, hoping I didn't dig my own grave with every word I said. "I know they went to call off my wedding." I hoped I sounded brave, but with the rabbit wreaking havoc inside my stomach, I was sure I sounded more like a terrified child.

"Yes, I gathered that. But what I want to know about is afterward. According to Levi, your pa started a fight. Took most of his men to get him off. And you know men—they couldn't leave it at that." He looked knowingly over at Newton, eyeing the bruises along his cheekbones.

I blinked in surprise. That was wrong. "They didn't start the fight!" I argued, desperately glancing between all three of the men. "Levi and Luke did."

"So you *do* know something of what happened today. But don't you worry, I will be comparing both of the stories." His eyes wandered to the cabinets, his eyes looking like a hungry child.

"Would you like something to eat?" I reluctantly asked. Maybe if I could make my way into his heart through his stomach, I wouldn't go to jail.

"Oh, yes, please." The smile lit up on his face, making him look like some sort of gleeful mascot for a pastry company.

I took a plate from one of the cupboards, tucking the knife back behind the other dishes as I did so. The blade safely hidden,

I grabbed a few pieces of bread and put them on the plate. Not sure what else to do, I grabbed a jar of jam and handed it all to him. He took it gratefully, putting one in his mouth before the saucer fully rested on his lap.

"Men get into fights, as I'm sure you know." I eyed him levelly. Perhaps he was simply there for the fight, and nothing else. The pesky, queasy feeling in my stomach didn't subside with that possibility.

"Well, of course," he said, licking some of the crumbs off his fingers. "We have one hitch in that story." He reluctantly set the plate on the table and stood up, groaning as his muscles protested.

"A hitch?" I echoed, glancing nervously at Elliot. His sickly expression hadn't changed. Newton's had slowly grown more pale.

"You see, when out ridin' the property line, Levi came across your pa. Do you have any idea what he mighta been doin'?" He raised an eyebrow.

"No?" I had somehow backed all the way up, the small of my back pressed hard against the counter.

"Your pa was out messin' with a body. And I'm real sorry to tell you this, ma'am"—he cleared his throat, a sign of his procrastination—"the body was Lucas."

My heart sank. Somehow, I had hoped he would say something else. Anything else. But it was what it was. I was going to go to jail for the murder of Luke Barnette. The sheriff was studying my every movement, waiting for a response.

"Oh," was all I could manage.

He didn't hesitate before continuing. "Levi accused your pa of killing him. And now I have to take him into custody."

My entire body froze. I hadn't expected that. "No, no! It wasn't him. He didn't do that. I—"

"He was hurting my daughter. I did what I had to do to protect her." Newton said each word clearly, as though he was already in the courtroom.

"But . . ." I stared at him, trying desperately to read his expressions. There weren't any. Just simple sadness, and slight queasiness. "You don't have to do this."

"I did, and I will do what I can to keep you safe," Newton said. His mind was made up, and we all knew it.

The sheriff made a sympathetic face and looked me over. "I don't want to take him in. Do you have anything to add to the story that might help?" His eyes were pleading, hopeful. The toast long forgotten.

I couldn't take my eyes off Newton. Was he really doing this for me? Why? Why would *anyone* do such a thing? He gave a brusque nod, solidifying the choice.

Bile rose in my throat. My heart rate wouldn't slow down. But I couldn't destroy everything of the façade he had created.

"No," I finally creaked out.

The sheriff took in a sharp breath. "That's that, then." Shaking his head slowly, he turned back to the door. "Say your goodbyes."

I ran to him, slamming against him like a brick wall. He wrapped his arms around me, squeezing out as much of the panic as he could.

"You don't have to do this," I repeated.

He rested his forehead against the top of my head, taking breaths to steady himself. "But I do."

"But *why?* I'm not her." A painful sob hitched in my chest.

"You're all I have left."

CHAPTER TWENTY-THREE

The sheriff took him then, leaving Elliot and I to stand in shock. Neither of us moved, let alone spoke, until the sun was quite far down in the sky.

Only when the clock struck the hour did I finally burst. "Why'd you let him do that? They would have been more kind to me. There's no telling what they'll do to him!"

"I didn't have much of a choice in the matter," Elliot muttered. "Pa had pretty much admitted to the whole thing by the time they reached me."

"And where were you? I thought you would have gone to help!"

"I had some things to sort through with your grand ole confession earlier, now, didn't I?" He crossed his arms and glared at me.

"You went to find her?" I couldn't imagine the emotional turmoil digging up a loved one could cause. It would have been impossible for me.

"No, I went and found Sam."

"Okay, then, if you believe I'm not her, why didn't you simply turn me in anyway? Screw what Pa thought. You're not gonna want me here."

He pinched the bridge of his nose. "Really? You think we're gonna simply throw you out? You're the closest we have to Elizabeth. You may not *be* her, but you're obviously family in some way."

"It doesn't make a difference," I snapped. "They wouldn't hurt me if I went to jail instead."

"Yes, they would. They would call you insane almost immediately. More than likely, they'd ship you off to an asylum somewhere."

I threw my hands up in the air. "They wouldn't do that! I'm not insane!"

He listed things off on his fingers. "You don't remember anything, you have sudden refusals to things you previously looked forward to, you swear, you haven't been to church in God knows when, and many of them saw that outfit you wore whenever you showed up."

I rolled my eyes. "Not enough to call me mentally unstable."

"And you killed your betrothed," he finished, one eyebrow raised, daring me to challenge him.

"It's ridiculous."

"No, it's not. It would be an act of sympathy. To everyone else, at least. 'Bless her heart' would be uttered all around town."

"I'd be able to get away in time. Right? They still wouldn't hurt me as much as Newton."

Elliot sighed. "You would be tied up more than he is right now, I can guarantee that."

"What if they hang him, though?"

Silence greeted me. I'd hit on the real reason for the sickening, pale expression.

My heart skipped a beat. "Elliot! Please!" I begged. "They can't do that!"

"They can," he said, voice tense and wrought with emotion. Before he could break, he left, the door slamming shut behind him.

There was no sign of him for over twenty-four hours. His horse was gone, but there was no other sign that he had planned on a long-term holiday.

I did my best not to worry, spending all my time making the house spotless. So clean, even Elliot's room smelled like cleaner. No more musty man smell.

Newton's room was the exception. When I stood outside the closed door, I could do nothing more than cry. I had never entered his room, and I couldn't force myself to take even one step inside.

Eventually, there weren't any more tears to cry. Each time the misery hit me, I stared off into space, my eyes turning to stone.

It was in one of these episodes, sitting under the drying laundry as it flapped in the wind, that Sam came.

It was impossible not to hear his horse approach, or his feet as they hit the dusty ground. Before I knew it, he had knelt beside me and wrapped me into a bear hug. I relaxed slightly, allowing the warmth and calm to engulf me.

"I'm sorry," he said, rubbing my back.

I hardly heard him. "Do you know where Elliot is?"

He let out a sigh as he figured out how to answer. "He's fine. I guess. He's in town, working hard to forget everything at the saloon."

I didn't blame him. I almost wanted to join him. "I killed Luke." The words popped out of my mouth without my permission, so silent there was a chance I didn't actually say them.

Sam stiffened. He'd heard me. "You did?"

"He had a knife! And he was trying to . . ." I shook my head rapidly to dislodge the memories. "I somehow got the knife and . . . well . . ."

"Shh," he said, holding me closer as if he could squish out everything. "You didn't do anything wrong."

"I did, though." I pulled away from him to search his face. "I *killed* someone, Sam. *Killed!* I'm the murderer. Not Newton."

"Shh." He rested his pointer finger on my lips. "You didn't have much of a choice, did you?" When I shook my head, he continued. "We don't know what's gonna happen yet. The court date's tomorrow. Anything could happen."

"They'll kill him," I said miserably.

"We don't know that," Sam protested. "Everyone likes him around town—they'll probably let him go."

"They won't. I know they won't."

Sam narrowed his eyes at me. "Stop. You can't help him if you're that negative about everything."

"I tried to help him. He wouldn't let me tell the truth."

"And there's a damn good reason for that."

"Why? Really, why? Elliot said they'd send me to an asylum."

Sam shrugged. "He's not wrong. Everyone has been questioning your sanity since you arrived. It wouldn't take much to set them off."

"You'd help me get free though if that happened, wouldn't you? I'd be fine."

He rubbed his temple, stress lines crossing from one side to the other with more force than he could erase them. "Being tied up in the back of a wagon is a bit different than running from a wedding, Ellie."

I fell quiet, picking at a sprig of grass in the dirt. At least the plant didn't have to worry about a loved one being killed because of something it did.

"Are you going to the hearing tomorrow?"

I sighed and let my body fall into him, leaning my head against his chest. "I need to."

"Good." He rubbed my shoulder. "Would you like me to take you?"

I nodded pathetically and let him hold me.

We sat there in silence after that, letting the laundry go from damp to completely dry. When the sun set on that second day, he helped me up to my feet.

Without even asking for help, he got down the laundry and brought it inside, assuming I'd follow. Like a puppy I did.

He stood in the center of the room, contemplating his next move. When he'd formulated the best possible sentence, he turned to face me.

"Are you wanting to be left alone? For the night, I mean."

I blinked in surprise. "No . . . are you going to stay?" A spark of emotion formed in my head. A mere taste of excitement.

"If you'd like me to."

"Please." I wrapped him in a hug. "You'll stay downstairs, won't you?" The excitement was still there, even with such a probable condition. Even so, it was somewhat disappointing.

"Do you want me to?"

"No," I said, searching his face for any sign of his thoughts. He had a smirk on his face, but otherwise everything was serious.

He took me by the hand and tugged me toward the stairs. "Then come on, we have an early start in the morning."

The awkward feeling ended almost as soon as the door shut behind us. He untied my dress carefully and let it fall to the floor. He even went as far as folding it and setting it on the dresser.

His touches were tender as he helped me out of the corset and petticoat. Nothing sexual about it, just comfort. Just his nearness.

He didn't let me assist with his clothing. It only took a second for his pants to come off, leaving him in his shirt and long, somewhat equivalent of boxers.

I didn't expect anything from him, and he didn't offer anything. In reality, I didn't *want* anything special. The idea of such a monumental act at that point seemed wrong. All I wanted was the closeness, someone to hold me tight.

That was exactly what I got. We lay in bed together, his body curled around mine, arm holding me close. And we slept together. Truly *slept*.

It was the best sleep I'd had in a long time.

We took the paint horse to town. The depression still had a strong grip on me, but at least I was more alert. It might have had something to do with how hard I had to concentrate on not falling off the side of a moving animal. Or maybe, it was simply from the deep sleep the night before.

Everything felt brighter. The colors vibrant, the birds twittering merrily, even the fluffy clouds seemed happier in a way.

Newton was liked in town. There was a chance he'd be fine. There was a large possibility that everyone would understand why he did what he did. To save his daughter.

But my bruises were already beginning to fade. And there was no real proof that Luke had inflicted them. Unfortunately, I saw just as much chance of him being hanged for the murder.

It was just easier to focus on the bright side for once. It would all be okay.

Everything would all work out.

Even so, the second my feet touched the packed dirt road outside of the church, my stomach lurched. Everyone was there, for sure. Farmers, ranchers, both rich and poor. Entire families showed up. There were more people there than had been at my wedding.

The street was full of wagons and horses, a classic case of organized chaos.

As if rehearsed, everyone went in silence and stared right at me when I stepped onto the sidewalk.

Sam stood behind me and patted my shoulder. "It's okay."

"They really do think I'm insane, don't they?" Confusion covered many faces, interest on others. It was like I was a key character in the newest TV premiere. The crazy one that everyone expected to jump off a cliff in the end.

"Yep." Sam didn't try to sugarcoat it. Without waiting for me, he linked his arm with mine and walked me into the church.

Many of the decorations from the wedding were still there. A vase of nearly dead flowers on the altar and a few stray ribbons hanging from the pews. It wasn't much, but certainly enough to stab me in the gut.

Everyone in the room had been looking forward to that event too. Well, mostly everyone. There were plenty of people who looked like they never did such a thing as socialize.

"Everyone, everyone! Find your seats, please," a tall man at the front of the room announced. Everyone did as he asked without protest, as though the schoolteacher raised her voice, snapping everyone to action.

Sam snatched a seat for the two of us in the second row before the room got too full.

Within minutes, it was standing room only.

"Where's Elliot?" I whispered.

"I didn't see him." Sam looked around slowly. "He's out there somewhere, I'm sure."

Something in my gut told me otherwise. With his habit of disappearing all hours of the night, I doubted he would come back for something so heartbreakingly hopeless. With a sigh, I stood back up. "I have to find him. Save my seat?"

Sam nodded but narrowed his eyes. "Don't do anything stupid."

I shot him a quick, fake smile before hurrying out of the church again. Everyone I passed stared at me. Every gaze wondered what I was going to do.

I only relaxed when I reached the street. Everything had calmed down out there—the horses were tied up to the hitching posts, enjoying their relaxation.

It would have been nice to do the same, not give a crap about anything going on in the church.

But Elliot needed to be there.

I hurried down the sidewalk, looking for what I was sure would be an obvious building. I doubted it would be close to the church, and unfortunately, I was right.

CHAPTER TWENTY-FOUR

It sat at the complete opposite end of the street, small, shack-like, and with the classic saloon doors.

I walked right up to them and peered over the lower spot in the wood. As I expected, Elliot was there, sitting in the corner with a drink in his hand.

A girl sat in the chair next to him, looking quite happy about whatever her situation was. Her dress was quite low cut and colorful, though much longer than it would have been in the movies. The cigarette in her mouth and relaxed posture added all the more to the carefree appearance of the saloon girl.

"Elliot!" I called. He didn't even adjust his gaze from the drink in front of him. With an annoyed huff, I pushed through the doors and marched in his direction. It took effort to ignore the woman. In a world where cleavage was a very hidden thing, the amount of skin was startling.

No one else was inside the building. The bartender must have gone to the hearing. Even so, I had felt the gazes of the few outside as I walked in. Everyone would be talking about it. A female going into a bar couldn't be a good thing, after all.

With some kind of bravery, or I-don't-give-a-shit-a-tude, I walked right up to him and grabbed the clear drink from his hand.

"Hey!" he complained, reaching blindly for it. "I wasn't done with that."

"You're done now!" Bravely, I tipped my head back and shot the liquid. I wrinkled my nose. Not from disgust, but from confusion. It had no sharp smell, no burn as it went down my throat. No sign of alcohol.

Water.

"I wasn't drinking," he said, though he stared longingly at the line of liquor bottles behind the bar.

"Oh." I glanced at the girl again, my confusion growing to realization. "Oh!" I glanced between the two of them, feeling my skin crawl. So *that* was where he had been sneaking off to at night.

"Calm down, you look like you're going to be sick." Elliot nodded at the chair across from him. "She's a friend."

The "friend" tipped her head politely in my direction, a smile playing across her lips. She stood easily, moving in a swinging, cat-like fashion toward the back room. I had to shake my head to avoid watching her too closely. Every movement she made was fascinating in that oddly elegant sort of way as she sashayed to the back room.

She gave him one final glance before she disappeared, blowing a kiss in our direction.

"Is she who you keep sneaking off to meet with?" I demanded.

Elliot almost smiled. Almost. He didn't say a thing.

I made a grumbling noise. His love life didn't matter at the moment, anyway. "What are you doing here? You're missing the hearing."

He rested his forehead in his hands, tired eyes closing for a long moment. "Not going to do any good, being there or not." He looked a good ten years older than he had before. I estimated he was about twenty-nine or thirty, but now he looked like he belonged to the old folks home.

"It'll do *him* some good. How would you feel if you were up front of all those people, and you couldn't find your son?"

That struck the chord I wanted it to. He drummed his fingers on the table. "Why couldn't you have just gotten some help? Why did you have to go kill the man?" It wasn't a question. It was more along the lines of an outright demand. Not even a demand with me—more like one of the world.

"Because he had a damn knife and was going to *kill* me."

He ground his teeth as he mulled it over. He was even more pale than I had seen him last. He looked so ill.

"Please don't make me go alone," he said, sounding like a terrified toddler.

"I don't plan on it. You're my family. As far as I know, the only family I have here."

He downed the rest of his water and stood up with a resigned sigh. His back popped audibly as he did so. He threw a few bills at the counter before walking out into the sunlight, leaving me to follow along behind. It made me feel somewhat better to have him to distract the curious eyes away from me. Even though most people were inside the church, we were most definitely the main focus outside.

The kids of a murderer.

When we made it into the church, Elliot tried to stand toward the back, but I dragged him right up to the seat that Sam had saved for us.

Sam leaned over to whisper in my ear. "There are rumors you went into the saloon."

"Already? Well, they're not wrong." Wanting to avoid the topic, I turned my whole body to face the front of the room.

While I'd been gone, they had brought Newton in and sat him up by the pulpit. Where the pastor would sit as the choir sang, I assumed. He looked unconcerned, as though he belonged there. There weren't even shackles on his wrists. Nothing to tie him to the chair. As though he'd suddenly found the will to attend church regularly.

A tall, well-dressed man stood behind the pulpit itself addressing the congregation gravely. There was no telling how long he had already been talking. "The loss of Lucas Barnette came far too soon. Soon to be married, start a family, he was shaping up to be a fine member of society. It was a horror that someone cut his life so short."

I tried to ignore his words, but they made me squirm. Good citizen he certainly was not.

To make matters worse, at the end of his sentence, he gave Newton a pointed glance.

I sneaked a glance in the direction of Mable and her family. She looked gray, as though she might throw up at any moment. If anyone could help Newton, it would be her.

The crowd whispered among each other frantically, all deciding where they would really stand in the case. I squirmed, wishing it would all be over soon.

"Quiet down!" the man up front called. He didn't even have to bang the book he held against the pulpit. Everyone was so anxious to get things underway that the room fell silent almost instantly.

"Did I miss much?" I whispered.

Sam shook his head. "Not really. Mr. Trainer just talked about himself for a while."

The man up front, the Mr. Trainer, didn't miss a beat of silence before continuing. "Now, as I understand it, Levi Barnette found his son's body two days ago, on Thursday over by the edge of his property. The one between him and Newton Hersley here. Is that correct?"

Levi stood up, tall and dressed in what had to be his Sunday best. His hair was brushed neatly. He looked like he belonged to a big city in comparison to everyone else in the room. He cleared his throat before he spoke. "Yes, you have it right. As many know, Newton Hersley and I have had our differences ever since the run last year. We each have differing opinions on who owns what part of our neighboring lands. Before things could get out of control, we made a good ole agreement. His daughter was to marry my son, that way the land would always be family land."

He made it seem so simple. So normal to marry off their children. Though, I guess it somewhat was.

"When his daughter decided she was too good for my son"—he glared straight at me, and I flinched involuntarily—"he figured he'd take care of it himself. After he came to my own ranch to start a fight, and we put him back in his place, of course." He stood straighter at that statement. "Newton Hersley here decided to get revenge on his own. He *killed* my son in cold blood." He scanned the crowd, catching each eye as he said it. It made the desired effect—everyone gasped.

The makeshift judge stayed calm. "Do you have any proof that Newton was the murderer?"

A cold, calculating smile appeared on Levi's face. "Yes, when I found my son, I also found Newton. He was going to bury him somewhere that I couldn't find him. Where his ma couldn't ever get a chance to grieve!"

Several women gasped, and Helen sobbed into a handkerchief. Mable rubbed her back gently, cooing unknown, sweet words into her mother's ear. Despite how much the woman irked me, I felt sorry for her. Whether Luke was an awful man or not, he was still her baby boy.

"Thank you for that, Levi. You may sit down now," Mr. Trainer said. "Now, it's your turn, Mr. Hersley. What do you say about all this?"

Newton stood up slowly, his body probably stiff from not being used in the past twenty-four hours. "I agree with a few things that Levi said. Our property dispute, first off. Everyone's heard plenty about that through the months. I did help to call off Elizabeth's wedding, and I did go over there to talk peacefully with Levi and his wife. The peace was lost, but at no fault of my own." He shifted his weight from one leg to the other, working hard at looking more approachable. "But in the end, it was me who killed the boy."

Gasps echoed through the room again, accompanied by a few shocked shrieks from the women.

"So, you admit to killing the young man?" Mr. Trainer said, shock written all over his face. The sheriff was in the front row, forehead in his hands as he stressed over Newton's answer.

"Yes sir, but I had good reason."

"There ain't never reason for such a thing!" Levi shouted. Much of the room agreed in loud unison, fists pumping the air.

"Quiet!" Mr. Trainer shouted. "This won't be that kind of hearing. Now, Mr. Hersley, we might as well go into your reasons while we are here." He crossed his arms and waited for the response.

Levi had no plans of letting Newton explain. "We don't need those reasons. There's no good reason for killing a young man." He stood so fast it made his wife jump. He took his time looking around the room, making eye contact with every person he could. "Unprovoked, I might add."

I couldn't stay still anymore. Anger flaring, I stood.

Startled gasps pinged around the room.

"There's no reason to go beating up two men who come to *talk* to you, either!" I snapped at Levi. "All they did was come talk to you about how I didn't want to marry your son. And you want to know why—"

Mr. Trainer went stiff, his eyes betraying his surprise at my explosion. "Miss Hersley, I'll have to ask you to sit down. As you well know, this is not a place for such outbursts." Mr. Trainer glared down his nose at me.

Sam tugged on the edge of my dress to get me to sit back down. I reluctantly obeyed.

"Why can't I say anything?" I whispered into Sam's ear. "They're making plenty of outbursts on their own."

"Last I checked, that's not particularly ladylike. Besides, you're not on trial," he said.

"Well, Levi isn't on trial either, but look at him." I gestured vaguely in his direction. "Luke left bruises. If I can show that, maybe—"

"Shh, Ellie." Sam patted my thigh, earning somewhat of an accusatory and confused glance from Elliot as he heard the nickname.

Calmly, Newton continued. "What my daughter said was true. When I visited Levi, I was going to talk about some mistreatment done to her by—"

"That's madness. We all know the mistreatment was from *you.* Don't try to put that on my son." Levi shook his head slowly, angrily.

I stood up in a huff. "No! It was Luke!" Without much thought, I pulled the corner of my sleeve down to show both the stitches and some of the yellowed bruising. Everyone gasped. Whether from the inappropriate conduct or the wounds, I had no idea. Both Sam and Elliot grabbed for me, but I was faster. "And this whole thing is a load of crap! *I'm* the one who—"

"Get her out of here!" Newton demanded. His eyes sparked with irritation. "Before you make more of a fool of yourself."

"No," I said, shaking off Elliot's grip on my arm. "I won't go! This is madness. Some kind of witch hunt. On account of me, no less."

Elliot was calmly trying to get my attention, but it was as easy to ignore as an annoying fly.

"Mable! Mable can tell you!" I whirled in her direction. She met my gaze with terrified blue eyes. "You saw him the morning of the wedding throw me onto the step. Tell them! I know he hurt you too!" She glanced in her mother's direction, then shrank into her seat.

"Miss Barnette, do you have anything to add?" Mr. Trainer asked levelly.

Mable remained silent for the longest possible minute. She looked like she would start shaking and explode into a million pieces at the slightest breeze. "No, I don't," she finally choked out.

My heart skipped a beat. "But you saw him! Mable, please! You know he doesn't deserve this—"

"Elliot, take her out of here!" Newton bellowed, pointing at the door.

"I'll just come right back, and you know it! I won't let you do this to yourself!" I squared my shoulders and glared right at Newton. "None of this is lawful. This isn't how any of this works!"

He was doing his best to hide the panic, but every once in a while, it peeked through the angry mask. He looked to the sheriff, who reluctantly stood and came my way. Elliot held my wrist effectively, but with the least amount of effort he could.

Sam scooted out of the pew so Erik could get in. He took my wrist from Elliot, who led me out through the crowd. My face flared with embarrassment, but my anger overruled it all.

"Traitor," I muttered at Sam as the sheriff led me past. "Stand up for yourself, Mable! Come on!"

It made sense that Erik would simply put me outside and go back in. He had other plans. As he led me toward his office, a sinking feeling told me exactly what he had been instructed in that wordless agreement.

"Come on!" I put on the brakes in the middle of the street, sending a puff of dust flying about us. The crowd packed around the church watched every move I made, but for the moment, I didn't care. "Don't make me miss everything!"

"It's what your pa asked," Erik said, pulling hard enough to make me fall up the stairs onto the front porch of the town jail. "He instructed me to put you in here if you started causing a scene."

"But he didn't do it!" I protested, as he pulled me inside and shut the door.

"I know that," he said calmly, plucking the old, iron keys from the hook and marching me straight to the cell. "But he'd rather be the one to take the blame."

"Just let me go! They aren't giving him a fair trial, and you know it." He shoved me into the iron prison and closed it before I had a chance to push out.

"I know that." His voice was still patient, but the edge of stress threatened to break through. He turned the key in the lock. It clicked with a sickening finality. "It's no more fair than they would have given you." He gave me a sympathetic look before turning and walking right out, hanging the keys by the door.

"Stop! Come back! Please!" I shouted, shaking the bars. Trained in the art of trapping people in cages, he completely ignored me.

The ticking of the wall clock echoed through the room. Every. Single. Second. I considered throwing my shoe at it for a while. Until I figured I didn't want to explain being half-barefoot.

The jail was far enough away from the church that I didn't hear anything. No muttering of the crowds, no gasps, nothing. The only noises that made their way to me came from the happily chirping birds and the slight breeze as it made its way past the newly constructed buildings.

Whenever I did happen to hear a stray person walk past, I shouted for their assistance and shook the bars. No one acted like they heard me.

I stood on the bed for a while, standing on tiptoes to see . . . well, not much, out of the barred window. The window was small, and too far up for me to gather much from it. I could see a neighboring roof, and the fluffy clouds as they passed.

It would be a miserable life to be stuck in such a puny jail cell. After all, it was only the length of the bed, and then the width of two doors. A semipermanent dog crate for humans.

I'd given up and sat huddled on the corner of the bed when the door finally opened. It was Elliot.

That pale, sick look had returned in full force. There was even a hint of green involved.

He removed the keys from the wall and unlocked the door easily, not saying a single word. His entire body was defeated.

"Sheriff sent me to get you," he muttered, voice dull.

"Asylum?" I asked, pins and needles poking me up and down my leg.

He shook his head once, then froze. Without any warning, he grabbed the waste bin and retched. I winced and placed my hand firmly over my mouth. The smell hit me full force, and I had to swallow a few times to avoid joining him in his predicament.

When he was sure he was finished, he stood fully up, stiff as a board, body resigned to his fate.

"Headache?" I ventured out of the cell, every ounce of my body ready to escape. From him, from the puke, from the entire situation.

"It doesn't look good," he said, barely audible. It didn't matter. I heard it as though he shouted it directly into my ear.

"No. Just no." I shook my head violently. Everything had to be a dream. The sheriff wouldn't let him go through this, right? They seemed to be friends. He knew the truth.

"There'll be a hangin' in the morning."

And I bolted. I let the door slam shut behind me and raced to the church. They were already bringing him out, the sheriff holding his hands tied behind his back. Newton didn't struggle. There wasn't even any hesitation in his steps. His easy manner looked as though he was on his way to dinner.

"Dammit! No!" I shouted to the incoming crowd. "He didn't do it! Stop!" I looked wildly around for someone who would help. For Sam, for anyone.

Instead, I saw Mable. She was walking next to her mother, head down, steps shuffling.

My feet made a beeline for her. Without my permission, my hands grabbed her shoulders. "You can stop this. You saw the other day! Please, tell them!"

She stared at me, her eyes huge and terrified.

"Please! You can't let them do this. You know *why*. I know he hurt you too." I searched her face desperately, hunting for any sign that she might help.

There was nothing. Nothing but apprehension.

"Mable! Please!"

Helen pulled her daughter away from my grip and shoved me aside. "Don't get near her."

"You too!" I shouted after Helen. "I bet he hurt you too!"

The crowd split around me, following their prisoner to his last night at the jail.

I don't know when I fell. By the time the crowd had passed, I was sitting in a heap on the dusty ground, feeling numb. There weren't even any tears. Only the sense of utter defeat.

"Hey." Sam's voice. Compassionate, calm. He pulled me up to my feet and let me lean my entire weight on him. He wrapped his arms around me as I did the same.

I breathed in his scent, making note of each and every one. Sweat, leather, horse, hay. Him.

"We can't let them do this," I whispered into his shirt.

He trailed his fingers through my now-loose hair, making soft cooing noises as he would for a terrified child. "There's nothing we can do."

"But we have to!" I pushed back to stare at his face. "We can break him out! They do it all the time in the movies. The sheriff keeps his keys hanging beside the door. All we have to do is sneak in after dark, grab the keys, and let him out. It's so easy!"

Sam let out a long breath. "Erik will stay there overnight."

My shoulders sagged, and I relaxed against him again. "Fix it." The command came out of nowhere. It was one of those that was serious, pleading, yet I knew impossible.

"I wish I could," he said.

CHAPTER TWENTY-FIVE

It was to happen at sunrise.

No one slept that night. Absolutely nothing.

Elliot and I sat on the sofa, staring at the unlit fireplace. A whiskey bottle had been produced, and we had both taken large sips throughout the night. Not enough to become completely wasted, but plenty to remain in a comfortable state of numbness.

Short of telling the truth, the complete truth, I couldn't see a way to get him out of the cell alive. Even then, my story would most likely not be believed. I had no proof. Even my bruises weren't proof enough. Anyone could have caused them.

And Mable. She was the only chance there was. She'd seen Luke. She'd *seen* him beat me. Not just that, I was beyond positive he'd done the same to her. With that terrified glance she'd had at the wedding, recognizing him as an authority.

A captor she respected even after death.

The reality of where we were about to go slammed into me the moment Elliot left to hitch up the wagon. Panicking, I grabbed the rest of the whiskey. Though I downed it in three big gulps, I choked halfway through. The burn was almost too much, but I embraced it. The pain real, something to cling to, something to fully pay attention to. The pain made sense. I coughed and wiped my mouth on my sleeve. It made my throat burn. My mouth, even my nose where the firewater had attempted escape.

My body had hardly recovered before Elliot came back, beckoning me to follow. I did, feet dragging and head swirling with the alcohol.

It was still so early in the morning that the birds were sound asleep. All except for a single owl, hooting on the top of the sod shed. Stars shone brightly in the fishbowl sky, but the moon had other ideas. As if for the occasion, it hid in a small sliver.

The drive was quiet. No birds, no wind, nothing except warm, humid air, stagnant around us. My mind had sorted through so many options already, it was beyond numb. The alcohol certainly didn't help. Possibly the sheriff had a plan to get him out. Or perhaps Sam had made a plan.

There was still hope. We had two hours until sunrise. The invisible clock ticked by every moment with a throb in my head, driving in the finality.

Erik had been expecting us. When we arrived, he just opened the door and beckoned us inside. He looked just as exhausted as we were. The very moment I stepped into the room, the real-life, physical clock was sure to take precedence in my head. Two. Hours. Left.

Tick.

Tick.

Tick.

Newton didn't look much better than his captor. He sat on the narrow bed, elbows resting on his thighs. When he saw us, he perked up, putting on the lying mask. The one who tried to convince us all that everything was okay. He was good at it, but we'd all seen the worry and sadness gouged into each one of the wrinkles on his forehead.

"How'd you manage to get Elizabeth up this early?" he teased, shooting me a smile. His eyes remained dull, the happiness not quite reaching them.

Before Elliot could answer, I pushed past and placed my hands on the bars. "What are you doing?" I demanded, planting my feet in preparation for a fight. "I'm not some fragile creature. Tell them the truth!"

He sighed, the happy façade ruined. "I can't let you take the blame."

"I'm not even your daughter," I protested. A sidelong glance at Erik showed me he wasn't fully paying attention. Not just that, he had sat down in a chair and looked as though he was fighting sleep. If he'd just give in, I could grab the keys.

"You are to me."

"But I'm not. You've only known me for what, a month? You have no reason to do this for me. I have more of a fighting chance than you do in court at this rate!"

He went silent for a long while as he thought through his response. "You're my daughter. One way or another, my blood runs in your veins. It has to. Otherwise, why would you carry the same name? The same face? That means it is my job to protect you. I failed you once, sending you off to marry Lukas. I will never fail you again."

My heart skipped beats a few times, feeling the intense love flow through the bars. "You can't protect me if you're dead." My voice went soft, lessening the impact I had intended.

"I *am* protecting you by doing this," he said sternly. "You can have a full, complete life. I've had mine already."

I rested my forehead against the bars and shook my head feebly, feeling the cold iron as it cooled my skin.

"I'm more stubborn than you." I squared my shoulders and turned to check on Erik. As I had hoped, his eyes were glued shut, his mouth hanging partly open. I hurried over to grab the keys.

"Elizabeth," Newton almost groaned. "I'm not leaving."

"You *want* to die?" I asked, sticking the single key into the lock. There were only two options, but only one cell. As I expected, they were exact copies of each other.

The door opened with a creak, and Erik made a surprised snore mixed with a grunt. Either he was sleeping roughly, or he'd woken up. Newton held up his hand in a stopping motion for the sheriff, which pretty much meant it was the latter option.

"I worked hard on making this life for you, for your brother," he said calmly, taking both my hands in his. His hands had a clammy coldness to them, but they were strong, brave. "I didn't join in on the run, lose my best horse to the chaos, and build that home with my own two hands to run from it."

"But—"

"I claimed that land for us. For our family. *All* of it. Even you." He smiled, though certainly not genuinely.

It was the kind of smile my own father had given when he tried to make me feel better after we put my dog to sleep. "We have to let him go," he had said. "He did everything he could for us, and now he doesn't have to hurt anymore."

A cold tear betrayed my lack of strength as I tugged on his hands. "Please, please don't do this," I begged.

He pulled me into his arms, letting me press my face into his shirt like a child. He backed up slowly so he sat on the edge of the bed, me beside him. He let me become a child again, practically curled up in his lap, holding on to every ounce of comfort I could.

Elliot didn't need prompting. Before I knew it, he was on the opposite side, head leaning against his father's shoulder.

We made a sad picture, the three of us huddled together like children, hearts shredded and hung on the wall to bleed out.

We, or at least I, must have fallen asleep at some point. For that blissful time, the internal clock had stopped its ticking. For the briefest of times, everything was calm. There was nothing. No dreams. No stress. Just alcohol-induced, peaceful slumber.

The physical clock, however, had not halted its progress. The moment I opened my eyes, it was all I could hear.

Tick.

Tick.

Tick.

And then the sound of the crowd outside.

"No, no, no, no," I said rapidly, the single word blurring together to create some new, desperate sound.

There was no time left.

As Newton stood bravely, I grabbed on to his arm. It didn't matter how much I pulled, he walked with purpose through the door.

"Don't do this!" I pleaded, planting my feet on the solid floor.

Newton made eye contact with Elliot, a previous agreement being put into action without a word. Elliot pried my fingers off his arm, letting Newton slip into the main room.

"I want you to remember me as I was at home. Not like this. Stay here," Newton said. Pain sneaked into his eyes, but only for the briefest of moments.

My body dove for him, but Elliot had other plans. He caught me, and before I knew what happened, he had closed the cell door with me inside. I wasn't even sure how he'd managed it. One moment I was on my way to protect Newton, the next, the cold iron was in my way.

"No!" I shrieked, shaking the bars with all my might. "Don't do this! Dammit! No!"

Elliot turned the key with a sickening sense of finality. An angry, animalistic scream escaped my mouth as I shook harder. The solid room of metal didn't budge. The only thing that had any movement was the clock's hands.

Tick.

Tick.

Tick.

"Elliot, please!" I begged, making eye contact for one miniscule moment before he had to look away. Tears were already flowing down his pale face, coming to rest in his two-day beard.

Erik walked slowly to Newton's side and patted him on the back before opening the door.

That was when Newton hesitated. Not in the way I would have expected. There was no fear in his movements, in his voice. He turned slowly to look at both of us, his child and probable descendent. "I love you both."

Then, as though they were simply walking to the bar on a Saturday night, they walked out the door and into the waiting crowd.

"No!" I screamed. "Pa!"

When the door shut behind Elliot, my body gave out, sending me sinking to the floor like a sack of flour.

Everything seemed to freeze. The clock slowed, my heartbeat slowed to almost nothing, the crowd was somehow calmer. I shut my eyes against every ounce of reality.

All I wanted at that moment was to be home. Really home.

In my childhood bed, with my light pink walls, my momma holding me close as she read me a bedtime story. My brother, standing in the doorway, watching everything with a happy smile on his face. My dad, standing nearby to wait for his turn to pray with me before I fell asleep. It was all I wanted. All I really needed.

But that reality would never be possible again. Even in a grown-up way, it could never be.

They were dead.

They were *all* dead.

And the second family I'd been given was about to join them.

I choked back the sobs and listened closely, hopeful for any sign of the grand escape. The sheriff, suddenly throwing Newton on the back of a horse and running for it. A whole army of friends, taking him to safety with brute force alone.

Instead, the crowd babbled to each other. Excitement that got faster and faster with every moment, echoing my own breathing. They sounded like bees, buzzing all around the newest of flowers. Apart from the frequent brawls from the multiple saloons, it was the most excitement they'd seen since the run.

Suddenly there was a strange thickening of the air, accompanied with light gasps.

Then silence.

Total and complete silence.

No one said a word. I didn't even breathe.

But the clock continued.

Tick.

Tick.

Tick.

And I screamed, knowing it was over. Realizing I had lost yet again. Someone else died, and this time it was all because of me.

Someone I really and truly cared for was gone. It was the same thing all over again. My family dying, one person at a time. Fate flicking them off the earth like pesky flies.

The crowd didn't stay silent for long enough to truly mourn. After the few agonizing ticks of the masochistic clock, the low buzz of voices resumed. The quiet felt like eternity, but it wasn't enough. It could never have been enough.

The death of such a selfless, local man was simply the biggest spectacle they could have hoped for. They would talk about the murder of Lukas Barnette for years to come.

CHAPTER TWENTY-SIX

Though they tried, they couldn't get my sobbing to stop.

"It's all okay now," Sam cooed, holding me in the biggest bear hug imaginable.

I pushed back and glared into his tear-stained eyes. "All okay? What part of this bullshit is okay to you?"

He smirked. "Look around, why don't you?"

I narrowed my eyes at him but looked around regardless. Erik stood by his desk, arms crossed in what could only be exasperation. But he wasn't who held my gaze.

Newton stood in the doorway, just as alive as he'd ever been.

My mouth dropped open. "What?" My voice sounded like a squeak. Pulling away from Sam, I rushed to him, wrapping my arms around Newton's neck. He returned the embrace, smiling into the crook of my neck.

"You're okay! I thought . . . I thought—" I pushed away and stared at him again. "The crowd got so quiet!"

Newton pushed a stray piece of hair out of my eyes. "Mable spoke up."

I searched the faces of everyone, hunting for confirmation. They all nodded. That was the *last* thing I expected to happen. It certainly never would have been possible in the twenty-first century. Once sentenced to death, it pretty much seemed you were as good as dead.

"She decided to say something at the last possible moment, but she did it at least," Erik said. "Had the rope 'round his neck and everything, and she ran up onto the platform herself."

Newton finished the story: "Levi tried to grab her 'fore she could say much, but she was too quick for him. She even accused him of being a reason she stayed quiet. Said she was scared he'd hurt her if she spoke up."

None of it seemed real. "Where is he? Doesn't he get questioned or anything? He lied, after all!" I demanded, turning my full attention on Erik.

Erik shrugged. "Elliot's after him. I don't have anything on 'em, but I have to talk to him anyway."

Not the answer I wanted, but it was better than nothing. "How do we know Elliot won't kill him?"

Sam smirked again but stayed silent. Apparently, the thought had crossed his mind as well.

"I behaved," Elliot said, pushing the door open with his foot and dragging in a swearing Levi Barnette.

"That land is mine, sheriff, and you know it!" Levi shouted, shaking free of Elliot's grip with a huff. "They didn't keep to their end of the bargain!"

Erik looked almost bored. "We already talked about it. The land office has all the paperwork on it. The property ends at the river. Framing Newton here for murder won't change that."

"But he killed my *son*!" Levi bellowed, balling up his fists.

"Not according to your daughter. According to her, *she* did it out of protection. Do you want to press charges on that? On your own daughter?" Erik raised one fuzzy eyebrow with enough precision it would make any actor jealous.

I stifled a gasp. They'd left that crucial part of the story out. "Mable said . . . she did it?" I barely breathed the words.

Sam came to stand beside me, squeezing my hand reassuringly, likely to keep me from telling my own version of the story. "That's what she said."

Levi fixed his thunderous glare on me. "We all know she would *never* have the ability to do something like that—"

Erik held up his hand. "Years of abuse will change a person, Levi."

Levi practically screamed. "When I get home, that girl—"

"Now, now, I have some more questions for you. I don't think you need to go home just yet. If you'll sit down right here . . ." Erik nodded at the chair in front of his desk. "I'll walk the rest of you out."

Levi let out a string of curses that would be enviable by a sailor, but Erik ignored him.

The rest of us followed him onto the porch, the curses echoing behind us even after the door closed.

A whole crowd of people stood outside the jail, eyes and ears all trained on the building. At the sight of us, they scattered like a group of terrified pigeons. The only ones I recognized were the ones on the porch across the street. Helen stood in the shade, hand gripping Mable's upper arm as she stared us down.

"That land is *mine*, Hersley!" Levi shouted from inside.

"Oh, get over it!" Erik shouted back.

Levi shut up then, probably only so he could hear what Erik had to say.

"I'll give him a good threatening in there, hopefully he won't cross any boundaries," Erik said. "I don't have proof of him doing anything, so I can't keep him here. But hopefully threatening him will keep him from touching the girl. He knows full well the entire town will be keeping an extra eye out for her after all she said up there."

I glanced in her direction, wishing I had the power to run across the street and pull her away from her captor. She looked miserable.

"To the group of you, keep your noses clean. Stay on your own land, don't give him a chance to pin anything else on you. Don't want to do anything that would turn the whole town against you. They've had enough drama for the whole year."

"We'll stay put," Newton assured. "Thank you for all your help today."

The men shook hands and turned in their separate directions. Erik to go deal with the angry Levi, Newton to head to the wagon he certainly didn't expect to ride in again.

My eyes remained on Mable as her mother dragged her in the opposite direction, toward what I could only assume was their own wagon.

"Hey," Sam said, tapping me on the shoulder. "I'll keep an eye on her as well as I can. He knows if he touches her, the whole town will go after him."

"But what if he does anyway?" I asked.

"I don't think he will. At least not for now." Sam gave me a one-armed hug. "Go on, I'll come check on you tomorrow."

I let myself smile just a bit at the thought. "Promise?"

"Promise," he assured.

I knew Sam would follow through and come over the following evening.

What I hadn't expected was for Newton to stay home the whole day.

Granted, he'd been through a near-death experience and discovered his daughter was dead and replaced by some doppelgänger. He deserved a day of rest.

That didn't change the fact that I had plans for Sam that Newton *certainly* didn't need to know about. Sure, he probably wouldn't agree to my request, but I still planned on asking. Perhaps I'd get at least *something* to cure the ache in the meantime.

I waited for him all day, sneaking outside whenever I could so I could grab him before Newton could see. Thankfully, he chose the time when I was in the barn to show up.

He tied his horse to the fence, seemingly unaware that I watched his every move. As he passed by, I pounced, grabbing his arm and yanking him into the shadowed building.

"Whoa," he said, taking no time at all to figure out what happened.

I stood on my tiptoes and pressed my lips to his, smiling when he returned the kiss instead of pulling away.

"What'd I do to deserve that?" Instead of righting himself and returning to the sunlight, he wrapped his arms around me, hands linked at the small of my back.

I shrugged. "Probably nothing. Newton's been home all day. Though I'm glad he's all right, if I have to go grab him one more random thing from the house, barn, or wherever he can think, I might have to escape to the river and *really* try to get home this time. He's finally taking a nap, though."

Sam rolled his eyes but fell silent. His body stiffened slightly, his hands forming fists on my back.

"What?" I demanded, pushing back from him so I could hunt his face for the truth.

He sighed. "You'd still go back if you could, wouldn't you?"

I let out a long breath through my closed lips. Suddenly I didn't think I would. I didn't have anyone back home. Sure, I had running water, a nearly finished college education, and permission to visit a bar whenever I damn well pleased. But *who* did I have?

Not Newton.

Not Elliot.

I couldn't keep an eye on Mable.

And I wouldn't have Sam.

Chills traveled all the way up my spine, then down to my fingertips. "I don't think so. I think I'd miss everyone here too much."

I didn't expect his response. He glanced out the door and, in one movement, pushed me farther inside the barn and shut the door with his foot.

"What are you—"

He pressed me against the wall and let his lips find mine while his hands traveled to my hips.

My heartbeat took a second to catch up from the shock. "But we're not betrothed," I teased, as his hands tugged at my skirt.

He narrowed his eyes at me. "Is that a no, then?"

"Absolutely not!" I yanked up on his shirt enough to untuck it, but he didn't pull it over his head.

"The more clothes come off, the more have to go back on if we get caught," he whispered.

"I don't give a shit right now," I snapped with more force than I originally planned. I pulled my dress over my head and tossed it into the hay, startling our only audience, a chicken.

He smirked and let his hands travel beneath the shift, finding skin with more skill than I would have expected. I froze, the twinge of nerves starting deep in my stomach. The good kind that only added to the thrill of it all, but also made me wonder if he would actually care about—

"I'm not a virgin," I blurted.

He laughed, a thick, full sort of sound that echoed throughout the makeshift barn. "You wanted it so bad before, I assumed you weren't." He kissed me so tenderly, it had me on my tiptoes begging for more. "I'm not either."

"That's obvious enough—"

He cut me off by proving my point, finding exactly what he was looking for under my skirt.

I gasped despite my best efforts, shutting my eyes and trying not to fall.

The hen squawked, apparently irritated to have anyone sharing her space.

"Shoo, shoo," I said, moving away from the wall and waving my hands at the bird. Sam cracked open the door for her, grinning at my attempts to chase her out of the barn.

I had no desire to share the experience with a chicken. She shared my opinion, escaping into the spring air with wings spread wide as she ran to join her friends in the hunt for bugs.

Sam gave the yard one more quick check to ensure we wouldn't be bothered, then shut the door. "It's not too late to wait, if anything until we can have a bed of something other than hay."

I glanced pointedly at the bulge between his legs. "Nah, I don't think so."

He pulled on the front of the corset, popping the front of it apart, biting his lip in concentration as he did so.

"If you decide you don't want to, just say so," he whispered, as the corset fell to the ground.

"I already decided." I pushed the suspenders off his shoulders with one surprisingly smooth movement and pulled on the shirt again. He assisted this time, pulling it over his head and adding it to the pile forming on the floor.

I watched his every move, waiting for the unveiling.

His laugh made me realize exactly how focused I had been on what hid beneath his pants. I'd never been quite so invested in someone else's anatomy, and it surprised me.

"Perhaps I should make you go first?"

For one fleeting moment, I considered arguing with him. But I didn't really mind. With a quick breath to stifle any lingering nerves, I pulled the shift over my head and struggled out of the underwear.

Nerves flickered across his own eyes as he took in every curve on my body. I wasn't perfect by any means. I had more fat on my body than I wanted, my chest had never been perky. But he didn't have models to compare me to, social standards dictating what I should look like. No BMI scale. None of it.

"Your turn," I said, my voice coming out as a whisper. His eyes had glued themselves to me, making me want to squirm away. He didn't have social media filled with sexy women, but he did have experience. He could easily compare me to them.

"Beautiful," he said, reaching out to run his hands along every curve he could get to.

"Your turn." I reached down to pull on the button of his pants when he got close enough.

He sidestepped me and unhooked them easily, letting them fall off his narrow hips.

I let my eyes scan his body, taking in the muscles that could only be formed from many hours of hard work.

"Come here." He pulled me to him, lips finding mine. "You're mine now."

For once, I was happy with possessiveness.

CHAPTER TWENTY-SEVEN

S ex in a bunch of semi-clean hay isn't what it's cracked up to be in the romance novels. We laid out our own clothes to help with all the poking and prodding, and it took no time at all to forget the entire setting, but afterward, I was sure to have irritated skin on my back.

Even so, we remained curled up together for a long while, both of us dozing off.

At least, until the thud of the front door closing reached us in our barn hideaway.

We sprung to action, each of us throwing clothes at each other just about as fast as we could put them on. Thanks to our efforts, they hadn't remained in a neat pile.

"My dress! Where'd it go?" I squeaked, digging through the pile of hay.

"Over here." Sam tossed the worn fabric to me before struggling into his shirt.

"Go out this way." I cracked open the back door. "I doubt it'll be good if we're caught together in here."

"Good plan." He kissed me, hands cupping my face. "I'll find you in a little while, then we can go check on Mable."

For the slightest moment, I felt guilty. I had almost forgotten about her. "Did you check on her yesterday?"

"She was fine as far as I could tell." He pulled a piece of hay out of my hair. "Quick, get going before we get caught. He's bound to have seen my horse already."

As if on cue, Newton began his search. "Elizabeth! Where are you this time?"

I wrestled my tangled hair into somewhat of a braid before popping out the front door. "You're up!" I said, far too happy.

Newton narrowed his eyes in my direction and nodded to Sam's horse. "Where's Sam?"

"Sam?" I could hear my heart beating in my ears. "I haven't seen him. I was in the barn." As if he needed directions, I pointed at the building in question.

Newton raised an eyebrow and opened his mouth, likely to point out how flimsy my excuse was. Thankfully, before he could speak, Sam showed up.

He appeared from around the back of the house. "I've been looking for you!"

Newton turned his direction, nose scrunching in the slightest confusion. "We've been out here."

"Oh." Sam scratched the back of his head. Some hay fell to the grass behind him, but Newton didn't seem to notice. "I guess I didn't see you." He hesitated, glancing at me as he hunted for what to say next. "If you don't mind, we were going to run over to check on Mable this evening."

Newton paused, eyeing the two of us suspiciously. "Don't be gone long, and stay out of their way. Don't need Levi comin' up with anything else to blame us for."

"Yes, sir," Sam said, his shoulders visibly relaxing.

I glanced back at the barn, making a plan on how I would saddle a horse without looking like a complete idiot.

"Just ride with me. It'll be easier," Sam said.

Relieved, I let him help me onto his horse.

"Be back by sunset, or I'll send Elliot after you!" Newton called.

"We will! Promise!" I said.

I didn't relax completely until we were out of sight. When I did, laughter overtook me.

"Do you think he suspected anything?" I asked.

Sam grunted. "He certainly suspected *something*. It'd be a good idea not to give him anything more to add to it."

"Do you think he'd do anything about it if he knew? He's not my actual father, after all."

Sam shrugged. "If he did, he'd probably arrange a wedding for us, whether we liked it or not."

The word *wedding* didn't send chills up my spine as it had before. To Sam, I wouldn't fight it. Oddly enough, it sounded like a nice idea. A life with him seemed natural in its own special way.

The Barnette ranch was just on the other side of the river. We crossed over a rickety bridge, crested a small hill, and were there.

When we arrived, there was no sign of anyone. Either everyone had left, or they were all holed up inside.

Sam navigated his way to the front of the house slowly, head swiveling to anything that dared to move. We were almost there when the shouting made it to us. Helen's voice soared in anger, the words impossible to decipher, but the meaning plain. Within a few seconds, it all got louder. Mable's shrill, panicked shouts joined in.

Sam nearly vaulted himself off the horse, and I followed. He threw open the door and led me into the dark room.

Helen stood closest to us, blocking the exit of Johnathan and Mable.

Johnathan looked like a startled deer, a few feet from Mable, hunting for any escape route. Mable simply looked desperate. Her face red, eyes blue ice. Her mother mirrored her almost exactly, only with the furious version of her expression.

"What's going on?" Sam demanded, squaring his shoulders, ready for almost anything.

Helen gave him a glare that would send almost anyone straight to hell, but she still answered. "What does it look like? These *two* were holed up in her room. What kind of person do you take me for? No daughter of mine is going to turn into some whore! Especially with . . . with . . ." Her voice caught on the word, unable to spit out whatever derogatory term she had been thinking of.

Sam moved between the angry woman and Johnathan, giving him a nod to escape. The man gave him a grateful half smile and escaped past me, keeping as much space between him and Helen as he could manage.

She crossed her arms and glared at Sam. "And what is letting that savage out of here going to do? I need him to answer—"

Sam sighed. "I'm pretty sure Mable can answer whatever questions you have. Don't have to attack either of them. The sheriff is already keeping an eye on you all. I wouldn't give him any other reason to worry."

"Come on, Mable." I crooked my fingers at her, hoping we could at least get her out of the house.

She bit her lip and shook her head slowly. "I can't."

"What do you mean you can't?" The last thing I wanted to do was leave her in Helen's grasp.

"I'm not allowed to leave the house." Mable crossed her arms and narrowed her eyes at her mother. "After yesterday, I'm not allowed out of this house. Not even to feed the chickens or gather water. Nothing."

"That's just a little excessive, don't you think?" I demanded.

Helen turned her piercing gaze on me. "It's not your say what I do with my daughter! I think it's time for you to *leave.* You're not allowed in my house, or on this property. Same with you!" She included Sam at the last possible second.

"We just came to check on Mable," Sam started.

"Well, she's just fine as you can see! Get out of here. Go! Before I call for Levi!"

Sam took my arm and pulled me toward the door, but I planted my feet. "She's her own person! If she likes a boy, why not let her? Isn't it better to marry for love than for—"

"Get *out*!" she nearly screamed.

"Come on," Sam said.

"Mable, come with us," I pleaded, letting myself be pulled to the door only by an inch or two.

Mable shook her head slowly. "I can't . . ."

"*Go! You're not welcome here!*" Helen screamed, her shrill voice piercing my eardrums.

Sam pulled me out of the house and helped me onto the horse within a few seconds.

"We can't leave her there!" I protested, eyes glued to the house as we rode off.

"We don't have much of a choice," Sam said.

"There has to be something we can do to help her."

He sighed. "If we meddle any more, it'll only cause more trouble for us all. Johnathan knew better than to sneak into that house. There's nothing we can do about it now."

CHAPTER TWENTY-EIGHT

Elliot hopped on his horse a few minutes after midnight, waiting almost no time after Newton fell asleep to go see his girl.

Good for him, I thought. *At least his brain is calm enough to enjoy his night.*

My own brain wouldn't settle. I couldn't call Child Protective Services about Mable, though that didn't stop me from trying to figure out who to contact instead. The sheriff knew. The neighbors knew. They would have to be enough.

The house was as quiet as a graveyard by the time I finally fell into a restless, nightmare-filled sleep.

A rapidly approaching thumping noise woke me at some point. I sat straight up as soon as I placed the sound. Footsteps.

The door flew open, and a small figure rushed in, sobs choking her body as she fell onto my bed.

"Mable?" I froze, head tilting to the side like a confused puppy. The girl just cried, curled up at my feet like a broken child. "What happened?" I demanded, moving to my knees and prying her face from the quilt. "What's going on?"

"I tried . . ." She trailed off, a sob choking her words.

"Breathe! It's okay, what happened?" From what I could tell, she seemed all right. At least physically. Even so, I could only imagine the worst.

She took a moment to breathe as she tried to calm herself enough to speak. "I tried to meet him," she said as quickly as she could manage, sniffles interrupting her. "But Ma saw him first!" She fell into a wail, burying her face in my quilt again.

"Wait, what?" I pulled her back up to sitting again. "Where's Johnathan? *What happened?*"

"Ma . . . she saw him first. And she, or maybe Pa, I don't know for sure, shot him!"

The sharp intake of breath I took hurt. Perhaps I had been right to fear the worst. "Is he okay? Where is he?"

"He ran. I don't know where he went. I tried to follow a blood trail, but there wasn't one. I don't know where he went. Pa is sure he'll never come back!"

I let her fall back onto the quilt this time, focused on calming my own breathing.

Shot.

Missing.

"Stay here, okay? I'm going to get help."

Not bothering to remove the quilt to wrap it around myself, I raced out the door and down the stairs, ending up at Newton's door.

I didn't hesitate, just banged away at the wood. I'd wake up that sound sleeper one way or another.

To my surprise, it didn't take much.

I had only pounded a few times when the door jerked open to reveal a grumpy, and somewhat disheveled, Newton.

I almost choked on my own words before I could get them out. "Mable is here. Johnathan was shot. Come on." Before he could so much as react, I grabbed his arm and pulled him back up the stairs.

The grogginess in his steps were long gone in an instant. He nearly ran me over on the race back to my room.

"Where'd Johnathan go?" he asked, kneeling beside the bed and watching Mable closely.

She shrugged helplessly. "He could have gone anywhere."

"How did you get out?" he asked.

"I waited for them to fall asleep and went off the roof. They bolted the front door."

Newton took in a calming breath and patted her on the shoulder. Somewhat awkwardly, but the feeling was there. "Stay with her, I'll head out and find him."

Before he could make so much as two steps toward the hallway, the front door opened with a bang.

"Pa!" Elliot shouted, his rapid footsteps echoing him. We only had to wait a few seconds for him to appear in the room.

Newton didn't look confused in the slightest at him being fully clothed. Though, suddenly I wondered if he had known all along.

"Sam's here. He brought—" Elliot froze, staring at the sobbing girl on my bed. "Mable?"

"Who'd he bring?" Newton asked.

Elliot blinked, clearing his brain glitch as well as he could. "Johnathan. And he's been shot."

Mable jumped up, rushing ahead of us with renewed energy. We chased her into the yard where the two new arrivals sat on their horses.

Sam had led the way, still looking half-asleep, but fully clothed for the day. Johnathan sat on his own horse, looking a bit worse for wear with a torn shirt tied around his bicep. He sat straight and tall, though a slight grimace sneaked through every once in a while.

He breathed a sigh of relief when he saw Mable. He moved to get off the horse, but Sam stopped him.

"We can't stay around," he warned.

Johnathan sighed and leaned forward so he could touch Mable's cheek. "I'm glad you're all right," he said.

She nodded through her tears. "Are you okay? I'm so sorry—"

He pressed a finger to her lips. "I'll be all right. We're going home. *Ulisi* will take care of it there."

They stayed still, looking like a sad painting with the first signs of the sunrise creeping up behind them.

"We'll go with you," Newton announced. He glanced at his own knee-length nightgown, but otherwise ignored it. "It'll give you more protection. Elliot, saddle my horse. I'm assuming yours is already done?" He raised an eyebrow pointedly in his direction.

Elliot smiled sheepishly but nodded. "I'll get it done," he promised.

Newton bobbed his head and hurried back inside to change.

Sam reached down to play with my knotted hair. "You should probably go change as well. I certainly don't plan on leaving you here alone with Levi prowling around."

"He won't be out until later," Mable said. She had her head pressed to Johnathan's calf. "He's arrogant enough to think nothing could go wrong after locking me upstairs."

"Well, that's something," Sam muttered.

On that note, I squeezed his hand before rushing inside to put something more acceptable on.

I rode on the back of Elliot's horse, somewhat irritated that he wanted to walk behind everyone else instead of anywhere near Sam. I would have preferred it if they would have let me ride with him. But apparently it hadn't been up for discussion.

Mable, on the other hand, rode with Johnathan, her head pressed to his back and her eyes closed. I didn't have it in me to be jealous. She deserved every bit of peace she could get after the morning she'd had.

We remained silent for much of the ride to Johnathan's house. By the time we made it, the roosters were crowing and the sun had turned a beautiful shade of orange.

Johnathan hopped off his horse easily, as though he didn't have an open wound on his arm. He took a few steps in the direction of his house, but Newton cleared his throat to stop him.

"Levi won't leave you alone," he warned, his jaw set firmly.

"I know." Johnathan took a moment to breathe, steadying himself. He looked almost sick at the thought.

"As I see it, you have a choice to make. The first is, leave Mable alone."

Both Mable and Johnathan visibly flinched at that.

"I figured that'd be your response. The second option," Newton continued, "is to leave."

Johnathan gnawed absently at his lower lip while Mable fidgeted with her skirts.

After a long moment, Johnathan stood a little straighter and spoke up. "It would mean taking away any kind of security she has."

Mable's shoulders slumped, and her eyes were trained on her feet. "There isn't much left."

The door to the house opened, and Johnathan's grandmother bustled out. Already dressed for the day, it wouldn't have been surprising if Rachel already finished half the morning chores.

She didn't pay much attention to the rest of us, just took her grandson by his good arm and dragged him inside. She didn't ask any questions. Even so, Johnathan quickly filled her in on the morning's events. She nodded slowly, not surprised in the slightest.

After he'd been shot, he had ridden as fast as he could to the Holmes ranch, knowing Sam would be there to help him. Sam had just been waking up and brought him to Newton to get some more assistance.

We all followed into the tiny house like lost puppies.

Rachel removed the knotted shirt and began cleaning the angry wound with ease. Like some kind of magical being, Johnathan hardly reacted as she poked and prodded.

"It looks like it just grazed you," Newton said approvingly.

Elliot snorted. "Doubt it feels like that."

Johnathan's half smile turned to a grimace as his grandmother poured something onto the wound. He recovered himself, putting the superhero façade back into place.

"I packed you a bag," she said suddenly. She sounded so confident, as though she had just told us the number of eggs the chickens had laid that morning.

Johnathan sighed. "I don't want to take her back to the reservation. They won't accept her there, either."

"No." Rachel shook her head steadily. "Make your own life. Your own beginning."

Satisfied with her speedy yet thorough cleaning job of his arm, she bandaged it back up and patted on his good shoulder. "Go, before he comes to look for you here."

Johnathan shut his eyes for a long while, letting himself reach the same conclusion. With a long sigh, he turned to face Mable, his eyes searching every inch of her face. "What do you say? Will you go with me?"

She didn't hesitate. "Yes!"

He nodded, a grim determination crossing over his face. "We'll go back to your place and get your things."

"No!" She waved her hands wildly, some of her energy returning. "I don't need anything. If we go back, they won't let us leave."

Newton nodded. "He's right. Levi won't miss the mark next time."

"I don't think he fully missed this time, either," I muttered. They ignored me.

Decision made, Rachel grabbed a cloth bag from the cabinet and threw all kinds of food inside. Jerky, dried fruit, bread, and anything else she could get her hands on. Once satisfied that she had emptied her own food stores, she held it out to Mable.

"Write when you can?" she asked, the slightest sign of emotion tracing into her voice.

Mable nodded. "As soon as we get to the next town, we'll write."

"Good." Rachel squeezed Mable's hand and looked one more time at her grandson. "They will know she's gone—the sun is long up. Go, now."

I glanced out the tiny window. It was still sunrise in my book.

Johnathan turned to encompass us all with his words: "Thank you. I'll keep her safe from here on."

Newton nodded. "That's all we ask. We'll keep him away from you for as long as we can."

"I'll ride to the sheriff to let him know what's happening and what to watch for," Sam said.

Elliot said, "I'll go shoot Levi myself if he steps one foot—"

Rachel tsked her tongue. "There's no need for that. Just go before they come here looking."

The departure was sweet, though relatively silent. Johnathan helped Mable onto his horse, gave his grandmother one final nod of farewell, and hurried off.

Newton didn't wait to watch them go. "Come on," he said gruffly, hauling me onto his horse without much effort. "If we don't get going now, Levi will get here before they make it two miles."

"I'll alert the sheriff. Stay safe," Sam said, his eyes lingering on mine for just a moment too long.

They were right about Levi, though I had hoped beyond anything they would be dead wrong.

We had hardly made it a few miles ourselves when the galloping horse came into view.

"Get ready," Elliot said, sitting forward on his horse as he readied himself for a probable battle.

"Don't let go for anything. Unless I push you off," Newton whispered into my ear.

"Push me off?" I echoed, eyeing the ground far below. The very idea sent shivers up my spine. "Give me some warning if you're going to try to kill me like that, all right?"

It was as though they didn't hear me. They kicked their own horses to a gallop to intercept Levi. I held on, praying they wouldn't throw me to the ground like a discarded sack of trash. The dirt looked a very long way away.

Levi's horse moved to dart around ours, but Elliot reached for the reins.

"What are you doing?" Levi roared. He resembled a dragon—his body so tense, the veins in both his neck and arms were visible. His nostrils flared.

Elliot's fingers barely brushed the reins but didn't manage to grab a hold of them. It was probably a good thing for the sake of his arm. I couldn't imagine trying to stop a moving horse would do much good for the state of his bones.

"Stop right there!" Newton shouted, rounding his own horse so he rode beside Levi. "Where do you think you're going?"

Levi shot him what could only have been described as a "go to hell" look. "You wouldn't be trying to stop me if you didn't know where I was going! That damned savage kidnapped my daughter!"

"He didn't kidnap her!" Newton shouted, cutting in front of Levi's horse, effectively slowing him down.

Elliot grabbed the reins easily this time, pulling the horse completely to a halt. "You know quite well she went willingly! There's no telling what kind of horrible things you've done to her in the past."

With a growling noise as his only warning, Levi drew his gun.

He pointed it at me.

Everything after that happened in an instant. Newton shoved me with enough force I tumbled toward the ground, unnervingly close to the horse's hooves as they pranced near my face.

The ear-shattering bang came at the same time as I hit the dusty earth. As I got my bearings and scrambled away to safety, I watched as Levi's body tumbled off his own horse, blood gushing out of a wound on his head.

"What did you do?" Newton vaulted to the ground, glancing at me to ensure I wasn't dead, before rushing to Levi's side.

"He was going to kill her! Or you! You know he didn't care which!" Elliot shouted back. He hopped off his horse and gathered up the reins of all three, keeping them away from the body so it wouldn't be trampled.

I scrambled to my feet, running my hands down my arms and legs to make sure nothing was broken. As far as I could tell, I'd only have a few extra bruises in the morning. I could live with that.

Elliot looked sickeningly pale as he stared at the body at his feet. Newton, on the other hand, had vengeance written all over his face.

"What are we going to do with him?" Elliot asked, the earlier fury replaced with the whisper of a child.

"Throw him into the river like his child did Elizabeth. Fitting, don't ya think?"

The anger flowed back over Elliot immediately after that. "Let's do it."

CHAPTER TWENTY-NINE

T he sound of galloping hooves thundered toward us.

"Quick!" I ran for them, wishing I could be of some sort of help. "Pull him into the trees!"

"No time," Elliot grunted, leading the horses so they might shield Levi's body from the oncoming rider at least a little. Newton sighed and turned to face his returning fate.

We all knew who it was. Sam had said he would alert the sheriff to keep us safe, after all.

Erik came into view, face red and sweaty from the panic. "What happened?" he demanded, leaping off his horse with surprising ease for a man his size.

I didn't dare answer. I stood there like a lost puppy and watched as Erik took one deliberate step after another to stand by the body itself.

"He was gonna shoot Elizabeth," Newton said, his voice strong, unapologetic, like he didn't care about the potential repercussions.

Elliot made a strangled sound to get him to stop. "You're not doin' that again! It was me. I shot him to keep him from firin' at Elizabeth."

Erik stared for a long while, chewing the inside of his cheek.

"I won't fight ya. I'll go with you to the jail now if you'd like," Elliot said.

Erik sighed. "There's no need." He took a few steps back and looked at all of us. "Let his horse go, put the body on mine. I'll put it somewhere where no one will find it."

Elliot's eyes went wide. "What?"

"Don't make me think again, Elliot Hersley. Go! I never saw any of you here. Got it?"

Newton nodded slowly. "Thank you."

Erik just grunted in response.

Elliot leaned his head back, staring straight up at the sky for a long moment. He almost looked like he might pass out from the relief. After a moment, he scooped up the large body as though nothing happened and plopped it on the front of the horse.

And that was the last anyone saw of Levi Barnette.

Helen bothered Erik almost every day about her missing daughter and husband. He never told a thing, and no one ever found the body. Somehow, the town slowly calmed down.

Sam came over nearly every evening to check on us and eat dinner. It was debatable sometimes whether he came for the free food or to see me.

One evening after we'd finished cleaning the dishes, he had other plans.

He nudged my side with his hip to get my attention. "Hey, come on a ride with me?"

Elliot glanced in our direction, an unspoken question hiding in his eyes.

Sam nodded in response but otherwise ignored it.

"Okay?" I wiped my hands on the dish towel.

Sam had hardly waited for my answer; he had already made it halfway to the door. I discarded the towel on the counter and hurried after him, giving Elliot a curious glance. He just shrugged.

As usual, Sam helped me onto his horse, and we started off. Instead of our usual chatter, he remained silent as we traveled down the dirt road. The only sound came from the horses' hooves as they sent puffs of dust into the air around us. The sun was beginning to set, sending all the shadows spewing across the green earth.

I ignored his mood as well as I could and breathed in the cool air. The weather wouldn't remain comfortable, and I knew it. Within a few weeks, I'd wish I had air-conditioning.

We were almost to town when I realized Sam had grown stiff. My own veins turned to ice. Something wasn't right.

"What's wrong?" I asked.

No response. He bypassed the town, turning the horse to go just north of it, behind the line of buildings that made up Main Street.

"You're starting to worry me," I said, trying to lean and get a view of his face. Every one of his features was rigid, apprehension flowing from his body. "Sam! Tell me!"

"I have to ask you something first," he said, jaw locking.

I sat back before I could fall. The horse's smooth movements had changed to something more choppy, nervous.

"Sam!" I protested. "What are we doing? Where are we going?"

He didn't answer.

We were at the old, wooden bridge. No one was around us, as the sun had almost slipped under the horizon. He hopped off, reaching his hands up for me.

"What are we doing here?" I demanded, gripping the saddle instead. The horse sidestepped and blew through her nose.

Sam sighed and left me there, tying the horse up to the first post of the bridge. "I'd never hurt you, you know that."

"Yes," I said cautiously. "Doesn't answer my question."

"I just wanted to talk to you about something," he said slowly. "You do trust me, right?"

With an irritated sigh, I slid off the horse. "Yes." It was true. I knew he'd never hurt me, at least not on purpose. But the nerves radiating off his body made my stomach churn. Made the horse's stomach do the same, based on her nervous movements.

"You have bad news, don't you?" I asked, keeping my eyes narrowed on him. My mind was swimming around all the possible conclusions. It found a specific one. It made so much sense, it had to be the one.

They hadn't made it. The news of Johnathan and Mable's death had to have arrived. What else would it be?

My heart ached at the horrible idea. Sure, we'd received word that they had made it to a tiny town in Kansas, but the mail could sometimes be delayed.

"You know something about Johnathan and Mable, don't you?" I demanded.

He stopped short, turning slowly in place to face me. "Why—"

"I know we got their letter yesterday. That doesn't mean you didn't get a *different* letter today. What happened? Don't drag it on! Just tell me!"

He didn't laugh at the idea, just stared blankly at me. "No. Why would you think that? Johnathan said he wanted to settle there since Levi won't bug them anymore. Close enough to visit if Helen ever calms down. You read the letter yourself."

I let out a breath, my shoulders dropping with relief. "Then what are you here to tell me?"

He took my hand and led me to the middle of the river. It was much higher than the last time I'd seen it, rushing smoothly along its path. There were no rapids by any means, but the water was on a mission nonetheless.

"Why are we here?" I asked, staring down into the water.

"If you had a way back home, would you take it?" he asked.

I glanced at him in surprise. "Home?"

Hope must have flittered across my face, as he narrowed his eyes. "Do you want to go home?"

I stared at the flowing water again, feeling the cold grip it would have on my body if I was to drop down, feeling the tightening of my chest it would give me as I drowned.

"It's what I'm supposed to do, isn't it?" I asked, unable to move my eyes from the water. "Stories are meant to go full circle. They don't just abandon a person in a strange time and place, right? There's always a way back."

He didn't fully gather the references, but he understood enough. "Do you not want to stay here?" When I didn't say anything, he continued: "I need to know, Ellie. Please."

My body felt like it was going into panic mode. It wasn't a decision I particularly wanted to face. "Are you sure you aren't planning on moving away yourself?"

He crossed his arms in my peripheral vision. "Of course not. I have a job here. Besides, a single person shouldn't be your deciding factor in anything. You are the decision. I don't matter in this."

I dragged my toe across the wood. I was so close to the edge. So close to simply falling forward. It would be easy to tumble into the water. I would either make it home, or join my parents, brother, Trish.

"I had college there. I was almost done. I would be able to get a job as a college professor, if they'd let me take the final. At least that was my hope." The drop in my voice at the job title was obvious. It suddenly sounded like a prison sentence. "But I'd have a job, an income. I could get my own house. I had electricity, instant food, bathrooms."

A picture of my life was being painted in my mind. A tiny apartment in downtown Oklahoma City, or rather on the edge. I wouldn't be able to afford anything as fancy as downtown. The noise, the lights, the crime, the sirens—and that phone. My eyes ached just thinking about it. I would spend most of my time worrying about the device. Worrying about all my devices.

But who would I really have? Really and truly have? I had no true friends. The one I did have was dead on the riverbank. My brother had died. My mother. My father.

There was nothing.

Here, it felt so safe. Sure, it was wild, but everything was quiet. I could see for miles and miles without any light intruding upon the natural view. I had Elliot, who I knew would never let me be hurt. He'd never pawn me off on some random suitor. I had Newton, who had taken me in as his own.

And I had Sam.

Without meaning to, my toes had made it to the edge of the wood, wiggling there in the unknown.

My breathing hitched, and I felt my body falling. A penalty of not paying attention, it was making its own decision. My body tipped forward, my arms swirling around in panic.

Weightlessness, dizziness, soon to be death.

Sam's hand grabbed my arm and yanked me fully onto the wooden panels before my feet could really leave the safety of the ground. I fell roughly, gasping for breath again as the fear trickled away.

"I don't want to leave," I told him desperately. He nearly lay on top of me, arms on either side of my head, body hovering just a few inches from mine. His blue eyes were wide with panic.

"I thought I'd be able to let you, to do this for you. But I can't," he said in a rush.

"I know my answer," I said firmly. "I don't want to leave. I don't want to go. I'm tired of running."

His lips met mine for a short, grateful moment. "Then I need to ask the second part of my question," he said, his breathing ragged and out of control.

He slowly got off me and helped me to my feet. I stood in the middle of the bridge, knowing there was no way I would accidentally fall from there.

"I talked to Newton," he began, his voice clear, rehearsed.

"What?" My heart jumped in surprise before picking up in a completely different kind of fear: anticipation.

"I know he is not your father, but he was the best I have."

"What?" I said again.

Sam reached into his pocket and removed something tiny. As he brought his hands forward, he went down to one knee.

I felt dizzy. Chills ran up and down my arms. Every other breath was catching in my throat, terrified. Of what, though? Scared he wasn't doing what I hoped he was doing?

"He said yes. But I'll only do this if you say yes first." Sam's eyes found mine, pleading, hopeful, scared. "Ellie, my dear from the future. I don't know why you're meant to be here. Maybe because you were needed to help Mable. Maybe because you needed a new start. Will you make your new life with me? Will you marry me?"

My mouth was hanging open, my tongue completely dry already. I closed it quickly. For once, my conclusion wasn't wrong. It was completely and totally correct.

"Really?" I whispered.

He nodded, a pale sheen taking over his features, heightened by the fresh moonlight that fell over his face.

My mind swirled with the new pictures of my future. A little house. Our house. Built with our own hands, blood, sweat, and tears. Something we put everything into. A tiny child. Maybe land, maybe not. It didn't matter. It was all the middle of nowhere to me. I'd have the freedom to do what I really wanted, as Sam wouldn't shove me in a corner somewhere.

He had no money, no land. But it was a time when he could work through that. There were things he could do.

To me, it sounded like paradise.

I would live in a cardboard box, if it was with Sam.

Tears pricked at the edge of my eyes, and I sniffed to keep them at bay. "Yes." I had never been so sure of an answer in my life. "Please, yes."

He stood up, his skin going back to its normal color almost instantly. He took the hand I offered him and slipped the delicate wedding ring onto my finger. I didn't even look at it—my arms immediately wrapped around him. He hugged me back so tight my back felt like it would pop.

"Do you like it?" he finally asked into my hair.

"Yes," I said.

"Did you even look at it?" I felt the smile against my head.

I reluctantly pulled back from him and looked down at my left hand. It was very simple. A single, small diamond sat in the center, with delicate swirls of silver that spread away from it and down the band. It looked like it belonged to a fairy. "It's beautiful. You didn't need to spend this much on it."

He laughed, the sound knocking away any remaining tension in the air. "No, I didn't. Elliot gave it to me. To us."

"Elliot?" I squinted at the ring in confusion.

"It was his mother's. When I told him my plans, he wanted to be sure it was passed on to you. He said his girl won't marry, so it might as well go to someone."

I stared at the ring, even more in shock. I wondered how long it would go on through the family tree, if it would one day make it to my own time again.

"I love it," I said, wrapping my arms around him again, refusing to ever let go. "I can't wait to spend the rest of my life with you."

He bent his head to kiss me then, sealing the deal.

AUTHOR Q&A

1. How did you get so interested in the late 1800s?

I'm not completely sure. In school, I'd research the 1800s instead of studying. It got me into plenty of trouble, but hey, it came in handy.

I think in some ways, it was a way to escape reality. Going back in time provides an escape that doesn't feel attainable just by writing current fiction.

It's probably why I've dabbled with fantasy as well.

Essentially, the 1800s feels like a different world.

2. Which character did you come up with first?

Elliot. 100 percent Elliot.

Back when I was probably thirteen or so, I wrote a lot of *Bonanza* fanfiction (totally normal for a millennial, right?). I wanted them to have a little sister. The characters migrated from those little episodes to several NaNoWriMo stories, then finally to *Twins in Time*—their rightful place.

3. What were some of the funny or intriguing things you found in your research for this era?

Sod houses were frequently constructed first, then they were transformed into sheds or barns after the actual house was completed.

All I can imagine is how hard it would be to keep a sod house clean.

4. Why did you choose Woodward, Oklahoma, for your setting?

I wish I could say that was a groundbreaking decision. When plotting the story, I wanted Ellie to be a college student. For some reason, I didn't want it to be in the Oklahoma City metro.

Northwestern Oklahoma State University is up there. Her college career was supposed to be a big part of the story, but the further I got into plotting, the less important it became. So, it just sort of stayed in Woodward.

This did cause some research challenges with everything being closed in 2020 and having to drive a good two hours to get up there.

5. What is the main thing you hope readers will leave with after finishing your novel?

I should probably say something monumental like, "Don't run from your problems."

But in all honesty, I want readers to keep shooting for the stars and to never give up on their dreams. People might harass them or explain why something isn't possible until their faces turn blue.

Don't listen to them.

If you love what you're doing, it's worth it.

Keep going.

6. What were some of the obstacles you had to overcome in writing this story?

Researching little details in 2020 was next to impossible. I spent weeks researching the Cherokee Outlet and if the Cherokees actually lived there in 1894. This might sound like an easy question to answer, but trust me, it was not.

No one would answer their phones.

Google would dodge the question.

Museums were closed.

I almost gave up on the subplot entirely.

Another one was the dirt.

"Dirt? Why dirt?"

When they find Elizabeth, she's on the riverbank. The part of Oklahoma where I live is covered in red clay. It never crossed my mind that Woodward would have a different sort of dirt.

Well, it does.

Originally, she was partially hidden under some of the little shelves of clay that the water had created over the years.

At the end of the *second* draft, my husband told me the ground was sandy up there.

I had no earthly idea how to fix my plot after that discovery. After all, why hadn't the coyotes eaten her yet? Why hadn't someone found her?

It was a mess.

7. Who is your favorite character and why?

In the long run, I love them all. But Elliot is probably my favorite. Years ago, when I first started playing with this story idea, his name was Sam and he was the big brother I always wanted.

8. A tornado has a major scene in this story. Have you ever encountered one?

Yes. Just yes.

I was born and raised in Oklahoma, so I could probably write a book about my tornadic experiences.

The closest call was back in 2011. It was the night of my senior band performance. Spoiler alert: it didn't end up happening.

A mile-wide F5 tornado dropped down right outside my hometown. My mother, brother, and I all rushed into the claustrophobic, nauseatingly hot storm shelter to wait. The next thing we knew, it sounded as though someone had bass music on way too loud across the street. A deep booming. Over. And over. And over. The sound was the tornado leveling houses.

When we opened the shelter a few minutes later, we didn't expect our house to be standing.

Somehow, it was still there. The sky swirled in this gray/green. It looked like something you'd see in a deep, deadly whirlpool from a pirate movie. It didn't look natural.

I distinctly remember two leaves circling directly above us.

The air felt like we'd stuffed our heads into plastic bags. It was hard to breathe. It was so hot, the air itself felt like sweat.

The TV didn't have any signal, so my mom called my dad to find out where it was.

"It's on top of you! The storm trackers can see the tornado, but I can't see the house!"

To say she shoved us back in that storm shelter would be an understatement.

The wind and popping returned almost before we got the door closed.

Our house survived. We ended up with a stranger's photos in our yard. Wheat clung to our windows as if someone had glued them there.

Sirens were everywhere. As we checked for damage, the giant tornado cycled back down. It was huge. Again, it didn't look natural.

It then went to destroy the next town, killing way too many people.

ACKNOWLEDGMENTS

To my husband, Gavin, who has worked his ever-lovin' butt off to ensure I get every chance I can to make my dream a reality. This would have been impossible without you.

To my friends, Shayla, Felicia, and Janey, who were always there to drag me out of a meltdown when I was sure I'd never make it. I'm positive there'll be more, don't worry.

To my darling Annaleigh: when I first started this story, you were still a far-off dream. And now that it's done, you're the cutest little toddler around. The last draft was completed only two weeks after I found out I was pregnant with you. One of the names we considered for if you were a boy was actually Elliot. Though you weren't around for the conception of this story, you certainly were here to help it morph into its final form. And I wouldn't have it any other way!

To my dad, who helped me edit all those little books when I was only seven or eight, who kept every recording he possibly could of me spouting off tall tales before I even knew how to write. You were probably my number one fan from the very beginning. I would never have been able to stick with it for so many years without you.

And last, to everyone who's always believed in me. There are so many people who never doubted me, who hyped me up every step of the way.

Thank you!

NATALIE GRIFFIN

Natalie Griffin is a historical fiction author, dog mom, and pianist. She started a mobile dog grooming company at age 19, where she still works part-time to keep her furry clients in tip-top shape.

As a toddler, she'd scribble illegible words on paper, then recite her fanciful stories to her mother.

Born and raised in Oklahoma, she can't stand the triple-digit heat, but she does enjoy the excitement that comes from tornado season. If you talk about the storms, you're guaranteed to have a long, animated conversation ahead of you.

She mainly writes stories set in the 19th century, believing she always belonged there, with corsets and log cabins. She's a sucker for anything involving fairies. Anything.

She stays busy with her hunter husband, daughter, three dogs, and two cats.

Connect with the Author

Nataliegriffin.com
Instagram.com/natalieogriffin
TikTok.com/@natalieogriffin
Twitter.com/natalieogriffin

Leave a Review

If you enjoyed reading *Twins in Time*, please consider leaving a review on your platform of choice. Reviews help self-published authors finds more readers like you.

9 789898 687381 7